COLORS IN ME

COLORS IN ME
STRENGTH, LOVE, RESILIENCY

C.M. DILCHER

Colors in Me
Copyright © 2020 by C.M Dilcher

Book design by Danna Mathias

ISBN 978-1-7357903-0-5 (paperback)
ISBN 978-1-7357903-1-2 (ebook)

DEDICATION

When I think of who to dedicate this book to, I have many people that come to mind. First, I would like to dedicate this book to Debbie Roush, the teacher who made a difference in my life. She inspired me to be the counselor and educator that I am today. Next, I would like to dedicate this book to my students, past, present, future. May you always have teachers with kind in their eyes. I can't leave out administrators, may you take the time to build meaningful relationships that make changes. Also, to the real Dorothy that loved so many and whose contagious laugh lit up a room. And of course I want to dedicate this book to teachers. You make a difference in every child, hopefully in a positive way, and your words matter. May you always love your students unconditionally and set out to make a difference, aiming for a good one. And lastly, to those who believed in me and inspired me to keep writing, thank you.

CHAPTER 1

DARK AND HOT. IT BUBBLES IN MY TUMMY and hurts. The dark grows when I hear the screams and his voice filling the house. I plug my ears. The floor is cold and hard in the closet. It is smelly and sticky. I am hidden by boxes and musty clothes hanging in front of me. The screams bounce around my head like a small rocket that jabs my brain. I squeeze my teddy bear tight, keeping him close. He is my friend, Teddy, he helps me stay quiet. I hear him, my dad, Don. Well, he is not my real daddy. I don't remember my real daddy much, except he laughed a lot. Sometimes I try to close my eyes and hear his laugh, or what I think I remember his laugh sounding like. Dad's voice forces me to open my eyes and it is mad and he is yelling bad words. His voice is loud and strong and his voice can hurt me and Mommy.

"You Dumb Fucking Bitch, I told you not to talk to him!" Dad's voice bounces off the walls.

"I only said hello. NO! NO! Please!" Mommy begs, her voice is squeaky and weak. I hear a painfully loud smack followed by a dull thump. The darkness grabs me, and I grab Teddy. Mommy. I hope she is ok. Dad's footsteps are moving. Coming closer. Oh no. I stay still and quiet.

"Where are you, you little shit?" Dad is looking for me. He opens the door. It squeaks as it opens and slams into the wall. I freeze, trying to not make a sound. I can feel the beats of my heart spread throughout my body and my breathing stops. He turns on the light and I can see the shadow of his legs under the closet door. Oh no, please don't let him find me. I close my eyes and try to think of my favorite cartoon to keep my mind off of what is about to happen, again. I can hear the words and music in my head. For a moment I can't hear him open the closet door. When I open my eyes, I see the light from the room cast shadows in the closet. There are boxes and a lot of trash piled up. I hide in here a lot and sometimes I sleep here with Teddy. Knowing what is about to happen to me, I wait as the hot bubbles start to boil in my tummy. Then, I see the clothes move as he reaches for me.

I try to make myself small. I hug Teddy, pull my knees close and back myself into the corner. I watch as his scarred, dirty hand reaches for me. I turn to avoid him touching me. I move myself away but he grabs Teddy. I hold on tight as he tugs and starts to pull me out of the corner using Teddy's arm. I don't let go as Dad pulls harder on Teddy's arm. I hear a slow snapping sound followed by a quick rip and then I fall back onto the floor. Oh no, not Teddy! I look at my friend and his arm is missing. I feel red burn inside me. I hate him.

"No!" I cry out when I see that Teddy's arm is gone. "NOOO!" I am crying, and hot tears slowly fall down my face. I don't like to cry. He thinks I am weak and he hurts me more. I must stop my eyes from crying. I use my pajama sleeve and wipe off the tears while taking a breath into my chest. Dad's hand grabs my hair and his grip is painful as he tangles his grimy fingers in my hair. With one quick, swift movement, he pulls me from the closet. I do not fight him because it makes it worse if I do. I stop crying and hide the darkness and the bubbles. I need to be strong. I must be brave. I must be brave. I try to shield myself as he throws me into the wall. It hurts and knocks my teeth into my lip. I hit the floor like a brick as I fall next to Teddy's arm.

I close my eyes, trying to think of a happy place where I am invincible. Somewhere where he can't hurt my mommy or me anymore. I picture a place like the superhero cartoons I watch on television. I picture myself as big as Ironman and strong. I am Ironman. I am Ironman and his armor will protect me from Dad. I open my eyes. When I look at Dad he is staring at me with mad in his eyes. I don't look away, I must not be afraid. I am Ironman protected by my armor, and I take in a breath of strength. I close my fists and stand up. I try to look as big as possible as I take a step to separate my feet to stand like Ironman. I stare at him and the darkness fills my eyes. I hate him. I want to hurt him like he hurts me, I tighten my fists preparing to fight.

"You worthless shit, I told you to pick up your cars!" He is close to my face and his breath smells of beer and complete grossness. I continue to look at him, showing him that I am strong. The darkness bubbles in my tummy pushing down the red and I feel sick. He is tall and strong. His jeans are worn and dingy from his job, and his shirt is stained. His hair is greasy and he has a big nose. He has a tattoo on his arm and scars on his face. Dad looks down his nose at me then his eyes move to the toys on the floor. He bends down and picks up my white car. It is my favorite car and is bigger than my other ones with doors that actually open. He looks at it for a brief moment, then at me. His mouth opens a bit and he pulls his arm back and the car flies out of his hand like a rocket.

I tried to move but the car was very fast and I didn't have much of a chance to avoid it. It finds its target and lands right in the middle of my forehead then falls to the floor. It hurts. I grab my head and fall to the floor. I want to cry and yell for my mommy, but she never comes when I need her. I pull my knees close to me trying to make myself small. Maybe I will disappear if I can become small enough, maybe the floor will swallow me up and take me away. I drop my eyes to my feet. I am not Ironman. I am not brave, I am not strong. I am a shit and I am worthless. I let the darkness turn to cold and it feels like ice in my throat as I think of what a terrible kid I am.

Dad's footsteps become faint as he walks away from me, I cannot see him because I closed my eyes. I hear the twist of a doorknob and the front door slams closed knocking pictures from the walls. The house shakes as he stomps down the stairs of the front porch. I hope he never comes back, I wish he never moved in, and we were still in my house where my real daddy lived. I rub my head and look at my hand. It is red. I must be bleeding. I am glad he didn't punch me again. I don't think of moving in case he comes back in. I feel weak and I am shaking. What if he comes back in to hurt us more and I can't protect Mom? I couldn't even keep Teddy safe.

The room lights up from the bright headlights of Dad's truck. It sounds like a tractor that I have seen on T.V. The light starts to move across the wall, and I hear the tires rolling over the gravel on the road. Once the light is gone and the gravel is quiet again I know he left and the darkness left with him. I let out what little breath I have in my lungs, not realizing I was holding it, and with that breath I let the tears fall down my face and onto the floor. I stand, still crying, and go check on my mommy. The blood is trickling down my face and I try to wipe it off. I walk into the living room and I can't see her.

"Mommy, are you ok?" My voice sounds soft. "Mommy, where are you?" I walk into the kitchen and she is on the floor with blood on her face and head. I hurry to her and shake her trying to wake her up. "Mommy, wake up, I need you!" I feel her chest and it is moving and I can feel air blowing from her nose, but she is not waking up. I want to call for help, but there is no one and I need to take care of her. I walk into the bathroom and grab a washcloth and get it wet with warm water. This is what she used to do for me when I had boo-boos. Of course, this was before she changed. Before my life changed. After I grab the cloth, I go back to the closet that I was hiding in and grab a blanket.

As I turn to walk back to the kitchen, I spot Teddy's arm on the floor. I feel this cold hardness swirl in my throat. I will have to find a way to fix his arm, but first I need to go back to Mommy. When I return to the kitchen, Mom is sitting up and has her face buried in her hands. I can hear her crying and her nose is all snotty. I take the cloth and wipe the blood in her hair and then she looks at me and I wipe her face. She doesn't say anything, but her eyes move to my head where I am bleeding. Her eyes look sad and empty. I take the blanket, wrap her in it, and climb into her lap. I need my mom. She holds me. When I feel her touch around me, I melt and tears drop onto her hands rolling down her soft skin. I cry as I hold onto her. I wish I could keep her from getting hurt by him, protect her, but I can't. I look up into her eyes, "Mommy, let's leave here and not come back." My voice sounds broken. She doesn't respond but squeezes me a little tighter. Deep down, I know she won't leave, but I hope she will.

After a few moments, she shifts her weight and moves me to the floor before she stands up. I look up at her wanting and needing her to take care of me, but she doesn't look at me. She picks up her phone and I have lost her again. My heart hurts. She walks around me and opens the cabinet door, pulling out a glass. She pours some of the "adult only" drink into the glass and drinks it down fast. She leaves the bottle and the glass on the counter and continues to walk around me. I am invisible again. She continues to look at her phone. I hate the phone. Sometimes I wish I could be the phone, at least she would see me. Mom puts the phone to her ear, then walks to her room and closes the door. It was only a few minutes, but I had my mommy back for those few minutes. It was wonderful. I close my eyes and try to remember her touch and her scent around me. It was brief. When I open my eyes again the darkness is back in my tummy poking at my heart. I am alone. I am worthless.

Mom is thin and kind of short. Her hair is blondish brown and curly. She loves to sing when she is happy, which does not seem to happen very much. I remember enjoying watching her sing and dance while she cooked for me. I liked it when I could smell the food cooking. It always made my tummy smile. She used to play with me and giggle a lot. I miss her smile. When she would smile, her eyes would squint. I loved to make her smile. I really miss it. Now, as I sit alone on the sticky floor I can see how much she has changed. Her hair is always a mess and sometimes even dirty. Her once bright beautiful eyes are now surrounded by dark rings and bruises. I haven't seen her smile in a really long time, and she doesn't hug me very much anymore. I try to make her giggle sometimes, but the giggles never come. She is always on her phone or watching television. I am invisible to her most days, especially when he is around.

He is not my dad. I really don't like to call him Dad, but he makes me. When he first started coming to my house I didn't call him Dad. I called him Don. He seemed okay with it then, but after he moved in I had to, or he would hurt me. He is tall and strong. He has dark, dark hair and cold eyes that hide under bushy caterpillar like eyebrows. His nose is big and sharp looking. It reminds me of Gru from the Minion movies I watched. He has scars on his face, too. I don't know where they came from. He works a lot and is always grumpy when he comes home. After he gets home from work, he starts to drink his beer, the ones in the blue cans that he keeps in the fridge. He is mostly quiet until he gets drunk, then he gets mean. I try to hide and stay out of the way but sometimes it doesn't work. As I think of him, I can smell him, and he always stinks of old beer and cigarettes and sweat. Yuck. The thought makes me get a cold chill. I decide that I need to clean myself up and get out of the kitchen in case he comes home. He doesn't stay gone for very long. I am guessing that Mom was probably trying to call him on the phone.

I wipe my tears away from my face and stand up. My head hurts. I pick up the dirty washcloth and walk to the bathroom. After rinsing the cloth, I climb onto the bathroom counter and look in the mirror at myself. It must be me, that is why Mom doesn't like me anymore. I frown and try not to think about it. I clean the blood from my face and see the cut. It is on my forehead and kind of to the side above my eye. It is the shape of the car's mirror and not very big. I am glad it is small because sometimes it is hard to think up stories about how I got the cuts and bruises. I don't like to be asked about it. I have gotten pretty good at remembering what to say when people do ask. School was the worst about it. Teachers and the principal would ask me over and over again. It was very frustrating. I did not like school. I try not to think about it. I start digging through the cabinet to find an old Band-Aide to cover it. After sticking the Band-Aide on, I pull my lip out to see where my teeth cut it when I hit the wall. It is puffy and hurts. I take a big breath and let out a sigh, I am tired. It must be late because it has been dark for awhile now. I grab my toothbrush and brush my teeth, then head back to my closet.

I pause outside Mom's door and put my hand on it. I miss her. I can hear her talking on the phone, but I am not sure what she is saying. Her voice is soft and sounds nice. I think about knocking or just walking in, but I know she doesn't want to see me. My hand slides down the door slowly. I continue to walk to the other room, it is a room full of stuff. Stuff that is piled up and needs to be moved somewhere else. I asked Mom once to move the stuff and when Dad heard me he got mad and said to leave it alone. Everything makes him mad. We moved here awhile back, and it was going to be my new room. My bed must still be at our old house because I haven't seen it in awhile. I miss my old bedroom and my bed. I made a bed in this new room over by the corner. I made it out of my blankets and put my Ironman blanket on top. My real dad bought it for me, the thought makes me frown. Sometimes I don't sleep there and feel better in the closet. Picking up Teddy and his arm, I climb over the boxes and find my space. I am going to sleep here tonight in case Dad comes home again. I cover Teddy and myself with my blanket. I close my eyes and picture my happy place as Ironman keeping the town safe. All the people would be smiling at me, even my mom and standing with her is my daddy, my real daddy.

I take a breath and hear my real daddy's voice and his laugh. I try to remember the last time I heard him or saw his face. He always hugged me tight and would call me his favorite little man. It is getting harder to remember. I can remember him playing with my little basketball hoop and picking me up on his shoulders. He had light hair, like mine, and happy, fun eyes. Why did he have to go? The thought makes me cold and sad. Mom was always smiling with Daddy and they would sometimes take me places to play together. I enjoy those memories. Well, at least I think they are memories or I just made them up. Either way I like to think about the three of us being together again and happy. No darkness, no hurt. I wish he didn't leave. I try not to think about it much but it is hard not to. Everything changed after that, everything except for Teddy. Until now anyway. I hold his arm up and feel the ripped stitches. I need to fix him. "I will figure out a way to fix you Teddy." I tell him this with a warm hug. I bet the nice neighbor will help me. She is nice to me. The thought of Dorothy and asking her to fix Teddy makes me warm. I start to snuggle into my pillow, I will go see her tomorrow. Holding Teddy close, I think of her and her nice smile and fall asleep.

CHAPTER 2

WHEN I WAKE UP, I HAVE A HEADACHE. I am still very tired. It is bright outside already. The summer sun is hot and the house is warming up fast. I stand up and stretch and climb out of the closet. I freeze at the door of the cluttered room before walking to the hallway. I try to listen. I want to know if he is here and what kind of mood he is in. I can't hear much over the T.V. I hear a low growl that echoes in my stomach and realize I am really hungry. I start to get excited thinking that maybe Mom made breakfast, but I take a breath into my lungs and know that probably didn't happen. I walk down the hall and into the living room. No one is in there and I start to feel very alone. I check the kitchen. Only the blanket that I covered Mom up with last night is tossed on the floor. The bottle that Mom left on the counter is empty now and the glass is in the sink. Definitely, no breakfast made. Oh well. I open the freezer and grab the last frozen waffles and put them in the toaster. I am glad that mommy let me get them when we went shopping. They are yummy, and I know how to make them. It beats toast. I should ask Dorothy today about showing me how to make eggs. The thought makes my tummy growl.

I walk back to the door to Mom's room and listen. After a minute or so I can hear snoring, and I am relieved that I am not home by myself again. I am not sure if he came home last night. I decide to look outside for his truck. The living room is large. There are two recliners and a couple end tables that are all cluttered up with stuff. The pictures that fell from the wall when the door was slammed shut last night are still laying on the floor by the door. Beer cans are all over the floor where he sits to watch his shows and the news. The carpet used to be this off white color but now it looks gray and dirty. What I like best about the living room is that it has our couch from the old house that sits against the window. I walk onto the coffee table and then hop onto the couch to look out of the window. The parking spot where his old pickup usually sits is empty and this makes me smile. I always seem to have more energy and my head feels lighter when he is not home.

The familiar sound of the toaster popping fills my ears and I jump off the couch and trot off to the kitchen. I climb onto the counter and stand up so I can reach the cabinet above the toaster. I grab the peanut butter and smear it on the waffles and pour some juice into my favorite cup. I relax and sit on the counter. I gobble down my breakfast quickly and think about making more, but remember that they are all gone. I want to go see Dorothy. I hope she is home. I put my plate in the sink and then head to the bathroom. I want to clean up and brush my teeth before heading out.

I squirt some toothpaste on my toothbrush and start scrubbing. I glance at the holder on the sink and see his toothbrush. As I rinse my mouth I get an idea and grab his toothbrush. I look at it for a second. When I think of what I want to do, the darkness swirls as I picture his pissed face. It doesn't stop me, he will hurt me whether he finds out or not. I look at the toilet and it is quite dirty, it kind of looks like Mom may have gotten sick last night. Using his toothbrush I start to scrub at the stained toilet and clean all those spots that catch all the dirt and other ickiness. I giggle to myself and pull off a hair that is stuck to the toothbrush. That would have been obvious. I carefully place the toothbrush back into place, and wash my hands. I quickly leave the room in case he gets home.

After putting on my shoes and socks, I scoop up Teddy and his arm and quietly walk out of the door. The sun is bright and high in the sky and it reminds me of my mood. I am not sure if I feel good because he is gone or because I get to go to Dorothy's home. She is an old lady that lives down the road. She is loud and giggles a lot. Many times, when she giggles she puts her hand over her mouth. Her hair is short and curly, and she wears glasses. She is not fat but she is not skinny either. She can be gruff sounding when she talks but it is normally in a funny way, but I wouldn't want to make her mad. She is one of those people that seems to know everyone and loves everyone. She always has a way to make me feel special and happy. I met her when I ran away from home one afternoon and she was working in her front yard. Dad had come home early from work and Mom was talking on the phone to someone and he became very angry. He hit me in the stomach and I ran outside to puke and just kept running.

I walk down the dirt road feeling the gravel move beneath my shoes with each step. There is a slight breeze that is much needed. It is going to be a hot and humid day. My mind is relaxed, and I am enjoying the sun and the fresh air. But I hear it. It is loud and sounds like a tractor. The sound sparks the dark fire and it shoots up from my tummy to my heart. I freeze and hold my breath, feeling every beat of my heart. I look over my shoulder and can see a cloud of dust. My eyes turn dark and I start to feel panicked. I hold onto Teddy and the arm tight. Quickly, I look for somewhere to run but I am frozen, the darkness has me. I fight it back down and gather my thoughts as I jump across the ditch and into the woods. I run, not stopping until I know I am far enough away. I duck behind a tree and drop onto my knees. I am hoping the brush will hide me. I am not sure if he spotted me or not. I squeeze Teddy and hold him close. Oh please don't find me. The bubbles are filling my chest and the darkness is choking me.

As the truck slows down the brakes make piercing squeal sounds that echo through the trees. The gravel becomes silent and the truck pauses. My heart beats echo through my body and I don't dare to make a move or a sound. The window rolls down and I can make out his big nose and messy hair as he leans out of the window. There is cold in my throat and fire in my chest as the darkness makes me feel sick.

"You little shit. I saw you and know you're fucking close. Run from me, you're a pussy, boy." His voice is angry and hurts me. I am a pussy, and weak. I should have stayed on the road and faced him, but the thought makes me tremble. He turns back to the windshield of the gray truck and rubs his chin like he is thinking about something. He then yells out, "I'm sorry. I need to work on being better for you and your mom. Come out and I can give you a ride." His voice changes. It is his fake voice he uses when he is forcing himself to care about me and pretending to care about Mommy. I don't trust him and know he doesn't care. I close my eyes and try to listen to the leaves blowing around me to keep my body from freaking out. After a couple minutes his voice is mad again and it forces me to look in his direction. He slams his hands onto the steering wheel. "Fuck you then!" And with his last stabbing words, the old truck spins gravel all over as it takes off down the road toward our house leaving a large dust cloud in its wake. Mommy. I hope he is nicer to her this morning, even if it is in his fake, I have to like you, voice.

I don't dare move. Not even after the dust settles I stay behind the large oak tree. I start to relax, and my body begins to not feel my heart thumping all over. The weight that was in my chest lightens and I continue to take breaths. He may be waiting a little way up the road and I want to be sure he is gone. After a little while, a couple of cars drive by and I decide that I need to get moving before the day is gone. I make sure I have Teddy and his arm and stand up. Instead of walking on the road I think I will stick to the woods. Dorothy's backyard will be visible from the trees and I can walk out and to her house then. I continue walking and I actually enjoy the stroll in the woods. It is beautiful here with the luscious green leaves filling the rustic trees. Birds are chirping and flying around. It really is a nice summer day. Besides it is not very hot in the shade.

A few minutes later I can see Dorothy's back porch. It has a table and set of chairs with warm welcoming cushions. The porch is surrounded by flower beds that have red flowers that she called Impatiens. Dorothy told me that they are her favorite and like to grow in shade. She let me help her plant them and she took the time to teach me how to take care of them so they would grow nicely. The memory makes me smile and I get excited. She is the one person I enjoy being around and she likes to take care of me. I know she won't hurt me and I know she is not a fake nice person. I meet a lot of fake nice people. People who say they care and say they will help me, but they don't mean it. A lot of these people get annoyed with me and give up on me. Last year at school I met many fake nice teachers and people who worked there. I didn't mean to be a bad kid, but it happened. I tried to be good for a little while but sometimes the dark and hot just took over and I couldn't help it. I try not to think about it and turn my attention to Dorothy's house.

Walking up the back porch, I hope she won't be angry with me for knocking on the back door instead of walking around. With a couple knocks, I hear faint footsteps that gradually grow louder followed by the sound of the door handle opening. The door opens and I see her face. She instantly lights up and her smile warms me and I feel at ease. Her eyes are full of kindness and caring. For that moment I forget my horrible night and morning, and my heart fills with smiles.

"Oh sweet boy, you frightened me when I realized someone was at the back door. But, what a wonderful surprise. I'm so glad you're here." Dorothy's voice was such a comfort to my ears. Then she quickly reaches for me and I jump back, the hot bubbles form in my tummy and freeze. "Oh, hunnybun, come in, come in. Can I make you some food?" Her voice is calm and she pretends she didn't notice my retreat. I walk into her kitchen, it is small and cozy. The table is a golden brown and is surrounded by four chairs. It smells sweet and welcoming. It is clean but not too clean and is a relaxing room. She walks in behind me and walks over to the fridge, picking up a pitcher of sweet tea. It is my favorite. She makes the best, it is not too sweet and is perfect.

She looks at me with knowing eyes, "I knew you would want some and made a fresh batch last night. And I have cinnamon rolls. Fresh this morning with my homemade frosting, made with love of course." She pours a cup, the one I always use, and then grabs a plate and puts a roll on it. She hands me the plate and cup and sits down at the table across from where I am standing. "Please sit and enjoy yourself." Her words are so kind, and I sit down and take a bite of the cinnamon roll. It is so soft and warm with such a yummy frosting, I can taste the love. "This is delicious, thank you," I tell her as I gulp down the cool refreshing tea.

"I ran into your mom the other day." Dorothy watches me over her coffee cup as she takes a sip. "I asked her about school and if you would need some clothes. My grandsons are about your age and I have some nice clothes for you that they don't wear anymore. And of course, I was out shopping and found some I knew you would like and bought them. Your mom said it was okay for me to give them to you. School starts in a few days so it's perfect you came over today." Dorothy waits for a response and sips her coffee. She is so kind. I think about how it would feel and how it would be to have her as my grandma. I picture it and it is warm and full of love and no darkness.

"Thank you, I haven't thought of school much. But Dorothy, I have a question for you." My voice sounds my age. I hold up my Teddy and the arm to show her. When I look at Teddy, my throat turns cold and hurts, I hope she can fix it. "Can you fix him? He is all I have," I sound desperate.

"Well, let me take a look at him." She grabs Teddy and the arm and gets a serious look on her face, then looks up at me. "Oh, well, I think I can. Yes. Yes. Come on, I'll show you." She quickly stands up and walks out of the kitchen into her dining room, then living room, and then off to the side is a smaller room. It is a bit bigger than a closet but not big enough for a bedroom. It is filled with fabric, and white envelopes with pictures of clothes on them. On one side, there is a table with drawers and on top sits a white machine. The room smells clean, and is warm, but very crowded.

"This is my sewing room, come in and we'll have to perform surgery on Teddy, but don't worry he won't feel a thing." She looks at me and giggles. I love her laugh. It is contagious. I giggle with her. She then takes out a doohickey with string on it and holds it up to Teddy. "This is a spool of thread, and it matches his color very well. We will put this on the sewing machine and feed the thread through here, and here, and here." She works fast and puts the thread through a few loops and holes and it ends up through a needle. "Now let's get him fixed." She grabs Teddy and the arm and starts the machine. She makes quick work of him and after a few minutes she holds Teddy up and he is all put back together. The sight of him makes me smile and before I know it I throw my arms around her and give her a huge hug. She hugs me back and says, "Well you are welcome my dear."

When I let go of her I grab Teddy and give him a squeeze. I am full of warmth with him in my arms, then I hear the doorbell. I jump and back up into the plastic totes full of fabric. "It is ok sweetheart, you are safe here." She looks at me with knowing eyes. Her words keep the darkness down, but I don't move. I hope he doesn't find me. Dorothy stands up and walks into the living room to her front door, I hear the door open, but I don't move. I continue to hold Teddy tight. Then I hear it. Her voice.

"Hello Dorothy, how are you today?" My mom sounds kind. "I was wondering if my son is here, he was gone when I woke up and I was worried." Mom sighs. Well I really don't believe that she is worried about me. She doesn't worry about me when he hits me. The thought brings the fire back to my chest and I feel the dark tugging at me.

"Oh, well yes he is here. We just fixed up his bear. But I was hoping to have him try on the school clothes I spoke with you about. Do you need him now or can he stay awhile and I will

give him a ride home after lunch? I really do enjoy his company." Dorothy's voice is serious and kind of sad at the same time.

"Well, I suppose. If he is bugging you just send him home.
Don and I are running to do some errands and will be home
later," Mom replies. I can't help but think of her words. Do I bug
Dorothy? I hope not, but I can make people crazy and mad, then
they leave me. The thought makes me cold and I frown, squeezing Teddy. I stay where I am, I don't want to see Mom.

"Oh believe me I thoroughly enjoy having him here and
he would never bug me. He is in the restroom. Are you okay
dear? Your face looks bruised." Dorothy's voice is serious and it
is that knowing voice I heard earlier.

"Yes, I am so clumsy sometimes and I slipped while washing dishes and hit my face. Banged up my elbow too," Mom
responds quickly and sounds very believable. "Ok, well Don is
waiting on me so I better get going, thank you Dorothy, I really
appreciate your help with the school clothes and for being so
kind to my family."

I hear footsteps and the door closes. I let go of the air that
I was holding in my lungs and take in another big breath. I am
glad that I didn't have to go with her. I hate going places with
them. They put on this fake act in front of others. They pretend
we are a happy family and that everything is perfect. I have to
act the part too and if I don't it makes him quite mad.

I remember one time we were at a restaurant and
the waitress made a comment, "I love how families spend time together, and it is obvious that

you guys are such a good family. That is hard to find nowadays." Her voice was all bubbly and annoying. After her comment I let out a laugh at the table and rolled my eyes. His eyes went cold and dark and as soon as we got to the car he smacked me across the face and threw me into the back seat. He told me not to pull a stunt like that again, and he didn't appreciate my attitude. It was awful. Dorothy's voice brings my attention back to her.

"Austin, I take it you did not want your mom to see you." There it is again, that *I know what is going on*, tone of voice. She looks at me with warmth and happy in her eyes. "You do not bug me, I love having you come see me. I get lonely sometimes. My kids are all grown and gone and I don't see them as much as I want to." Dorothy seems a bit lost in thought too.

"No, I didn't want to leave and I was worried she would make me go shopping with her," I tell her as I roll my eyes and smirk as I say shopping. She giggles. It makes me smile. She gestures for me to walk with her to the other room. "I want you to try on the clothes. But first, when was the last time you took a bath?" Her tone was serious and gruff. "Don't get me wrong, I don't mind having you here but you stink, and you do not need to be the stinky kid, especially when school starts." She smirks at me and laughs again. "And what happened to your head, you have a Band-Aide and there is some dried blood on your face?" Dorothy asks in a softer voice.

"I fell," I respond quickly. She looks at me with that knowing look. "I really don't remember the last time I had a bath," I say changing the subject. I take a sniff of my armpit and I do smell pretty bad. I need to remember to take baths. My real dad used to help me and we would have so much fun throwing bubbles at each other and I hear his laugh, it makes my heart warm. I try to hold onto the memory but remember that I am talking to Dorothy and need to pay attention. "Could I clean up here? I do stink," I tell her as I giggle.

"Are you sure you fell? It looks painful, after your bath I will clean it up and put some triple antibiotic on it for you." She doesn't give me a chance to answer her and walks into her bathroom and starts running water. I follow her and she asks me if I want a shower or a bath. I tell her a bath and without thinking I ask for bubbles too. She smiles and opens the closet door, pulling out a bottle of bubble bath, a towel, and a washcloth. She pours some soap into the water and starts sloshing the water around with her hands to make the bubbles bigger. After a few minutes, she turns the water off and turns to look at me.

"Be sure to wash all of your bits, including behind your ears. I will get some of your new clothes for you to put on when you are done." She turns and walks out of the bathroom returning with some jeans, a shirt, and some underwear. "These are new," she says as she holds up the underwear. "Now I want you all clean and smelling fresh! I am going to go start lunch, let me know if you need me. And here is the shampoo and the soap, use lots please." She smiles at me and leaves the bathroom, closing the door behind her. I take off my clothes and hop into the tub, the bubbles are so fun and I pick them up and blow them off my hand. It has been a really long time since I had a bath. Don says it is a waste of water and that I have to shower to save money. The last bath I had was before my real dad left I think. I really miss him. I close my eyes and remember the memory of him playing in the bubbles with me. He would grab the squirting toys and spray water on me. He had happy eyes and a big smile. I blow the bubbles again and a tear starts to fall down my face. Thinking of him is hard because it hurts my heart but also makes my heart happy.

I grab the washcloth and the soap and wash up, being sure to remember behind my ears. I pick up the shampoo and squirt some on my hand. She said to use a lot, so I dump out a bit more. The last time I used this much shampoo I emptied the bottle. Then Don tried to take a shower and the shampoo was gone. He came out of the bathroom in his towel screaming at me. He threw the empty bottle at me and called me a lot of cuss words. Mom just stood there and watched. I am sure she didn't want to get hit either. I finish up washing my hair and stand to grab the towel to dry off. I reach down to pull the plug and the water is a dark brown color. I was really dirty. I grab the clothes and start getting dressed. The shirt has a picture of Ironman on it. It is perfect.

I walk out of the bathroom and Dorothy smiles. "Oh goodness you smell so much better now," she giggles. "Let me have a look at that head, come on let's get it cleaned up." She takes me to the bathroom and dabs my head and puts some medicine on it and a new Band-Aide. "Hmm, must have been a hard spill because it looks bruised too," she responds without looking at me. I have the urge to tell her what happened but stop myself. I remember him threatening me before. He said that if I told anyone about him that he would kill my mom and me. The thought makes my tummy hurt and I try not to think about it. I decide to not answer her. She takes me into her extra bedroom and on the bed, there is a pile of clothes. "Well, now try this stuff on and if something doesn't fit or if you don't like it let me know. I am going to finish up lunch." She casually walks out of the room.

I try on the clothes that Dorothy says she got from her grandsons but most of them had new tags on them. I am guessing that is what she told my mom, so she would let her help with clothes. I am glad, I needed some new clothes. My pants were starting to look like shorts on me, and my shoes had holes worn in them. I love all of it. I don't get new stuff very much. I pick up a shirt and smell it, it still smells like the store. Dorothy bought everything I needed for school including my supplies. I am so excited about my new stuff. She even bought me an Ironman pencil box. A thought pops into my mind and I remember being in kindergarten and the kid next to me told me to shut up and I threw his pencil box across the room.

Suddenly, the darkness fills me and I sink onto the floor. I feel sick. I don't want to go back to school. School did not work for me. I am too much of a worthless shit to be in school. All the angry eyes and scared faces looking at me. I try to take a breath, but the air doesn't come. I close my eyes and think of Ironman. He could go to school and be a good kid and would have friends. I will be like Ironman in school and be good. I open my eyes and stand up. I really don't like school. I had what my teachers called a "challenging" time, at least that is how they told my mom. The look on her face made it worse for me. I don't want to be a disappointment to her, but I am. The thought fills me with a blue bubble. I am done looking at this school stuff, besides I am hungry.

"Thank you for all the clothes and school stuff," I tell Dorothy when I walk into the room. She smiles at me.

"Did you like the clothes? And I was excited to find an Ironman school box, I know how much you like him," she told me as she gestured for me to sit down. "I hope you are hungry. I made beef roast, fried taters, green beans from the garden and fresh sliced tomatoes. I also made homemade tapioca pudding for desert," she said as she handed me a plate and turned around to make her own. I look at the food and smile. I haven't had a meal like this in awhile. Mom doesn't cook much anymore, and I usually eat something from the microwave. I take a bite of the potatoes and they are so yummy. "These are delicious," I tell her as I take another bite of beef roast. She sits down and starts to eat. We don't talk much during the meal, I think my mouth is constantly full of food. It is the best meal. The tomatoes are sweet and juicy, I think they are my favorite summer food.

After we finish the yummy pudding I am so full I think I am going to pop. I ask her if I could have some food to take home to eat later. "Of course you can, I made extra just for that reason. I will get the kitchen cleaned up and then we will have to get ready to go. I told your mom I would have you home after lunch," Dorothy tells me with what looks a little sad in her eyes. "Here dear, take this bag and gather up all your new clothes in it. And here is a new backpack for you, you can put your supplies in it." She hands me an Ironman backpack with a smile.

"Thank you." I walk back into the bedroom and gather my new stuff. Maybe school will be better this year. I am going to a new school. I am glad. But it is scary too.

> I remember when my mom walked into the office to tell the office lady that I wouldn't be back. My teacher was standing in the office at the time. "Excuse me, Austin will be going to a different school next year, we are moving. Do I need to fill something out or do anything?" Mom asked them. When I looked at my teacher, it was the first time she had happy eyes. It hurt. She wanted to get rid of me. I knew she fake cared but to see it hurt me. I am a shit, and in the teacher's words "a dirty little rat." She called me this after I had what they called a meltdown. She was angry with me and her voice hurt. The thought bothers me, and I try not to think about it. I grab my stuff and walk back to the living room.

"Sweetie, are you ok? You don't look well," Dorothy's voice is soft. I want to tell her no I am not and that I don't want to go home and get hurt again. But I can't or he will kill us.

"I am okay, just tired. I didn't sleep well last night," I respond trying not to sound weird.

"Well, we better get going. I don't want you to get in trouble. Don't forget Teddy, he would be sad if you did, and I will carry this stuff," she picks up the bag of school clothes and the leftover food. I grab Teddy and squeeze him and grab the backpack. We walk to the car and without talking, she drives me home. As we pull up to my house, my heart sinks when I see his truck sitting there. He is back. I let out a sigh and open the car door. Dorothy walks to the porch and sets the bag and food down. She asks for a hug and I throw my arms around her. I try to put my thanks into that hug. Besides, I don't know when I will get another one. When I let go I feel like crying, but I hold it back. She waves as she climbs back into her car and drives away. I wish I could stay with her and take Mom with me. I have a feeling Dorothy could protect us from him. I turn to face the door. I hope he is in a good mood. Maybe he won't notice me, I will be as small as I can, and quiet. I take a big breath and open the door to the house.

CHAPTER 3

I am alone. Mommy is bleeding and isn't moving. "Mommy!" I yell for her. I can't move. I feel alone. Where is he? Why can't I see him? I close my eyes to listen for him. I take in a breath and it smells of beer and smoke. I hear it. His low raspy breaths. The darkness has me and I am surrounded by it, it hurts. I am cold. I open my eyes. All I see are his brown eyes, dark, mad. They wrap around my throat. "Mommy, help me, help me!" I can't breathe. "No! No!" My voice is faint and weak. I see my mom lying there empty, alone. I am cold. I am wet. I can't breathe.

I SIT STRAIGHT UP IN MY BED. MY TUMMY is full of bubbles, and I feel like I am going to puke. My heart is pounding as fast as John Henry in the books my real dad read to me once. I realize I was asleep and it was a nightmare. I close my eyes and go to my happy place. I am strong. He can't hurt me in my happy place. I focus on my breathing. My heart begins to slow down and the burning bubbles begin to disappear. When I open my eyes, I realize I am cold and wet. Oh no. I peed my bed. I hate when this happens to me. It seems like nightmares always end with me peeing the bed, especially the ones that have him in them. I think about going to check on Mommy, but I talk myself out of it because he might wake up. I climb out from under my covers and walk over to the pile of clothes on the floor. I can't turn on a light because I do not want to wake up anyone.

Well, I wouldn't mind my mom helping me right now. The thought makes me feel colder and I let out a sigh. I dig around until I find a t-shirt and shorts. I change out of my wet clothes and put on the shirt and shorts. I don't feel like looking for underwear. I decide to grab the top blanket that isn't wet and try to go back to sleep in the closet. I have less nightmares there. I pick up Teddy and climb over the boxes to my little cave. Squeezing him, I try to focus on my happy place. I am glad the nice counselor at my old school taught me to go to my happy place. After a couple minutes I doze off as Ironman flying through the clouds, strong and untouchable.

His voice pierces my ears and I jump up. He is yelling about being late for work. His voice is strong and fierce. "Where in the hell are my keys?"

I can hear a lot of shuffling followed by my mom's voice. "I am not sure, but Austin needs a ride to school today."

"That is not my problem. The little shit can walk. I am sure his ass will be kicked out by his lunchtime, and I ain't going to get him either, even if the fucking school calls, they can deal with him." His words stab right through my heart. He is right. I shouldn't try to go to school. I am shit and a terrible kid. The new school probably knows this by now.

"It is a new school and he needs to go. I start my classes today too," Mom's voice sounds hopeful.

"You don't need to go to class. I think it is bullshit and a waste of time. You will be just like your bitch son and quit after it gets hard." He sounds so hateful. Mom doesn't answer him. The door slams shut after a couple minutes and I hear his truck start up and leave. I feel sick again. I don't want to go to school. I hate it. I am just a disappointment to my mom, and school makes it worse. The thought makes my throat feel tight and cold. I know she is going to make me go and fighting it will make it worse. I walk over to the bag of new clothes and find the Ironman shirt and a pair of jeans. I put on the new shoes and go to the bathroom to clean up. Dorothy's words come to mind, "You do not need to be the stinky kid and need to bathe." I am glad I remembered to shower last night. I grab my toothbrush and brush my teeth. Looking in the mirror, my heart sinks. I have a bruise on my cheek. It was a couple days ago when he hit me last, but the bruise is still there. The thought brings the darkness to life and it crawls up my ribs.

He was drunk again. I was putting my school supplies in my pencil box and backpack trying to be quiet, but he got up and looked at me with hate in his eyes. He started yelling at Mommy for spending his money on me and he went after her. I am not sure what happened to me. I felt the darkness when I heard her screams but then it turned to a red hot fire in my chest and eyes. I watched him hit her. I went after him and kicked him in his nuts, and then I don't remember what happened. Next thing I knew, I was on the floor and my face really hurt. When I looked at him, his arm was bleeding. "You little fucker, you bit me," his voice was scary. I do not remember biting him. He came at me again, but I managed to get out of the way and I ran outside. I hid in the woods until the house was dark and snuck back into my room. By that time, he was lying on the couch surrounded by blue cans and my mommy was on the floor. She must have had too much of her mommy drink. She smelled really bad, but I covered her up with a blanket and made sure she had air blowing out of her nose.

"Austin, you have to hurry up and get ready for school," Mom's words bring me back from the thought. I answer her and finish brushing my hair. Looking at my face, I decide that I wrecked my bike and hit the handle bars. Yes. I think that will be believable, maybe no one will notice. I know better. The thought makes me tense. I did not like being questioned about it last year, and besides they didn't care what the answer was anyway. I picture my teacher's cold eyes and how when I walked into her room she would glare at me with them. Then she would walk to me with disgust and look down at me with her cold eyes and tell me she cared about me and was glad I was back. Her words always hurt me. I hope it is better this year and maybe they will not know how worthless I really am. I take in a slow breath and try to be strong. It is a new school and I picture it as a happy place where I can help others. This thought blocks the gray prickles in my tummy.

I walk out into the living room and look at my mom. She is clean. She looks different today and is dressed in her clothes she used to wear before she met him. I can smell bacon. The smell makes my tummy happy and my mommy is happy today too. This makes me smile. She is singing to herself and seems excited. I walk up to her and I am hoping for a hug from her. She looks down at me with happy in her eyes and my heart warms up. This is my mommy. The one I used to know. I stand still and wait for her to hold me and snuggle me like she used to do. I can almost feel her arms around me and her kiss on my cheek, I can't help but smile at her as I wait to have the familiar touch that I miss.

"Oh excuse me honey, I am making some lunch for my class today." Her words pierce my heart but when she steps around me, my heart breaks. She ignored me, again. I am invisible but the pain I feel is not. I feel myself turn cold and my eyes fill with tears. I quickly wipe them. Be strong. Be strong. "Here, there is enough for you to have some breakfast, and I will make you some eggs to go with it. I think we have eggs, let me check," she tells me as she fumbles around in the fridge. I am not hungry anymore, and my tummy feels like butterflies are flying around.

"Thanks Mom, but I am not hungry," I try to hide any sadness in my voice. "I need to get to school, are you taking me?" I watch her and wait for her answer.

"I can't, your dad left and I am going to be late for my first class today if I don't hurry. You can walk there, it is not far, just walk past Dorothy's home and keep going until you see it." Her voice is rushed. "And you should probably get going so you are not late." Her voice seems distant and she doesn't look at me. I can't help but feel alone. My throat is cold and blue and I turn away from her and let the tears fall from my eyes. I haven't seen my mom's smile in so long and then I do and it hurts me. I need my mom back. The thought is a spike in my brain and then I remember that, really, it is my daddy that I need back. If he was back then none of this would be happening. The thought sparks a fire in my heart and it hurts even more.

I turn and walk back to the room where my stuff is at and pick up my new backpack. I unzip it and stuff Teddy inside. I need a friend, and just knowing he will be close will help. I am not sure what time it is, and I can't tell anyway so I quickly head to the front door. Mom doesn't look up when I walk by and I try not to let it bug me. "Bye, Mom," I wait for my words to reach her. Her back is to me and she tosses up her hand in what I think is a wave. Oh well. I knew it was not going to be a good day, I just need to get it over with. The gray prickles are still in my tummy, and I can't help but want to run. I open the door and my feet take off and I do not slow down as I run down the driveway and onto the road. It is quiet and still kind of dark out. It is a crisp morning. The wind is calm outside. All I can hear are my feet moving the gravel on the dirt road. All I can feel is my heart thumping and my legs burning. My tears flow freely off my cheeks, and I don't try to stop them. Sometimes I feel better when I let myself cry, I can't very often but when I do it does feel good. I push myself as I run as fast as I can down the road. My legs are aching and hurt and my lungs are starting to sting, but it helps me to forget the morning and the thought of a hug from Mom.

Finally, I stop. My chest hurts and I try to slow my breathing down. I bend over with my hands on my knees. I feel it coming and puke all over the road, the gray prickles mixed with an empty stomach and running too hard put me over the edge. After a couple minutes I stand up and take a long breath in and feel a little better. I start to walk up the short driveway and when I see lights on I feel the prickles disappear. She is awake and I am relieved. I hope she doesn't mind me stopping by on my way to school. I will just tell her I wanted to show her the clothes. Then she won't know about my morning. I walk up the steps and take another deep breath as I push the doorbell and wait. My heart is still beating fast and I am thankful my tummy is feeling better. The door slightly cracks open and I can see Dorothy's face peek around to see who is knocking on the door. It only takes a couple seconds before the door flies open and her smile and happy eyes fill me up. Seeing the warmth on her face makes all my coldness and butterflies disappear.

"Sweet boy, what are you doing up so early today?" She peers down at me and pauses before speaking again. "Oh, nevermind why, come in, come in, I was just about to make some breakfast and drink my coffee. Please join me," Dorothy opens the door wide and gestures with her hand for me to come in. Her house smells like biscuits and it is warm and comfortable. I feel my muscles relax and the thumping of my heart lightens. I take in a deep breath and turn to look at Dorothy.

"I would love some food, but I need to get to school. It is the first day and I wanted to show you that the new clothes fit me," I tell her and pull out my shirt to show her. "I really like them, and I have all my stuff ready in my backpack. I am feeling nervous about school." The words are out of my mouth before I realize I said them. I didn't want to tell her how I was feeling. I need to be strong. Ironman doesn't feel nervous about stuff, and I can't be either.

"Oh, well of course you're nervous! You're starting a new school and it's a new year. And If I remember correctly you told me you didn't like school last year. I always feel nervous when I must go to new places and meet new people, it's normal. And I know just what will make those butterflies in your belly feel better, sausage gravy and biscuits! It's too early to go to school right now, and besides it's a long walk from here, and I'll take you." Her words are kind and she smiles at me as she leads the way to the kitchen and starts cooking. "It'll be a few minutes before the gravy will be ready." She turns and starts breaking up the sausage in the pan, it smells delicious. She starts to add some white stuff from a blue tub and then some flour. After a few minutes, she pours in some milk and continues to stir it. I love gravy. But the smell and the thought of it reminds me of the first morning that Don stayed at our old house, before we moved in with him after Daddy left.

Mommy was rushing around the house picking up all my toys and cleaning. I was watching cartoons and she told me that she had a friend coming over to meet me. I just sat there ignoring her watching my show. She asked me to be on my best behavior and that she didn't want to see any fits or I would have to go to time out. "Ok Mommy," I told her. The doorbell rang and Mommy said he was here. I remember being surprised when she said he. I moved the curtain on the window to look outside and there was a truck with stickers all over it. It was black and shiny. I quickly sat back down to watch my show. He walked into the living room with my mom.

"Honey, this is Don, he is a friend of mine that you will be seeing a lot of," she was smiling, more than I had seen her smile in a long time. I said hi to him and he walked up to me and peered down at me. I looked at his dark eyes and they were full of hate and seemed cold. I just looked at him. It was the first time I felt the darkness. It was like a warm swirly strange feeling that was new to me. I did not like it. I did not like him, but I froze and all I could do was stare at him. He was very different from Daddy and was scary looking. He spoke first and his voice was deep and strong. He asked how old I was, and I showed him three fingers. He continued to look down at me and the darkness started to hurt and finally Mommy asked him to come to the kitchen to help her cook.

After dinner was finished cooking, Mom called me to the kitchen. I had to eat at the table with Mommy and him. Mommy kept staring at him and smiling. The way she looked at him made a fire grow in my tummy. I did not like it. She looked at my daddy that way and I did not want her to look at Don. I remember him talking about his job. He worked to build houses and stuff for people who needed help. He told Mom he was driving the company truck so he could leave for work from our house. Mom giggled and replied, "I was hoping you would want to stay so I bought sausage for gravy and biscuits in the morning." Her words made the fire get hot and grow in my tummy. I didn't want him to stay here, I didn't like him. This was not his house. This was Daddy's house. Don needed to leave.

"You need to go home now," my voice was loud and I gave him a mean look. I felt hot. "Mommy, I don't want him to stay with us, this is our house not his. He needs to go away and not come back," I told her with a serious face.

"Austin, this is our house and he can stay if he wants to stay, and you will be nice." She used her "I mean it" voice. I let out a sigh and started crying and when I looked at him I remember seeing the mad in his eyes. They were scary and seeing the mad made the new dark in my gut grow and move up to my heart. Then he used this weird fake voice and he asked my mom if he could talk to me alone. I quickly looked at her wanting to tell her no but the words did not come out. My heart hurt when she said of course and left the table. He stood up and walked over to me. I was still crying. I looked at him and his eyes were dark and made me feel small. The new feeling swirled in my stomach and it made me cry more.

He bent down so only I could hear him. When he spoke his voice was different than the voice he used when mom was at the table. His words were slow, "Listen. You little worthless shit. I am staying. I am not going anywhere. You need to stay out of my way and stop the crying. Only pussies cry, so shut the fuck up and be a good boy, or a 'talking to' is not the only thing you will get from me." His voice was strong. His breath smelled like yuck and I wanted nothing to do with him. I stopped crying and didn't dare to move. It was the first time I felt small and the first time I was called bad words. He sat down and had his fake voice back when my mommy walked into the room.

I felt shocked and hurt and the new darkness took over me. I did not like it and I did not like him. The only words that came out of my mouth were, "I am tired." I just wanted to get away from him, I didn't want to look at him again. Mommy told me it could be bedtime and to go ahead and brush my teeth. She said she would come tuck me in and read me a story. I walked to my room without a word and brushed my teeth and waited. I picked out our favorite story to read together and waited. I picked up Teddy and held him and waited. She never came. I did not get tucked in. I did not get a bedtime story. And it was the first time that I cried myself to sleep since Daddy left. The first time I was on my own. Alone. Hurt.

"Austin, I think it's ready, will you grab the orange juice from the fridge and a couple of glasses?" Dorothy's voice brings me back from my thoughts and I realize I am super hungry. I grab the glasses and the juice and sit back down. She dishes up a pile of gravy and biscuits and sets a plate in front of me. She pours some juice in the glass and sits down with me and has a wide happy smile and caring eyes. "I'm glad you stopped by, but it worries me that you're walking to school when it's such a long walk for a young man," she says in a questioning way.

"Don left for work and Mom said she couldn't drive me because she was starting classes today too. I don't mind the walk, it isn't too far. Thank you for breakfast." I tried not to sound upset with my words.

"Well, how about this, you can walk here and I'll feed you breakfast and drive you to school," Dorothy said with a *this is not a question* tone in her voice. "I enjoy the company and I like to cook and it's hard to cook for only me."

"Ok, well I don't want you to be lonely," I giggled in response. I will enjoy my mornings more if I can look forward to having breakfast and talking to Dorothy. I warm at the thought and dig into my food. It is delicious and filling. I drink my juice and start to take my plate to the sink when Dorothy starts talking to me again. I was so focused on eating that I didn't think to talk during breakfast.

"Oh, well I suppose it's 'bout time to head to your school. First grade this year, do you know who your teacher is?" she asks.

"I don't know." The thought makes me start to have gray prickles in my tummy again. I don't want to go. I hope I can behave and not get into trouble. I don't want to be a bad kid, but I am such a worthless shit that it just happens that way. I think about how my kindergarten teacher would glare at me when I had a meltdown and I had to apologize to her. The thought makes yellow in my throat and I start to feel scared. "I don't want to get into trouble like I did last year." The words just fall out and I look at her. I don't want her to know the real me. I have never told anyone that before. I look down and hope I don't sound like a pussy like Don says I am. I don't want to go. I think about Ironman and his armor. I need armor to protect me too. I picture myself covered in steel and how I would be invincible from pain, angry eyes, disappointment, and from being a bad kid. I take in a long deep breath and look up at Dorothy hoping she doesn't see the real me. The worthless little shit I am.

CHAPTER 4

THE RIDE TO SCHOOL IS QUIET, BUT MY stomach is not. I try to distract my brain by looking around outside and try to focus to slow my heart. It feels like it is going to beat out of my body. With every thump, my body aches and I feel weak. I wish the school was not so close to my house. I can't do this, school is awful. Dorothy pulls up to the front of the building and I look at it through the dirty car window. The school seems big and made of red brick. There are a lot of kids with their parents walking. They all look happy and this makes me feel worse. The sidewalk is wide and leads to the front door. A hand railing and bushes are on one side and part of the building is on the other. The grass is green and the school looks clean and welcoming on the outside. But I know what is waiting for me inside, disappointment and angry eyes.

"Austin, you'll be fine. No matter how the day goes, I want to hear about it. Focus on the good stuff and I see your backpack is full. This tells me you're not alone today, and also I believe in you." Dorothy's words are shocking. She really doesn't know me very well and I will be a letdown to her. I don't want to hurt her and see her sad eyes look at me after she finds out about me. I don't have words. I feel small and worthless. I manage a smile for her and get out of the car. She waves to me as she drives away. I watch her leave and I wish I would have asked her to walk in with me. I don't want to be alone. I try not to think about it and turn back to the school.

I stand still, frozen to the spot. I watch as all the kids and parents walk past me. The more smiles I see the smaller I am. I can't hear anything but my heart beating. The darkness starts to grab me and tighten around my throat and I can't seem to move. I have the thought of running away and finding somewhere to hide. Just as I start to convince my brain to run, I feel something touch me. Don't touch me. Don't hurt me. The touch goes straight to my heart and hurts. I jump trying to get away, but I fall to the ground. My heart beats all over my body and the darkness fills my tummy and throat. Mommy. I need her. I close my eyes trying to make myself small and take in a deep breath. I hear someone talking to me and before I open my eyes, I shield myself like Ironman. I am strong. I can do this.

When I open my eyes, I look up to see who is talking to me. But no one is there, not standing up anyway. How weird. I look at this lady who is kneeling beside me. She is blonde and has green eyes. Her eyes seem different, not like ones I have seen before. They seem warm and caring. Not fake caring but like she cares about me. She doesn't even know me. What else is weird is she is wearing a red cape with a shirt with a lightning bolt on it. I just stare at this lady for a few minutes, she doesn't look like a teacher. What kind of crazy adult person would have a cape on? I am feeling mixed up and I want to say something to explain my reaction to her touch, but no words come to me. She smells good like flowers and yummy. I like this lady, and I am not sure why. Anyone who wears a cape must be a nice person or a little crazy. But I like it.

"I am sorry I frightened you, are you okay?" Her voice is soft and calming to my thumping heart. The darkness turns to gray prickles and lets go of my throat. Her voice seems to be safe, and she continues to look at me with her kind eyes. I have no words. I manage to nod my head yes and then she reaches for me again. No, don't touch me. I scoot back and try to keep the darkness away but it swirls up my throat again trying to choke me. Calm down, I tell myself as I take in another breath, continuing to look at the lady in a cape. I stand up and brush off the dirt from my new jeans and pick up my backpack. Teddy, I give the bag a squeeze and the thought of him pushes the darkness back down. I look at the weird lady and she is still kneeling looking at me. She stands up and takes a step back from me, but doesn't leave me. Her eyes continue to be kind and caring, and I think they seem to be more caring after my reaction to her.

"Hi. Welcome to Portland Elementary!" she says this with a giggle and a big happy smile. I can't help but smile back at her. "I am Ms. Jennie, the school counselor. Can't you tell?" and with her words she stands in a super hero position. I think this lady is crazy and I laugh at her. I like her. "I think you're new to the school this year, what's your name?" She smiles again and her eyes squint, like my mommy's eyes used to do. Her smile and her squinty eyes make me feel warm inside. I smile back at her, but I still can't get my words to come out. I hope she doesn't think I am stupid for not talking, I try to answer her, but my voice has left. "Well, since I am not sure of your name and our schoolwide theme this year is be your own superhero, and you have an Ironman shirt on, I shall call you *Ironman*!" Her voice changes when she says Ironman, making it sound deep and echo, it makes me smile more. She is funny. I have never met anyone like her before. "Ironman, class will be starting soon, can I walk you to your classroom and show you the way?" Her words make all my gray prickles go away and a weird bubbly feeling fills my heart. It feels purple and is snuggly. She slowly holds out her hand, but she does not try to touch me. She waits and I look at her hand and reach up and grab it with mine.

Ms. Jennie. This seems like a strange name for a teacher. Her hand is warm and firm but not too tight. She starts to walk into the school through the large gray metal doors. The doors open up into another room that leads to another set of doors. The second set of doors are old looking and wooden. She walks me through the wooden doors into the school area. It is big. Ms. Jennie stops to talk to some other students but does not let go of my hand. In front of me is a long hallway with a lot of windows and to each side of me are two more halls that do not have as many windows. This school feels huge and there are so many kids walking around me. The floor is shiny and almost looks like ice. It smells clean and feels warm. I start to feel small. As I look at the new school and the kids around me, I feel sick to my stomach. The gray prickles poke at my lungs. I feel the prickles move to my heart and into my chest and they hurt. I need to get away from here. I need to run and find somewhere to hide. As my body begins to move, Ms. Jennie's words reach my ears.

"Do you like the decorations? I made them myself to show off our theme. And show that everyone can be a hero!" She uses her other arm to show me the decorations around the area.

Her words seem to freeze my body to the spot and I squeeze her hand to see that she still has mine. I feel her squeeze back and the prickles shrink. Above each hall there are a lot of decorations that relate to superheroes. I really like the capes and lightning bolts that dangle from the ceiling. I can see that there are letters that dangle with the other decorations, but I cannot read them. To the side of the window hall a large bulletin board has pictures of superheroes with people's faces taped to them. It is funny looking. All over the walls are superhero word bubbles that I have seen in books. I wish I could read them, but last year I didn't learn much. "What do those words say?" I don't mean to ask that out loud but the words come out without hesitation. I look up to Ms. Jennie and she does not have a reaction to me speaking.

"Oh, well let's go have a look." She walks closer to the words and points to them. She said words like "Pow" and "Wham." Then she reads the words that hang from the ceiling: "Find the superhero in you," and "Be someone's hero today." I really like it. Maybe this would be a good school after all. I feel strong and she did call me Ironman. I am strong. The thought makes me smile and stand tall. I can be a hero like Ironman and be safe. I look up to Ms. Jennie and smile, "I like it." She smiles back at me and lets out another giggle. She seems to laugh a lot for a teacher. She seems happy. And she has happy eyes.

"Well, Ironman, I am not sure what grade you are in or whose class you are in. Do you know?" she asks me with kind eyes.

"No, I don't. I have never been here before," I say as I shrug my shoulders. "I am in first grade. I keep talking to her and she looks at me like I have important stuff to say. "My name is Austin."

"What a great name! Let's go to the office and find out who your teacher is this year, then I will give you a tour while I walk you to class," she says as she turns toward the door that leads into another room. The office I got to know well in the last school. I spent most days there, the idea of me being in here a lot makes me frown. As we walk into the office there are many kids and parents talking, smiling and looking excited. There is a long counter that is taller than I am and a small space to walk around it. Behind the counter is a lady sitting at a desk that has a bunch of stuff on it and the desk is really big. Ms. Jennie lets go of my hand with a gesture for me to wait on her and walks over to talk to the lady behind the desk. After a couple minutes, she walks back to me. "It seems you are in Mrs. Roush's class, room 22. Let's start to head that way and I will show you a couple things on the way."

Ms. Jennie starts to walk out the door of the office and I follow her. Many kids are hugging her and giving her high-fives while we are walking. She shows me the cafeteria and gym, then shows me where the bathrooms are. We continue to walk down the longest hallway and then she turns and says, "This is your hall, where your classroom is, but it is the last one waaaayyyy down there," she says the word way really slow and giggles again. She starts to walk, and I keep following her. I hope she can stay with me for a little while. When she stops we are standing outside of a classroom door, and she turns and looks at me with a smile. "Here it is, the best class in the whole school. You have the best teacher, but don't tell anyone I said that!" her smile is kind. She pushes open the door and walks in, and I follow her closely.

The room is bright with bulletin boards that go from the counters to the ceiling. The boards are colorful and have many characters all over with more words and letters. The room followed the superhero theme like the school lobby. The bulletin board by the door has words over pictures of superheroes with fluffy colorful flowers in the corner. As I am looking at the board, I notice my name. I did learn how to read and write my name. It is written on a little superhero character with the hand pointing up like it is flying and the cape is blue. I love it. I can't believe my name is on there. I smile and look around the room some more. The floor is wooden and shiny like the hallway. There are many desks that are wooden, and some kids are already sitting at them putting away supplies. In the front of the room there is a huge table and many white boards, and another table toward the back of the room. Farther back it looks like there is a rocking chair and the carpet area with tons of books all around.

I see Ms. Jennie talking to a tall lady with short brown hair. She is older and kinda looks like a grandma. She looks up and over at me and a smile fills her face. She reminds me of Dorothy and I smile back at her. I can't help but hope she doesn't see the worthless shit that I am. The thought brings the gray prickles back to my tummy. Behind where they are talking, the teacher desk is covered in papers and books. It looks like the lockers are behind the messy desk and many students are back there with some parents helping them put their stuff away. Watching the moms with the kids brings a blue bubble to my throat and I feel like I am going to cry. Mommy. I wish she would have brought me to school. I picture her smile from the morning and the thought of getting a hug from her. It makes me feel empty and I try not to think about it. I start to walk to the lockers to see where mine is so I can start to put away my stuff.

I am walking toward the lockers and can feel my heart beating and my head starts to hurt. Suddenly, a kid runs past me, pushing me into a desk and I fall to the floor. The darkness grabs me. My chest tightens and heart quickens. He is reaching for me. I can smell yuck and cigarettes and I don't know where Mommy is. I am alone. Mommy. The hand comes closer and I try to get away, but I am frozen to the spot. I start to see red. Please don't hurt me again. I am not sure what to do, I need to get away. I try to kick him. "Get away from me!" I scream as the darkness continues to push the air out of my chest and flames fill my eyes. "Don't touch me!" My heart is thumping in my head. I need to get away from him. I grab my backpack and Teddy. I don't want him to get hurt and I run. I run fast and don't look back.

I need to hide where he won't find me. I run as fast as I can to the end of the hall. I find a closet and run into it. There is a large garbage can on a cart and some boxes around it. I quickly climb over the boxes and get behind the garbage can. I pull some of the boxes to block me in and hide. I wait and listen. I need to be quiet. I pull Teddy from my bag. I hold him close. I try to take in a breath but the darkness blocks it. I hear footsteps. Oh no. Please no. There are voices. I hold my breath and stay very still. I squeeze Teddy and listen. I hear someone talking outside of the closet.

"I am not sure what happened," the first voice sounds scared, "he kicked at me and just ran, and I didn't see where he went."

"Something must have happened to cause him to run, and we need to figure it out after we find him." The second voice is new and sounds worried and in a hurry. "Goodness, the school day has barely started, and already a runner."

"I will keep looking in this hall if you want to check other areas of the school and the office," it is the first voice again.

I hear footsteps and they disappear. Then I hear a big sigh, and some movement. I close my eyes and shield myself. Ironman. I am Ironman and I just kicked a teacher. I am such a worthless shit. Now they know the real me. The terrible bad kid I am. The thought makes a tear come to my eyes. I do not want to see anyone. I do not want to see angry eyes and disappointment. I hope they can't find me. I squeeze Teddy and let the tears fall. The darkness is gone, and I am left empty and blue. I feel cold inside and try to take in deep breaths. As I am thinking about my breathing, I hear someone enter the closet. Oh no. Please no. The darkness grows, and I squeeze Teddy. I stop breathing again and freeze. Then I hear a voice. But is it not angry. It sounds a little sad, and maybe a little something else and I am not sure what.

"Ironman, are you in here? This is a good hiding spot, but it is a cleaning closet and is not so clean. And kinda smelly," she moves some of the boxes. "There is a handsome face. Can I sit with you? I am not going to touch you or hurt you. I just want to sit with you." Ms. Jennie's voice is calm and almost a whisper.

Her words are strange, I have never had an adult tell me they were not going to hurt me. I have a weird feeling about this and I am not sure what it is. I hear some more boxes move and I see her face. I look at her and she is on her knees. I look for the angry eyes, but they are not there. Her eyes are still kind and they look like they care about me. She slowly moves toward me, crawling, and sits next to me. She really is crazy. Her cape is still on and she just sits, and no words come. I am not sure what to say or do. I look at her and she smiles. As strange as it is, I like her, and the darkness disappears, and that bubbly purple feeling comes back to me. What a weird teacher, in all the times I ran and hid last year, no one ever sat with me. I remember them grabbing me and picking me up to get me out. But to sit? What a weirdo.

"You are a weirdo." Oh no, I didn't mean to say that out loud. I look at her and wait for her reaction.

"Yes, I think I am," and she starts laughing and I laugh with her. I like her laugh. It makes me smile. "Can you tell me about what happened?" Her voice is concerned, and I have to think before I give her an answer. How do I say that I thought that Don was about to hurt me and I had to get away so he wouldn't hurt me? I do not want her to think I am crazy. I am not sure what to say so I choose the easy answer. "I don't know," I say with a sigh. "I'm sorry." And I mean this, I really am.

"I am sure you are. How about we head back to class and you and your bear can get settled into your desk. I will stay with you for a little while before my class starts." Ms. Jennie holds out her hand and I glance at it and put my hand in hers.

"Teddy," I tell her. "This is my best friend, Teddy, my daddy bought him for me." The memory is vague, and it always makes me feel blue, but his smile when he gave me Teddy was the best. I picture his smile and it makes me feel warm.

"What a great name for him. Thank you for telling me." She squeezes my hand and we walk back to class without saying any other words.

When we reach the classroom door, I start to feel the gray prickles again. I really don't want to go in and see scared faces and angry eyes from the teacher. Ms. Jennie doesn't give me a chance to wait because she opens the door and pulls me through. The class is sitting around the carpet area and the teacher is looking at the calendar. The kids turn around and look at me and then the teacher stops. I hold my breath and wait for her to turn and show me the, "oh great here he is," look in her eyes. She turns and when I see her face it is filled with a smile and her eyes are happy and kind. This is not what I thought I would see and I let out my breath. I feel my body relax and I smile back at her. She starts to walk over and as she does, she starts to talk to the class.

"Class, I am so excited to have another new friend in our family. This is Austin and he will be joining us for our superhero activity I was telling you about! Austin, we were waiting for you to start our craft and get to know you activity. Ms. Jennie, I was just showing the class the calendar and explaining the routine, would you be able to take over calendar time while I visit with Austin?"

"Of course, I will, but I do not know the routine, so we will figure it out together," Ms. Jennie answers as she starts to walk over to the carpet area.

Mrs. Roush is tall, her hair is short, and she has on a dress that looks like jeans with apples on it. She continues to smile as she walks around some desks toward me. My heart starts to beat faster, and I feel the gray start to turn dark. I take in a deep breath and try to stay calm. There is nothing to be afraid of, she looks so nice. I repeat this in my head as she stops in front of me. She kneels down next to me, her eyes are kind, and they look caring. She smells good too. My kindergarten teacher had yuck in her mouth and when she would get close to me to talk, it smelled really bad. I hope Mrs. Roush doesn't have smelly breath and this thought makes me giggle and I smile at her.

"I was worried about you when you left the room. I am glad you are safe and came back to me. Can I show you your locker and help you get your things in your desk?" I am surprised at how much she seems to care about me, she didn't even meet me yet before I left. Her eyes are so kind and calm. My heart beat slows down and the dark turns back to gray prickles. Prickles I can deal with. I nod to her, she reaches for me, it surprises me, and I move away. She then shows me her hand, I reach for it, and we walk to the locker area. My name is on another superhero and it is taped in a locker, Mrs. Roush shows me my book box that sits in my locker. I take out my supplies and Mrs. Roush holds them while I hang up my backpack and put Teddy back inside. We walk to my desk and she shows me my name tag and then pulls out a book from the desk.

"This is a welcome to my class gift, I hope you like it." She says this with a smile. I look at the book and I can't believe she gave me a gift. The thought makes the bubbly purple feeling grow in my chest and I can't feel the gray prickles anymore. It has a picture of P.J Masks on it and it has a number one in the corner. I wish I could read it. The thought makes me frown.

"Thank you, I love it!" I tell her, and I have the urge to give her a hug but the darkness stops me. She smiles at me and puts the book back in my desk with my Ironman pencil box.

She then looks at me with a serious look that makes her eyes shut a little and talks. "I am glad you are in my class, Austin. I look forward to getting to know you and us learning to trust each other."

After her words, she stands and starts to show me the class and goes over her expectations and rules. I must have missed all this when I was gone. I didn't think I was gone very long but she has a lot to say about her rules and routines in the classroom. Man, I need to come back faster next time. She finishes telling me the bathroom procedure, which involves a cup on the desk and hand sanitizer, then she asks me to join the class at the carpet. I have a special spot on the letter D, which is on the carpet, and I sit down with the class. I don't feel like I missed anything, and it makes me feel like I am a part of the class.

"We are going to start our superhero activity. You are all going to get a blank paper and can draw yourself as your favorite superhero. Then, I want you to share with the class what part of the superhero or the superpowers would you want to have if you could. When I say the word go, I would like walking feet and safe bodies back to your desks to get started. Ready, and G-O spells go!" Mrs. Roush gave the word, we all get up, and I make sure to walk and be safe like she says.

I do not want her to see the real me. I need to hide what a bad kid I am. When I reach my desk, I get out my new crayons and they smell good. I don't want them to break so I leave them in the box. Last school year I didn't have my own supplies and had to use the teacher's all the time. I get my paper and know just what to draw. I start with red and then add in the yellow and the details. I am really concentrating on my drawing when I hear the teacher's words again. It is time to share our pictures and what we would want if we could have it. The first kid talks about Superman and how he wants to fly, and the next was

Spiderman and wanting to stick to stuff. I can't think of what I would want, and it is almost my turn. I didn't hear the last student and gray bubbles are in my tummy and I feel sick. "Austin, would you come up please?" Mrs. Roush asks me.

I stand up and walk to the front. I hold my picture up so the class can see it. "This is Ironman, he is my favorite cartoon and superhero. I really like to watch him when I am allowed to." A student in the class raises their hand and I do not know why.

"Gavin, do you have a question?" Mrs. Roush asks.

"Yes. I really like your picture. It is really good and really looks like Ironman. I have the action figure that I got for my birthday and I play with it a lot." Gavin's voice is excited.

"What a kind thing to say, Gavin, thank you. Austin, what is it about Ironman that you would like to have and why?" Mrs. Roush looks back at me with happy eyes. He likes my picture. I smile.

"I would want to have Ironman's armor because it would keep me from getting hurt." I say this before I can tell my brain to stop and look at the teacher hoping she didn't notice. She looks back at me. Knowing eyes. It is like she can read my mind, like Dorothy. She smiles and calls up the next student. I sit back down, and I am glad she didn't ask me anymore questions. I need to not say anything about home.

At my desk, I picture his mad face and angry eyes when he tells me not to tell anyone. "You little fucker, you better not tell anyone about what happens at home or I will kill you and your bitch mother." His voice is scary, and the darkness fills me up. Mommy. Is she ok? I hope she is ok. I can smell the yuck and his cigarettes. My heart is beating faster, and I put my head on my desk. It is cold on my face and it distracts me from the thought. I look up at the next student and the teacher is looking at me. Her eyes are kind and seem to really care, she likes me. I want to be a good student and not "challenging." She smiles at me and I hope her smile doesn't disappear when she sees the real me, the bad kid that I try to hide inside.

The day seems to go by really fast and I only had the one time I ran away, and I didn't hit anyone. I did notice that Ms. Jennie seemed to spend a lot of time with me. We laughed a lot and she helped me during class and played with me at recess which was my favorite. She even ate with my table in the lunchroom. Mrs. Roush is a great teacher and I really like her. As I pack up my backpack to go home, I am excited to come back, which is a new feeling when it comes to school. I only checked on Teddy a couple times today. Last year I wouldn't let him leave my desk and this made the teacher crazy, so a couple times in my locker is a good thing.

When it is time to line up to leave, Mrs. Roush says that every kid has to leave with a hug, high-five or fist bump. I watch as kids in front of me give her hugs and only one gives her a high-five. I am not sure what I want to do and when it is my turn I freeze. I just stand still looking at her. As she reaches for me the darkness starts to swirl and I quickly put my hand up for a high-five to protect myself. I want to hug her, but I can't. She says goodbye and I walk out of the room and head to the hall to walk home. It was a good day and I smile as I leave the school. Kids are running up to their parents and I can't wait to tell my mom about my new teacher and about my day. I am ready to come back tomorrow and as I walk down the road toward home I am feeling as strong as Ironman.

CHAPTER 5

I KNOCK ON THE DOOR AND I CAN'T HELP but feel excited to tell Dorothy about my first day of school. I only had the one time that I hid, and it really wasn't a big deal. They didn't even call my parents, which is the best part. I wait for her to open the door, but I don't hear anything, and knock again. Still nothing. She must not be home and it kind of makes my heart sink, but I can tell my mom. She hasn't heard a good report from school and I am excited to tell her. I hope she is still in a good mood like this morning. I turn and start to walk down the steps and out the driveway. It is a nice day because there is a little breeze that is keeping it from being too hot. My stomach growls and I realize I am super hungry and decide to walk a bit faster. A car drives by and the dust is thick and makes me cough, it is so dry this time of year. I step off the road and walk through the woods toward home. The trees and shade feel much better than the sun beating down on me.

I see home and my excitement disappears when I look at the driveway. It is empty, even Mom's car is gone. This is not normal, and it makes the gray prickles grow and swirl in my stomach. Oh well. At least he is not home, and Mom will be back soon I think, anyway. I go to open the door and it is locked. I do not have a key and it normally isn't locked. I will have to walk around back and climb through a window. I can't reach the window and need something to stand on, looking around I spot a white bucket and grab it. I carry it up on the back porch and flip it over. Carefully, I climb on the bucket and push open the dusty window. I can barely reach my fingers onto the window sill, but manage to get a grip and pull myself up and into the window. I fall through the window and hit the floor, scraping my stomach and legs on the way down. After standing up I see blood through my shirt and look at the scrape. It hurts. There must be a nail or something that I got stuck on. I get a paper towel and clean myself up then walk back outside to get my backpack. My tummy growls again and I am hungry.

I head to the kitchen and open the fridge. There is not much to eat, but it is full of the blue cans of beer. I don't even see any eggs or leftover food from Mom cooking this morning. I find a piece of sliced cheese and pull off the dried-up part and eat the rest. I give up on finding anything else in the fridge and walk to the cabinets. The cabinets are empty too, but I do find some crackers and some peanut butter. I grab a spoon and dig out the peanut butter from the bottom of the jar and spread it onto the crackers. I should not have eaten all the frozen waffles.

Oh well, these will work. I head to the living room to watch T.V. and enjoy the crackers. I like watching cartoons when Don is gone, I can't when he is home unless he is asleep from being drunked. One time he was drunk, and I pulled the remote from his hand and he never woke up.

It is starting to get dark outside and my mom is still not home. I am feeling tired and hungry and decide to go back to the kitchen and dig through some stuff to see what I can find. I open the freezer and dig around, most of the stuff I can't tell what it is but I find what looks like a Hot Pocket. I open it up and pop it in the microwave. I have no idea what is in it, I guess it will be a surprise. I grab Teddy and walk to the back room and find some pajamas to put on and change out of my school clothes. I hear the microwave beep and it makes my tummy growl. I hurry to the kitchen and grab it out and put it on a plate to cool off. I decide to get a glass and pour some water in it and eat in the back room. I am not sure where Mom is and I feel like it is getting late. I pick up the glass and the plate and start to walk when I hear a car pull into the driveway. When I see the lights, I run into the room and climb into the closet and close the door. I hope it is not him, but I can hear the sound of his truck.

I move some of the boxes and run back to the room to grab Teddy. I freeze when I hear the front door slam shut and the pictures fall to the ground. I really don't know why Mom keeps picking them back up when they fall every time he opens the door. I jump back into the closet and slide the door closed. I don't want him to see me. I move a box and try to block where the closet door slides to jam it closed. Then I move and do the same to the other side and hope he doesn't try to get me. I climb into the corner and hold Teddy while I listen. My heart starts to beat faster, and the darkness has its grip on me. Mommy, where are you? I need you. I try not to make a noise and I feel like the closet is spinning. His voice is mad, and it echoes in my ears. I can't breathe, and the darkness is choking me. I force my chest to inhale and try to be invisible.

"Where is that bitch! She is not answering her fucking phone. Damn it!" His voice is scary, and I hold Teddy. I can hear the fridge open and slam shut then his footsteps coming down the hall. Please no. No, no. My chest gets tight and I can feel the darkness continue to squeeze my throat. My heart is beating throughout my body and I can feel each thump. I close my eyes and go to my happy place and I picture Ironman standing on a building overlooking the city. He is strong and protected. I picture myself covered in his armor and I open my eyes to the sound of his voice.

"Are you here you little shit? Where is your mother? I got a call from school today. You worthless fucker. It will only be a matter of time before they kick you out." His words hurt me. I didn't think that the school called them today. "Always hiding in that closet like I don't know you are in there, stupid kid." I hear the closet door move and it hits the box and blocks it from opening. I gasp in air and try to make myself small and invisible. The door hits the box again and slams into the other boxes. "Oh, you fucker, I am going to get in there so open the damn door." I close my eyes. I am strong, I am strong. He tries again with more force and it squishes the box some and I can see his dirty grimy hand reach through. Don't touch me. Please don't touch me. He can't reach me.

"Oh, Fuck it!" These words are fierce and then I hear a smash of wood by my head. His fist breaks through the door and chunks of the closet door shatter on me. I am wet. Mommy. I need Mommy. Daddy. I need my daddy. I start to cry, and tears are falling when another hole comes through the closet with his foot. It smashes into me and the pain pierces through my body. His face is dark, and his eyes are empty and cold. "NO!" I plead. "I had a good day!" My voice cracks and I shield myself as his scarred face looks down on me. I can't breathe and this time it is his hand that is choking me. It tightens around my throat and he lifts me off the floor. I grab his arm with my hands to try to free myself. I kick him over and over and then he throws me into the wall. I hit hard and fall to the ground. I am not Ironman. I am a worthless shit. I look at him and he is scary. He picks up his beer to his mouth and drinks it gone, then squishes the can in his hand. He smells like yuck and dirt.

"Where is your mom?" he yells at me. "Fuck! Answer me!"

"I don't know, I don't know! She was gone when I got home," I plead. My voice is weak, and I am crying. I hope he leaves. I hate him.

"Shit," he yells and without warning he lifts his hand and I see hate in his eyes. I try to block the hit with my arm, but it doesn't help. The back of his hand hits my face and I hit the floor again. I try to make myself invisible and be small. I am crying, and I can't help it. "Stop crying you pussy and get up.

Get up!" He is angrier than I think I have seen him. I am not sure what to do and I freeze. He grabs my hair and closes his dirty fingers into a fist and lifts me to my feet. I stop crying and stand tall. I hate him. I feel the darkness turn to red. I run at him, kicking him in the nuts as hard as I can. He lets out a yell and punches me in the stomach, I hit the floor and puke. I don't dare move and he spits on me and leaves the room. I am a worthless shit and I start to cry. The tears flow down my face and I can't stop them. Mommy. I need my mommy. I curl up into a ball and don't dare to move. I don't want him to hurt me more. I wait. I wait, and it seems like a long time. I am cold, wet and I hurt. All over.

I hear him moving around and then I hear the slam of the door and footsteps down the porch. I am so relieved, but I hold my breath. His truck starts up and the sound echoes in the room as he drives away. When I can't hear his truck and I can't see the lights I let out my breath and continue to cry. I am hurt, and I have owies all over me. I am cold and wet. I stand up and I am covered in pee and puke. I am alone and cold. I take in a big breath and walk to the bathroom. I carefully take off my pajamas and climb into the shower. I let the warm water wash over me and I cry, I am so terrible. I should not have stayed here when Mom was gone. I quickly wash up and turn off the water. I wrap up in a towel and head to the back room. I toss the towel over the puke and find some clothes to put on. I try to clean up the puke as best I can. The towel is really gross, and it is now covered in vomit. I carry it to his room and rub it all over his pillow. I hate him. Then I toss the puke towel under his bed stand and leave it there. I hope it stinks up his room.

My closet is nasty, it is wet and smelly. There are sharp pieces of wood all over the floor and all over Teddy. I also peed my pants and the floor is covered in pee. I try to clean it up and get a splinter in my hand. Shoot. I am a mess. I go back to the bathroom and look in the mirror. Such a shit. My face is already bruising. I sigh. I have no idea what I am going to say to cover it up. I look at my side where he kicked me, and it is bleeding and scratched up from his shoe and the closet door. It hurts to touch it, and my tummy hurts too. I just sit in the bathroom and look at myself. I want to run away and hide where he can never find me, but I don't know where that would be. If I left, then I am not sure what would happen to Mommy. I climb down and walk back to the room. I pick up Teddy and put some new blankets in the closet. I move the boxes around to cover the holes in the door. I pick up my Hot Pocket. It is cold and covered in wood pieces. I clean it off and eat it. It is a pizza one, I like the pizza ones.

I cover up with the blankies and snuggle Teddy and try to go to sleep. I feel lost and alone. I don't understand where my mommy is, and I am alone. I hold Teddy close and I cry again, I will need to think of a reason for my face before I go to Dorothy's tomorrow and for school. I think I will say that I tripped and fell down the stairs and I hit my face on the stairs. Yes, that will work I think. I practice it in my head so that I sound believable and make sure my story doesn't change. After what seems like a long time, I start to doze off and fall asleep.

"Mommy, where are you? I lost my mommy can you help me?" I am in a large building with people all around me and they are all ignoring me and walking past me. Someone runs into me and I get knocked over. I hit the ground and the darkness fills me. A hand reaches for me through the crowd. "No, don't touch me, don't touch me! Let me go, let me go!" The hand grabs me, and I am being dragged across the ground through the crowd. The crowd disappears, and the hand throws me into a hole and I am falling, falling, I can't catch myself. I am empty, alone, and I hit the bottom. I fall in water and I am wet. I can't swim, please help me, help me. I go under and sink down, I can't breathe. I see dark and another hand. I am getting pulled up and when I get pulled from the water there is a person with a cape on and they disappear.

I sit up fast and gasp. Looking around me I realize that I am in my closet. I am wet. Again. Dang it. I hate nightmares. Ouch. I am really sore and ache all over. I can't remember being this sore after him hurting me. I stand up and a pain shoots through my side and makes me wince. I carefully and slowly walk out of the closet and find my school clothes. I am not sure what time it is, but it is still dark outside. I slowly take off my wet clothes and put on my school clothes. With every move I hurt, and pain is everywhere. Maybe I will stay home from school today. I could avoid the questions and avoid needing to lie. But for the first time in my life the idea of missing school makes a blue bubble in my throat. I take in a deep breath and grasp my side, even breathing hurts. I need to go to the bathroom, but I am not sure if I am still alone or if he is home.

I walk quietly and slowly down the hall and past his room. I can't hear anything and keep tiptoeing to the living room. I carefully climb on the couch and look out of the window. The driveway is lit by a light on the front porch. No cars. I am still alone. I don't know where my mom is. I hope she is okay. I am glad he is gone. I don't have to be sneaky and head to the bathroom. I turn on the light and use the bathroom then look in the mirror. My face is really bruised, and my eyes are puffy. I pull up my shirt and my side is bruised too and has scratches on it. My neck is red looking and I look rough. I am not sure that any story will be able to cover it up. The thought makes me blue and I try not to think about it. I don't want to stay home in case he comes back, and I am still here. But I don't want to go to school and get questioned either. Either way it is still early, and I want to go back to sleep. I walk back to the room and find some blankets that are not wet and make a bed on the floor. I close my eyes and try to think of good thoughts like my daddy's laugh and smile. It makes me warm and I fall asleep.

Mommy. Her screams bounce off the walls and shake my brain. I jump up and look around. I am not sure what time it is or what is going on. I hear voices, but I am groggy from just waking up. My body hurts, and I grab Teddy.

"You can't just do whatever the hell you want, and you didn't even call or answer your damn phone. Where the fuck were you last night? Answer me!" His voice is scary and angry. He sounds dangerous and the darkness wraps around me. Mommy! Please don't hurt her. The thought makes me blue. I need to do something. I feel frozen to the spot and squeeze Teddy close. Mommy's voice fills my ears. She is crying and sounds scared.

"I went out with new friends from my class and lost track of time, I am sorry. I drank too much, and my phone died. I didn't mean to be gone, I am sor..." Her words were cut short by a smacking sound followed by her screaming again. I hear some stuff fall to the ground and then a thump that makes the trailer shake. I have to help her. I have to protect her. I close my eyes and shield myself. When I open them, I am strong, and I can stop him. I look around the room to find something but there is not much. I look at the closet door and the wood is broken enough that I can pull off a stick from it. It will have to work. As I pick it up, her screams fill me and the darkness turns to red and a fire builds in my chest and my eyes. My hand grips the chunk of the closet door and I take in a deep breath and picture myself as Ironman. Strong. Protected.

I walk out of the room. I can't hear anything except my heart beating throughout my body. I see him, and he has Mommy shoved against the wall choking her. Mommy's eyes are big and scared, and she is trying to get him off of her, pulling at his hands around her throat. Her scared eyes see me, and they get bigger; I pick up the chunk of wood and run at him aiming for his head. The wood stabs him in the side, and he releases my mom. I watch her fall to the floor and tears slide down her face. She pulls her knees to her chest and holds them, crying and struggling to catch her breath. Don, holding his side where the wood stabbed him, turns and stares at me. As I watch him step toward me, my Ironman protection disappears. I am not strong. The darkness wraps around my everything and I feel burning in my chest. His arm moves toward me with hate pouring from his eyes as he picks me up. I am such as shit. I close my eyes and I can only feel black all over my body and my heart pumping. I am invisible. I picture myself happy and laughing in my head and try to not feel the pain of his hands, as everything goes blank.

The sun is hot and is peering through the living room window onto my face. I open my eyes and feel lost. I am not sure where I am until I look around. I am on the floor beside the couch and I must have landed here and did not move. I am afraid to get up. Mommy. Thinking of her scared face makes tears fill my eyes. I want to run away with her and never come back. I listen and can't hear any movement, I am not sure if I am alone or not. I kind of hope I am alone but my heart hopes my mom is home to take care of me. After a few minutes, I decide to get up and my whole body hurts. It hurts to breathe and to move. I move myself to look out the window to the driveway and it is empty. I am alone. I don't know what time it is, but I do know I am hungry.

I walk slowly to my room and pick up Teddy and squeeze him, replaying my mom's screams in my head. Tears fall down my face and I am scared and hurt. I decide I need to go to Dorothy's house and eat, and I walk out the door and start off the porch. I don't have shoes on and the rocks hurt my feet and I have to turn back and get my shoes. I can't believe I forgot shoes. I really am a worthless shit. I take a breath and it pierces my chest and back. I slip on some sandals and, carrying Teddy, make my way down the dry dusty gravel road. I can feel every step and hear everything around me. I hear a rustle in the tall grass in the ditch and I jump sideways, my heart thumping into my ears. A rabbit. I freaked over a rabbit. I am not Ironman, I am weak, and I need my mommy.

CHAPTER 6

THE SUN IS REALLY BEATING DOWN AND I am sweating all over by the time I can see Dorothy's house. It is really hot, and I am not sure of the time, but I think it is late. I probably should have looked at myself in the mirror before leaving the house to be prepared for what I look like. But I don't think that I care what I look like. A part of me wants to tell someone so they can take me away, but what would happen to my mom? I try not to think about it. My stomach is growling at me and my head really hurts. I reach Dorothy's porch and take a breath, hoping she is home. I start to knock, and I can hear footsteps walking through her house and I squeeze Teddy close. The door opens, and her smile lights up her face when she sees me and quickly disappears. I know I must look bad, and I have to tell her something because she is going to ask. Her kind voice fills my ears.

"Oh, sweet boy, you look awful. I'm so glad to see you though, I was getting worried. It's nearly noon, and I was wondering if you were staying home or skipped my house and went to school." Her voice is worried and sweet. Her eyes are knowing and caring.

"I had a rough night and slept in so long that I'm late and didn't have time to eat or clean up," I tell her with a smile.

"Come in, come in. I'll make you some food. What would you like? Breakfast or lunch?" She is asking this as she quickly walks into the kitchen and I follow her holding Teddy close.

"Both," I respond as I giggle. The giggles hurt, and I wince. She looks at me and I can see her concern and ignore it. "I'm starving." I try my best to smile.

"Of course, I'll make brunch! And while I'm cooking you need to go clean yourself up, and really you could take a quick shower. I have a few more clothes I found for you that you can wear. You smell a bit rough, and you know I don't like stink." She laughs and heads for the cabinet pulling a pan to put onto the stove.

"Thank you." Those are the only words that I can say, but I have so much to say to her. I stand there watching as she digs through her fridge and cabinets to make me food. She really does care about me. I turn and head to the bathroom dragging Teddy behind me. I set Teddy down and looking at him makes me feel thankful that my real daddy bought him for me. I close my eyes and think of his eyes and the love he had for me. I miss him. If he were still here I would not be getting hurt, he would take care of me. I feel a blue flame flare up in my heart

and it turns to red, why did he have to leave me? I try not to
think about it.

I look into the mirror and I can see why Dorothy's smile
disappeared so fast. I look terrible. My eye is black and swollen
and I have a cut on my cheek with dried blood. My ear even
has blood on it and I think it looks like I am missing hair
above my ear. I have no idea what to say happened. I feel like
a car wreck would explain how much I hurt, but I don't think
that would be believable. I close my eyes and hear Mommy's
screams and the darkness grows and consumes me. My chest
hurts and burns inside, and tears fall. I hate him. I do not remember much after he threw me into the wall when I stabbed
him with the stick. I do remember hitting the floor but I know
I did not move from there. My mind is full of gray bubbles and
I am not sure what happened to Mommy last night. I couldn't
keep her safe from him. I am not Ironman, and I feel weak and
helpless. I wish I had someone to take care of me. The thought
makes me fill with blue and tears continue to fall.

I am a shit and I wipe the tears from my eyes. No wonder
I get hurt, I can't even keep Mom safe. I deserve to be hit. The
thought hurts my heart and I turn on the shower to try to wash
away the pain that I am covered in. The water is warm and
calm. It rolls down my shoulders and does make me feel better.
I get all cleaned up and put on the clean clothes that Dorothy
left for me. I can smell the food from the bathroom and my
tummy growls at me. I look in the mirror again and take out
some of the stuff that girls put on to try and cover up my eye.
It is like mud and smells weird. Mom did this once last year to

cover up a black eye that he left on me. It did help then, but the questions still came. I layer up the stuff and then take in a breath, it hurts but the smell of food distracts me.

I pick up Teddy and walk into the kitchen and she has a lot of food ready for me. I smile at her but she doesn't say anything. I sit down and start piling food on my plate. She has cheesy grits and smoked sausage, creamed peas, warm rolls, fruit, and what I think is a cheese omelet. Words can't say how thankful I am to eat. Most of the time we have food at home but when we don't, it is awful. I shovel in the grits and they are perfect and delicious, and my tummy is happy. I think of my mom when she seemed happy about class. I can't believe it was only yesterday when it feels like weeks ago. I miss her smile, and when she took care of me. I look at Dorothy and she is watching me with a serious look on her face. I can't help but wonder if she would let me live with her. Her food is really good. I am starting to feel full but finish the food on my plate. Don gets really mad if you don't finish all of the food on your plate.

I chug down the chocolate milk that Dorothy makes for me and when I put the glass down I know the questions are about to come.

"Austin, what happened to your eye and head?" Her voice sounds different and I think her eyes look teary. I am not sure what to say and I just look at her. Mom's screams come back to me and tears start to fill my eyes. I can't let myself cry in front of her or she will definitely think something is wrong with me. I want to tell her about him, but I am afraid he will hurt us more.

"I was climbing a tree and grabbed a branch that broke, and fell, and my head hit the branch below it and fell." I have no idea how I thought of that story and I hope it sounds true. But then again, I hope it doesn't. I wait, and I continue to look at her. Knowing eyes. There they are again. She knows already, I should just tell her, and the words fill my mouth but before they can come out the darkness grips my neck and chest. I freeze, and her voice makes the darkness lighten and let go of me.

"Well, I'm not sure I believe you, but if that's the case then you need to stop climbing trees. And I see you found my make-up?" She is so serious, and this shows that she knows about him. I bet Dorothy would protect me from him, she seems like someone who has secret powers.

"Yes. My mom taught me about how to cover up a black eye. Thank you so much for the food. You're the best cook and I was starving," I tell her as I smile, hoping to change the subject.

"You were very hungry; do you have food at home?" Her voice seems warmer now. This is not a question that anyone has asked me before. I decided to be honest with this one.

"Not that much. Sometimes we do and then it's gone. I'm hoping that they go shopping soon." This is the truth and I feel lighter and my chest seems easier to breathe.

"Oh sugar, I'll be packing food for home. Now that you're fed, let's get to school. It's important to be at school, so you can get an education. Actually, how was your first day?" her voice is back to normal and seems happy.

"It was great! I tried to stop by to tell you, but you were not home. The teachers were all nice and friendly and Ms. Jennie went to recess with me and played with all of the kids. I only had one issue and it wasn't a big deal really. I'm ready to go back." I smile as I am telling her about it. It is the truth, I am ready to go back, I really liked it there. The thought of seeing Mrs. Roush and Ms. Jennie brings a purple bubble to my chest and I feel calmer. I am glad I came to Dorothy's today and smile at her.

"I'm so glad your day went well! And I bet today will be even better. It's getting late, but you still have time to go to school and before the afternoon recess! Maybe the teacher will play with you again!" Dorothy says, as she grabs her purse and her car keys and walks to the front door.

I grab Teddy and follow her. I realize I did not bring my school stuff and the thought brings back the darkness and gray bubbles form in my tummy. I start to feel sick to my stomach and try to calm my body down by taking deep breaths. I can do this, I can do this, I keep telling myself this. I follow Dorothy and close my eyes to shield myself as I climb into the car, my body aches as I sit in the seat. I let out my breath and feel a little better about going to school. I will just stick with my story of falling from the tree when the questions start coming. The car is musty, but clean and the seat feels soft under me. I look out of the window and there is a layer of dust stuck to it and it is hard to see through. I hope that I do not get in trouble for not having my backpack with me. I think I was kind of hoping to stay with Dorothy today and not go to school. I look at her and smile and she smiles back and I feel warm inside as we pull up to the front of the school.

I hug Teddy, open my door and turn to say goodbye to Dorothy, but she is out of the car and walking toward me. How strange, I am not sure what she is doing, and gray prickles start filling my tummy again and it hurts. I look up at her and she sees through me, I hope she doesn't see the real me, the bad kid that I am inside.

"I would like to walk you in today if that's ok with you?" Her words are happy and kind, and they make the bubbles start to go away. I have never had anyone walk into school before, unless the principal made them of course.

"Ok, I'll show you my room!" I feel happy as the words come out and I grab her hand without thinking about it and head inside leading her to the office to check in. The lady behind the desk looks over and smiles at us. Her smile is warm and makes purple fuzzies fill my tummy. She is kind of short and has big hair and a flowy colorful shirt. Her glasses sit on the end of her nose as she looks at me and her eyes are kind and happy. She seems much nicer than the office lady at my other school.

The other lady's name was Mrs. Ellenor and she was so mean to me. The thought reminds me of a time that I had a meltdown and the teacher said she couldn't deal with me anymore. She called the office and the principal came down and carried me out of class. The principal had dark angry eyes and she did not like me. Sometimes she would fake care about me when she was trying to get me to calm down. When the principal carried me into the office, Mrs. Ellenor let out a sigh and rolled her eyes at me and I heard her say, "Oh great, here we go again." It made my body feel blue and gray and then I remember her telling the principal that they should have a place to send kids like me and that I needed a good spank and I wouldn't act that way anymore. Which I did not need a spank, what I needed was my mommy back and to not get hit anymore. I was such a bad kid there and I had trouble with what they called "self-control." I hated going to school there and seeing the disappointment and anger in everyone's eyes. The thought makes me feel sick and I try not to think about it anymore.

The office lady's voice brings me back from my thoughts. "Well hi there Austin! I'm so glad to see you today! I'm Mrs. Marsha, the school secretary." Her smile is big and her voice is so sweet and really seems happy to see me.

"Hi! This is my friend Dorothy, can I show her my classroom?" I ask her with a smile.

"Of course, you can, here's a slip to let your teacher know you checked into the office." She hands me a piece of paper with words on it, but I can't read them. I really want to be able to read and the thought makes my smile disappear.

"Would I be able to talk with the principal or the counselor after I see his classroom?" Dorothy asks Mrs. Marsha. This question brings back the gray prickles in my tummy. Why does she want to talk to them, does she know about the true me? The bad kid, I am such a shit. I look at her and I want to ask her why, but I can't find my words, they are stuck in my brain. The gray prickles make my tummy sick and I let go of Dorothy's hand, and take in a deep breath.

"Yes, I'll see if I can find one of them for you." Mrs. Marsha's voice seems more serious.

Dorothy spun around to walk out of the office, but I was frozen. I couldn't get myself to walk and I am not sure why. I watch as she walks out of the office door and then she turns to talk to me and I am not there. She looks at me and her eyes are kind and caring, she walks back to me and kneels down.

"I only want to ask about the rules for me visiting and bringing treats since I'm only a friend." Her words are a relief to me and the gray prickles pop and start to get smaller.

I smile at her and start to walk toward my classroom. I show Dorothy the superhero things hanging on the walls and pretend I know what they say. I lead her down the long hallway and then show her where my classroom door is with my name on it. We walk in and the kids are coloring at the desks and the teacher is sitting at the front table with a student. Mrs. Roush looks up and I wait for the disappointment in her eyes that I am here, but when she looks at me a smile takes up her face and she gets out of her seat. Her eyes are kind and happy and they seem like they are happy because I am here.

"Why hello there sweet boy, I'm so glad to see you. I was worried when you were not here this morning." She is still smiling and reaches out to give me a hug. As her hands reach for me, I can see his slimy fingers and I can smell his stink and yuck of beer and cigarettes. The darkness quickly squeezes my chest and is wrapping around my neck, I feel like I am choking. No, don't hurt me, don't touch me. I quickly move backward away from his hand and I trip over a chair and fall. My body hurts all over and I can see the hate fill his eyes as he looks down on me. He disappears as Dorothy's words find my ears and her words bring me back to the classroom. Mrs. Roush and Dorothy are both looking at me with concern and care in their eyes. I have a hard time wanting to move because of the pain filling me, but I slowly stand up trying not to show it. I am not sure what to say. I take in a deep breath and the darkness lets go of me. I look at them and simply say I am sorry.

"Oh Austin, don't be sorry, I should always ask before I hug you, that's just good manners and sometimes I get excited and forget, so I owe you an apology." Mrs. Roush tells me this and she still has happy in her eyes and a smile on her face. I think she really does care about me. She turns to the class and in a calm voice says, "Class, class." Then all at once the students say "yes, yes" and freeze with their eyes on Mrs. Roush. I must have missed this instruction today while I was gone and I want to remember what to do next time she says those words. I really want to be a good kid this year and I don't want Mrs. Roush to see the shit I am.

The kids were all listening and seemed to be calm as she spoke the next directions. "You may clean up your areas and get ready for recess. I'll know you are ready when you're in line order and quiet." As she said this the class started to put away their supplies and head to make a line. I have never had a line order before and wonder what it is. I stand and wait because I want to introduce Dorothy to Mrs. Roush and I am not sure what line order is and need to ask her. As I watch the other students put away their supplies, it reminds me that I left my backpack at home and gray prickles form in my tummy again. I do not like my tummy to feel all yucky, but it seems to happen a lot. I take in a breath and tell myself it will be ok and that school is almost over anyway. I am focused on my thoughts when I hear Mrs. Roush's voice again and it reminds me to focus.

"Ok class, walking feet out the door and be kind at recess." She tells everyone this as she is holding the door. After she takes the class to recess she turns back to me and smiles again. "Austin you missed some important procedure things today so I want to catch you up before you head outside." She kneels down next to me and tells me about what I need to do when she says class, class. Then she explains that I am number 2 in line order and that will always be my spot unless it is my special day and on my special day I will be the line leader. This is different, and I find myself feeling good about knowing where I will be in line.

"Mrs. Roush, this is my friend Dorothy. She's here to see my classroom." I smile as I introduce Dorothy. Mrs. Roush reaches out and shakes Dorothy's hand and they say hi to each other and then she turns back to me.

"Austin, what happened to your face?" Her eyes were calm and full of care as the question that I knew would be asked reached my ears. I pause and am not ready to answer because my mind goes blank and then fills with my mommy's screams. Mom. I wonder if she is safe and where she is. Her face with tears in her eyes flash in my mind and the darkness swirls around my insides. I can see her fear as he chokes her, and my chest feels red. I feel a touch on my shoulder and I jump away from it. Don't hurt me. My breath stops, and I can feel my heart beating throughout my body. I look up and it is Dorothy's hand that touched my shoulder, her sweet look calms the fire inside. Her touch reminds me to answer the question.

"I fell. I'm ok, I heal up fast. Can I go to recess now?" I want to get away from getting asked questions, I don't like to lie to her.

"Of course, you can head outside, just line up in line order when you hear the bell ring." She smiled.

"Austin, I'll see you later and have a good day!" Dorothy tells me as I put Teddy in my locker and head out of the classroom door.

My room is the last in the hallway and it is close to the outside doors that lead to the playground. As I open the playground doors the gray bubbles return, and I can feel my heart pounding in my body. I have no idea who to play with and I am not sure if Ms. Jennie is outside or not. Maybe I should have asked Dorothy to come with me, but I wanted to avoid more questioning. As I look around the playground, there are kids everywhere. Everyone seems to be playing and I am not sure what to do. I walk over to the equipment area where the rocks are and I freeze. My heart is beating fast and I can feel my hands sweating. I sit down and pick up the small rocks in my hand. I let them fall slowly and I like the smooth feel of them. They are cold on my sweaty hand and I can feel myself calming down. I keep picking up the rocks and watching them fall to the ground. As the next handful falls, feet come running past where I am sitting and I remember I am on the playground. I look up and take in a long deep breath. I see a girl running away from a couple boys. They are chasing her and I am not sure if they are playing or not.

She is blonde and seems smaller than the boys. She is wearing a blue shirt and shorts and has glasses on. She turns and starts running toward me. I think she is in my class. Her eyes look sad and kind of scared, and then she lets out a loud scream. Her scream pierces through me and then she screams more. I can see tears falling from her eyes and her screams bounce around my head. Mommy. My heart stops and a flame grows in my tummy. I have to stop him from hurting her. I hate him. I run after him and I jump on his back. I am Ironman. I punch him and kick him. Mom's scream echoes in my ear and I need to protect her. I can feel his arms wrap around me and pull me. The darkness chokes me and squeezes my chest, I can't breathe. The darkness has me and I can't see very well. "Don't touch me, don't touch me, please don't hurt me or her." My voice is loud and I am the one screaming. My body hurts all over and his grip on my ribs stabs through to my heart. I am not sure what to do but I need to get away and run. I don't want to be hurt again. "Let me go, LET ME GO, DON'T TOUCH ME!" I try with all my strength to free myself from his grip.

I see his dirty arm and his stink fills my nostrils. His dark-hate-filled eyes look at me. I have no choice and I bite him to free myself and then bite him again. One arm moves enough for me to take a punch and then I try to kick him. Mommy. She is still screaming. I need her to help me. I need my mommy. I decide to yell for her, "MOMMY, I need you! Please don't hurt me. I need my mommy. I NEED MY DADDY, I hate you, let me go, let me go, DON'T TOUCH ME!" I can feel his arms on me and they won't let go. He has my arms pinned and I keep fighting. My body hurts but I need to get free. I am trying everything I know to get free, but nothing works. Where is he taking me? His cigarette smells and stink is all around me and I take another bite to free myself, I think it was his slimy hand. Finally, his grip loosens, and I escape to a corner of the room. I make myself small, I need to be invisible. I wrap my arms around my knees and squeeze myself small. I am not Ironman. I am a worthless shit and a terrible kid.

I start to cry, and the tears fall down my face to my arms. I don't want to move and maybe he will leave again. My body is really hot, and my clothes are wet from sweat. I try to picture the Ironman cartoon to take me to my happy place, I hear the music and I close my eyes to picture it. He is strong, not like me, the thought makes me cry harder. Mommy, I hope she is ok, I need to protect her. My heart beats throughout my body and all I can hear is the thump. I take in a deep breath and then another. I think he is gone but I am afraid of opening my eyes to see. I feel something touch me. No, no, not again. I move away from it and open my eyes. Teddy. It is Teddy touching me. I grab him and hug him tight. I let the tears fall and squeeze him. I close my eyes again and I hear my daddy's laugh and see his smile. I need him. I take in a few more deep breaths and the darkness swirls and disappears. Holding Teddy close, I feel blue. I open my eyes and I have no idea where I am.

CHAPTER 7

THE ROOM IS SMALL AND THERE IS NOTHing in it. It is hot and kind of smelly, I look next to me and there is Ms. Jennie and another lady standing by a door. I am at school. I am hot and wet. I think I peed myself again, and I become embarrassed, really embarrassed. I have no idea what happened or how I ended up in this room. I look at Ms. Jennie and she is bleeding on her arm. The other lady has a big reddish mark on her arm and her face is really red and puffy looking. I hope I didn't do this, but deep down I know I did. I had another meltdown. It is over, I am a worthless kid and now all I will see are angry eyes and hate. I start to cry again. I do not know what to say. I bury my face into Teddy and let myself cry. I feel like that is what my body needs. As I cry, I feel someone near me and I look up. Ms. Jennie is sitting next to me on the floor. I wait for the dark eyes, but when I look at her, they are not angry or hateful. Her eyes are kind and caring, and actually, I think she may be teary. I look up at the other lady, and her eyes are kind too. The other lady kneels down and introduces herself.

"Hi Austin, I'm Ms. Benson, the principal here. I'm glad you're feeling better. After you chat with Ms. Jennie I'll visit with you, ok?" She smiles at me and her eyes look calm and she walks away. They care. They really care. I take in a deep, long breath. My body starts to feel calm and the darkness disappears and leaves me empty inside. I hold Teddy and look at Ms. Jennie and think about how the principal didn't yell at me. Maybe they don't see the shit that I am, maybe I can be better. Maybe I am Ironman and I can be strong too. The thought makes me feel gold and warm inside. Ms. Jennie's touch brings me back from my thoughts. I look at her and I think she gets me, she seems safe. The counselor at my old school would always look at me and say she didn't deal with bad kids and would walk away from me. I try not to think about it. I see Ms. Jennie's arm and I need to apologize to her and hope she knows I really mean it.

"I'm really sorry." My voice is weak and tired. My body hurts all over. "I didn't mean to hurt you, I'm really sorry." I look at the blood on Ms. Jennie's arm and I am sick to my tummy. I didn't know I hurt her, I don't remember anything that happened. I close my eyes and try to remember and the only thing that I can think of is my mom's scream echoing in my head and his hate eyes and nasty face looking at me. I take in a breath and know what I need to ask next. "Please don't call him. I'll be better, I promise I'll be better, just please don't call him."

Her face is warm with kind eyes. She just smiles at me when I look over at her waiting for an answer. She just sits next to me and continues to be quiet. I hope they do not call him, it will make it worse and I don't think I can make it through another fight like last night. The thought brings back the screams and I can't help but worry about my mommy. I hold Teddy close. I hope she is ok. I don't understand where she went or what happened to her after I hit the wall. My chest starts to squeeze in on me and the darkness wraps around my heart. I try to take a deep breath and calm my body. I need to stay calm. I feel a hand on my back and I am surprised at how it feels. It doesn't hurt me and my breath starts to calm the dark and push it back. I look at Ms. Jennie and she is not looking at me, just rubbing my back looking in the distance. She really is a weird person.

"I think it's hot and stuffy in this room. Actually, it kind of smells and I think we need to go to my office for a bit. What do you think?" Her words make me smile. I stand up, taking Teddy with me, and follow her to the office.

It is small but cozy. There are a few rocking chairs and stuffed animals on the counters. I pick the coziest looking chair and I sit down and start rocking myself. I really like this chair. It is super comfy. She sits across from me in another rocking chair. She picks up a stuffed dog and holds it close to her, she gives the dog a hug and looks at me. I hug Teddy and start to giggle. I am not sure why I am laughing but I can't help it, it just happens. Ms. Jennie smiles at me and giggles too.

"What's your dog's name?" I ask her.

"Oh this guy, he is Fred and he lives here in my office to help kids and adults feel better," she responds with a smile. "I bet Fred and Teddy could be friends."

"I think so," I say holding back a giggle. "I'll be Teddy and you be Fred." Teddy starts to talk, "Hi Fred, I'm Teddy. Do you want to play?"

"I would love to play!" Fred responds. "What do you want to play?"

"Let's play cars!" Teddy grabs the box of cars off the counter and sits on the floor.

Fred sits on the floor and grabs a car to play with. "I like this one, Teddy. What one do you want to play with?"

"I like blue." Teddy picks up a blue car and starts to drive it. It is driving all over and then races off the counter to the floor with a crash.

Fred's car is red and it is bigger than the rest of the cars in the tub. He races the car off the counter too but it hits my car with a crash and then the doors on the red car open. This makes Teddy mad.

"Why did you hit my car Fred? You shit!" Teddy picks up the red car with the open doors and throws it at Fred.

"Wow! Teddy, that could've hurt me! I'm sorry I hit your car," Fred responds calmly.

I freeze and look at Ms. Jennie. I don't want to play anymore. I feel my heart ache and the gray prickles poke in my chest. I walk back to the cozy chair and flop down holding Teddy close. I rock in the chair and thoughts take me away to my mom again. I hope school is out soon. I need to take care of my mom. I wonder if she has her phone with her. Maybe Ms. Jennie can call her.

"Can you call my mom? I'm not feeling well. I think I'm sick and need to go home," I tell her with a soft voice. I really do not feel well, so it's not a total lie.

"Yes, let's give her a call." She doesn't hesitate and picks up her phone and dials the number. She sits and listens. I can't hear anything and I wait. I hope she answers, at least I would know she is ok. Ms. Jennie says hello and it brings me back from my thoughts.

"Hi, this is the school counselor at Portland Elementary School and I was looking for Tina." Her voice is kind. There is a pause and I wait, then I hear: "Oh ok, Don. Yes everything is fine. He is just not feeling well and wanted to call. Yes. I will check. Thank you and have a great rest of your day." She hangs up and looks at me.

The breath in my chest left when I heard his name. Why does he have her phone? Where is she? Did he hurt her again? The darkness forms again in my chest and I am not sure what to do. I need to find my mom. But if he is with her, I don't want to see him. As I sit rocking and lost in my thoughts I hear Ms. Jennie's voice and look up at her squeezing Teddy.

"Well, that was Don. He said your mom is at school and if you do not have a temperature do not call him anymore." She pauses. "Austin, tell me about yourself." Her eyes are still caring and warm. She smiles. I want to tell her everything but I know I can't. I will have to give her some info but be careful what to say. I take in a deep breath and hug Teddy.

"Like what?" I answer her.

"Anything you want me to know I guess." She continues to look at me with caring eyes.

"Well, I like tacos. But we don't have them much. I don't have any pets but I would love to have a dog. A big dog." I smile thinking about a dog to cuddle.

"Oh how about a dog named Taco! Ms. Jennie giggles when she says this. She really is a strange teacher. "Who lives with you?"

"Well, my mommy and Don, but he is not my dad. I don't like him much. He stinks like yuck and dirt and gets drunk a lot." I sigh thinking about him and I picture his grubby face and pointed nose. I hate him. I bet he hurt Mommy and took her phone. I fall quiet and I am done talking.

"Yuck never smells good!" she responds and then she seems to fall quiet too. I want her to know what happened but I need to keep Mommy safe and if I tell her I do not know what would happen to her.

"Can I go back to class now?" I ask, wanting to avoid telling her anything else. I stand up and hold Teddy.

"You asked me not to call him, were you talking about Don? She looks at me caringly waiting for a response.

"Yes, he gets angry when I get into trouble at school." I sigh and his face comes to my mind with his hate filled eyes. My mommy. I hope she is ok.

"What does angry look like for Don?" She continues to wait for an answer, as I picture him screaming and coming at me with his beer in his hand, my chest gets tight. I take in a breath and try to calm my body but the gray prickles take over and my tummy starts to really hurt. "I want to go back to class now please." I do not look at her when I say this. I want her to know but I can't and I can't tell her about him.

"School is almost out and we can walk down together to get your things if that's ok with you?" She smiles at me and stands up to move toward the door. I do not say anything to her, but start walking beside her toward the classroom. I glance over to her and see her hand, I want to hold it but the thought makes the darkness surface so I hold Teddy instead. I hope she doesn't see the real me, I am such a shit and so worthless. The teachers at my old school knew the real me. I don't want to see the same look in Ms. Jennie's eyes. I don't like that I hurt her, but I don't remember her even touching me. I sigh and my body is tired and hurts all over. I watch the floor move under my feet and I can feel pain shoot through my side and chest with every step. As I watch the white square floor move with my steps, it reminds me of when my dad left me, my real dad.

The building was tall and made of blocks, brown bumpy looking blocks. My mommy had tears on her face and she was scared. It made me feel scared too. I never saw Mommy act like that. She held my hand tight, it hurt. I didn't tell her that it hurt because she seemed lost. I liked her holding my hand. My body felt cold and lost. I don't know what happened but Mommy answered her phone and then scooped me off the couch and to the car. She didn't even buckle me and we drove here. As we walked closer to the tall block building, I watched as the large glass doors opened, they took a long time. Mommy dragged me in and she was walking very fast, my legs hurt trying to keep up. The floor was shiny and white. The squares, I think they were squares, went fast under our feet as Mommy pulled me faster. The smell of that place was weird but clean. I didn't like it, it made my tummy pokey. The people had on weird clothes and seemed to have lots of things hanging on them. The pokes felt bigger and my tummy hurt.

"Mommy, I.." her words made mine stop coming out.

"Not now, Austin." She was crying and her words were serious.

She pulled me up to a desk. It was tall and blue. It had green things stacked up and a lot of bottles of stuff. The desk wrapped around the corner and there were a lot of people messing around behind it. She stopped and started talking to the lady sitting behind a computer. The lady walked away and into large doors. We just stood there waiting, I felt scared and hugged Mommy's leg. After a few minutes, a person dressed like Doc McStuffins walked out, shook my mom's hand, and started talking to her. I could not hear the words but my mommy cried harder and put her head down on the counter. The person in the white coat put her hand on mommy's back and I heard her say something about being sorry for losing something. She just stood there with her head on the counter not moving. I did not want to say anything but something was wrong and my tummy continued to be poked and hurt. After a few minutes, Mom let go of my hand, it made me feel invisible, and I don't think she has held it since that day. I miss her holding my hand, it always made me feel safe. I feel blue and cold all over when Ms. Jennie's words bring me back from my thoughts.

"Do you have plans when you get home today?" She smiles at me as she turns down the hallway toward my classroom. Her footsteps echo on the walls and my words seem to have left me. I look at her and shake my head no, but do not say anything. In my head, I want to say I hope to see my mom but if I say this, she will have questions. As we get closer to my class, I think about the scared faces that the kids might have and I do not want to go in. Mrs. Roush probably won't want me back in her room anyway. I stop walking and freeze. I am stuck to the floor and suddenly the darkness starts to fill me. I can't see the disappointment in Mrs. Roush's eyes. I don't want to go back to the room. Ms. Jennie stops with me and she doesn't say anything, but waits next to me. I take a deep breath, then another, but the darkness doesn't stop, and it makes my tummy sick. I remember that I did not bring my backpack today and I don't need to go into the classroom. I don't have to go see Mrs. Roush, the darkness let's go of me, but a part feels like I want to see her. I look at Ms. Jennie and I'm able to find my words.

"I forgot my backpack today, the only thing I want is Teddy and I have him, see?" I try to sound strong and brave. She kneels down next to me and looks at me.

"I see, well let's walk back to the office, the principal wanted to speak with you. You will have consequences for today, but tomorrow is a fresh start and we all make mistakes. You made a bad choice but you are an awesome kid." Her voice is kind and she moves quickly to reach out to hug me but as her hands get close to me the darkness takes over. His eyes and dirt-crumb-covered arms fill my mind. I try to step back but fall and hit the wall. I shield my face with my arms. I try to not move and wait to move my arms away from my eyes. I feel a soft touch on my shoulder. It does not hurt me. Slowly, I lower my arms and remember I am at school. I stare at Ms. Jennie. I wish I was not me, I wish I was like the other kids. I am such a pussy. The thought makes me blue.

Her eyes are still caring and kind. She smiles and waits with me by the wall. Her hand is resting on my shoulder. "Are you ok?" she uses a soft voice. I don't answer her because I am not ok. "Let me help you up, sweetheart," she slowly holds out her other hand. She is calm and I put my hand in hers to stand up.

She thinks I'm an awesome kid, but I don't feel that way. Ironman makes good choices but can I? I hold Teddy close.

Can I do better? What does that mean anyway? I am the bad kid, but can I make better choices? I feel confused, but I have a purple warm place in my heart and I can try. Ironman can try, and so can I. I smile at Ms. Jennie and start to walk back toward the office with her. I don't talk, I feel like my words are stuck. I am ready to go home and go to bed. When we turn the corner to walk down the long hall with all the windows, a class is walking toward us, and a girl smiles at me. It is the girl from the playground. She steps out of line toward me and starts talking to me.

"Hi! I'm Jasmine. Do you want to play with me at recess tomorrow? I like your Teddy Bear. I have a unicorn at home that is my stuffie." She is excited and seems to be nice to me. I have never had someone to play with before. The thought makes gray bubbles pop up.

"Ok." I didn't know what else to say but I gave her a smile and headed toward the office. I have never had a friend before, what if I hurt her? I try not to think about it. I am Ironman and I can be a friend. I smile and hug Teddy.

We walk into the office and Mrs. Marsha smiles at me. "Are you feeling better sweetie?" I shake my head yes and Ms. Jennie walks me into the principal's office. I am in trouble. I hope she didn't call home and tell them. I got hit a lot last year when I got into trouble at school, and the worst was when I got kicked out of school and then I really got hit and hurt. I pause at the door and look at the floor. The darkness swirls around and I try to calm myself. I don't like being in trouble. I was in trouble all the time last year and so many people had scary angry eyes at me. I try not to think about it. I squeeze Teddy and take a deep breath. Ms. Jennie asks me to sit down and then says she will be in her office waiting on me. I walk over and sit at the chair she pointed to.

I look around the room and it is small but comfortable. There is a round table to the side with way too many chairs for such a small room. Against the back wall is a tall bookshelf full of books and papers. Next to the bookshelf is a small desk with a chair at it, that looks like a student desk with a computer on top. There is a stack of what looks like a weird type of pop on the floor in yellow and green boxes with bubbles all over. I am not sure what it is, I have never had that kind before. I hear a voice and it brings me back to the principal. She is sitting at a teacher desk that is covered in pencils, lotion, and papers. She is next to me in a twirly chair and is leaning back with her hands touching in front of her chest. She is sitting slouchy and her bright blue eyes are serious but not angry. Her hair is straight and really shiny. It makes me think of sunshine and flowers. She seems nice and she is pretty.

The principal I had last year was old and reminded me of a witch with a pointy nose and she always smelled like coffee and a weird flower. Her shoes made loud clicking sounds everywhere she walked. She always had her hair the same way and it smelled like glue. She yelled a lot and always sent me home. She did not like me and struggled to even fake like me. I remember telling her a couple times that she was an evil witch and to leave me alone. It never worked to get her away from me and only made her angrier. The thought reminds me of one time that she was in my face and her breath smelled so bad. She was yelling at me to sit down and I wanted her to get away from me. She would not listen so I spit on her smelly face and she left to wash it off. I felt bad but she really freaked me out and her breath didn't help, yuck I can still remember it.

"Austin, what happened at recess?" Ms. Benson asks as she looks at me over her folded hands. She waits and stares at me. I don't know what to say. How can I explain that the girl screamed and then Don attacked me? I decide to just sit and not respond to the question. I look down to the floor, shrug my shoulders, and wait.

"You were really upset, and yelling to not hurt you. Austin, do you get hurt at home?" Her voice is soft and kind, but her eyes are full of concern. She still has her hands in front of her so that only her fingers cross.

"No, I don't know what happened at recess, and I don't remember hurting anyone. I'm really sorry, I didn't mean to hurt anyone." My voice seems weak and I look at her as I respond. I lied to her, but I hope she can see it. I hope she can help me, but I can't tell her that.

"I know you didn't mean too but you did hurt a classmate and teachers. You are not going to be able to go to recess without an adult to supervise you. You have to learn to control your reactions to things, and make smart choices. We will work together to help you but you have to work harder than I do," her voice stays calm and kind as she tells me this. This is a weird way to get in trouble. I have always just lost recess or have gotten kicked out of school. Ms. Benson's voice brings me from my thoughts.

"Tomorrow, you'll start your day here in the office and we'll discuss what recess will look like. I'm glad you are back to being yourself now, I like this version of Austin instead of the angry one!" She let her arms fall to her lap and she scoots forward in her chair. "I know you're sorry, but making good choices and working to change behavior is how to show you're sorry. It's hard, but we will work together." She smiles and quickly reaches out for a high-five. As her hand comes close to me the darkness wraps itself on me and I jump away from her moving the chair backward on the floor. My heart is beating quickly and I try to slow it down. Ms. Benson stands up and kneels next to me.

"I'm sorry, I didn't mean to startle you. Listen, tomorrow is a new day and a fresh start, remember you're in charge of your choices and it will be a great day." She holds out her hand for a high-five, but this time she moves slower. She holds her hand out for me to take it and I do. She makes me feel green. "I will walk you back to the counselor's office." She smiles at me and we walk out of her office. I hate that I am jumpy. I am such a pussy. The thought makes me frown and feel blue. I try not to think about it. I let go of her hand and squeeze Teddy close. I want to go home. We walk past the small room where I had my meltdown and next to the room is where Ms. Marsha is sitting reading something on her desk. When I look over to where the counter is, a guy is standing there waiting and looking at his phone.

He is blonde and not very tall. He is clean and has a nametag on his neck. The nametag. That nametag. Oh no. No. Not again. I have seen these people before and their questions. They always make it worse and their questions are hard to answer because I have to lie. They can't take me, I have to keep Mommy safe. Who called them? Why? My heart races and my tummy fills up with yuck and gray bubbles. I feel sick. Not again. What will I say, what did I say? My heart makes my whole body thump and my words, my words leave me and I don't know what to do.

CHAPTER 8

The hall is dark and cold. My footsteps echo off
the walls and it makes a creepy sound. I feel like
someone is following me and turn around to look.
No one is there but the school is scary at night,
feels like ghosts are flying around. My legs feel
jumpy and I can feel every breath and heartbeat.
The moon is shining into the large windows of the
hall. The trees are lightly blowing outside and it
creates shadows on the floor in front of me. I am
lost and stuck. Mommy, where is she? Her scream
echoes in my ears and I need to save her. I take a
breath and I need to keep going down the hall toward the echo. My feet feel heavy and I am full of
gray prickles. I start to turn around and the feeling
that someone is watching me becomes bigger. The
darkness builds and grabs me. When I turn, there

are his eyes. Hate. Anger filled eyes. He grabs me
by my arms and lifts me up. I try to scream but my
breath leaves me and all I see is the brick wall and
I hit the floor. When I look up, there is another
shadow and they reach out for me. I see the name
tag hanging from the figure. I hold my knees and
make myself small. I am small, I am weak and a
shit. I am wet and laying in a puddle on the floor.
It is so cold, I start to shiver, and suddenly I wake
up with a huge gasp of air.

I am in my room. The closet is cold and wet. I peed again, I
hate this and now my blankets are wet and I don't know where
more are. I should just stop sleeping and then I wouldn't have
so many bad dreams. I am weak even in my dreams. I have had
a bad dream every night since that guy came to school to talk to
me. I try not to think about it. I need to change my clothes and
try to go back to sleep. As I am looking for clothes, I hear the
door to my mom's room squeak and footsteps. Maybe it is her
and she can help me clean up. I peek out into the hall and I see
her walk into the bathroom and turn on the light. She has been
so quiet since Don tried to choke her and DFS came to talk to
them. Actually, Don has been better too in the last week. Well,
he hasn't hit me anyway. The toilet flushes and Mom comes out
of the bathroom. I hold my breath and a yellow pokey feeling
pops into my tummy.

"Mommy," my voice sounds like I am three again. Her face
is pale and she looks very tired and blue. Her hair is tangled

and dirty. She is wearing an old t-shirt. That shirt, it used to be my dad's and now she wears it often at night. When she looks at me, her once loving eyes look empty and lost. She has a new bruise on her face around her cheek. They must have fought again when they went out last night. I heard them come in, it was late and they were loud but I fell back asleep. They have been going out a lot lately. It is nice because I have not seen Don much but I do miss Mommy, and being alone scares me. I wait for her to answer me, but she just looks at me.

"Mommy, I had an accident, will you help me?" I ask and continue to wait.

"Oh Austin, it's late and I don't feel good. You need to stop doing that all the time, what's wrong with you? Just change your clothes and go back to sleep." She lets out a sigh, drops her head and eyes to the floor, and walks back to her room, shutting the door between us.

My chest feels like a black spikey sea creature poking at my heart and everything else. Like one of those creepy things in the Octonauts cartoon. I take a deep breath and try not to think about how much it hurts me that my mom walked away from me again. I wish it didn't bother me but it does, and I need to just get used to it. Maybe I should have talked to the DFS guy last week. He was kind and did seem to have caring eyes. If I did talk to him, maybe my mom would pay attention to me. Or Don would have killed both of us. The guy was nice to me and tried so hard to get me to talk. He said his name was Charles and he even sat on the floor with me. I hid behind one of the rocking chairs. I did not say a peep. He even tried to get

Ms. Jennie to get me to talk. I was Ironman and strong. I didn't crack. Then, when they showed up here and questioned Don and Mom it was awful. I try not to think about it.

I go back to the room and take off my wet clothes and all I can find are a pair of dry underwear. I put them on and grab Teddy. I hold him close and walk out to the couch to go back to sleep. At least it is Sunday and that means I can go back to school tomorrow. I made it a whole day last week without a meltdown and it was such a good day. Dorothy said she was proud of me and it felt so warm and purple in my heart. I like her smile and I want to make her proud more. I am ready for the weekend to be over. Last week at school, even the days I was bad, I still liked it. When I get to go to recess Jasmine plays with me, and either Ms. Benson or Ms. Jennie, whoever is able to. The thought of playing shark tag with Jasmine makes me smile and feel warm. I close my eyes and start to fall asleep, hoping that I don't have another bad dream.

The room is dark. My eyes are open but I can't see. Smoke is filling up around me and the darkness is choking. It is hard to breathe. The flames grow and I yell for help. "Mommy, help me!" I am alone, and I need to escape, but I need help. I start to yell again for anyone who will listen. I fall to the floor to crawl under the smoke and start toward what I think is the door. I suddenly feel something in front of me, shoes, dirty worn shoes. Don. His laugh fills my ears and he looks down at me with evil in his eyes. He turns and walks away. He reaches out and grabs my mom by her hair and starts pulling her away from me. She doesn't even look back at me. Don turns and his hate-filled eyes glow through the smoke and flame. "You little worthless ass. Get up!" his voice is loud. "Damn it, I am done with this!" he screams and throws my mom to the side and comes back toward me. He reaches for me. I try to hide under the smoke but his grubby hands find me. Ouch, my hair, he has my hair.

Suddenly, I wake up and Don is pulling my hair and dragging me off the couch. "Wake your stupid ass up and get out of my way!" He finishes talking when I hit the floor beside him.

"You are the stupid ass!! I hate you!" I am shocked that the words came out of my mouth. I didn't mean to say them but it was too late. Gray explodes in my body as I look at him filling up with rage. He squishes up the blue can he has in his hand and throws it straight down to the floor. His eyes look like fire and his body tenses. He slowly closes each fist and starts squeezing his fingers tight. I have to shield myself and I take in a deep breath. I am Ironman. I am strong. The darkness is creeping up so I try to push it down but it takes over. I know what is going to happen next. I am so stupid. Why would I say something like that to him, of all the times why did my mouth have to open? I brought this on myself. It is my fault. I try to make myself invisible by squeezing my knees but it does not work. I am a bad kid.

"What did you say to me?" He is pissed. His face went dark red and he has this creepy vein that is throbbing out of his forehead.

"You little piece of shit, who do you think owns this house?" He pauses to take a breath almost waiting for me to answer him. I have said too many words already and know better.

"Well, let me remind you." He picks up his hand, pulls it back and my heart freezes and my breathing is stuck. It is like slow motion as his hand comes down and makes contact with the side of my face. I fall backward onto the floor and don't dare move. I try not to cry, it makes it worse. I hold my face. My head feels like a door shut on it and my brain is slammed around inside of my skull. I peer up at him. I hate him. His eyes are still cold and dark. He pauses and then mumbles something under his breath. I thought he was done and about to sit down. He then pulls back his foot and kicks me in the side, I can't hold back the tears and I let them fall.

"Get up you worthless pussy!" and with his words he grabs me by my hair and drags me off the floor to my feet. My scream bounces around the room and the pain shoots down my neck. Once standing, I see my mom watching. She is just watching. Standing there empty and hollow. I need you, I try to say it with my eyes but she doesn't move, not even a look at me. I give up. She doesn't care about me.

"Get out of my house! Now! You little bastard! GO!" His hate-filled eyes burn through me and all I can see is red.

I hate him, and what he has done to my mom. Before thinking about it, I pull my arm back and make a fist. I put all my strength into the hit and I aim right for his nuts. My mom used to tell me that if someone tried to take me to hit them in the nuts. It works and he lets out a loud groan and bends over. When he bends over his face is close to my foot. I kick him in the face using all the power I have left in me. With the kick, I make a break for it, run to my room, and grab clothes off the floor and Teddy. I can't go out the front door so I kick out the screen in the window, throw out Teddy and the clothes. His footsteps make the house rattle as he runs down the hall after me. My heart is thumping and I need to hurry up. I pull myself up and into the window. Looking down, it is kinda high and I start to change my mind. Don bursts through the door yelling and stumbling toward me. I don't have a choice and jump. I make it out just as he reaches the window. The ground is hard and my breath explodes out of me when I hit it. When I look up, his arms are out of the window. He is yelling and screaming inside. His arms disappear and I am not going to wait for him to come outside to get me. I jump up and grab my stuff. I look around and run into the woods as fast as my legs can carry me.

The trees fly past me as I keep running, I want to be sure to get away from him. My chest starts hurting. I push myself on, but my breath is starting to be hard to get. I slow down and watch to not trip on the sticks and things on the ground. I lean against a huge maple tree. I quickly glance behind me to see if he is chasing me. He probably went back to getting drunk. I put my hands on my knees and start to calm down. I pick up the clothes I grabbed and put them on. They are dry at least. It is a shirt and some shorts I wore last week. I realize I forgot my shoes. Oh well it is a nice day and I don't need them. I grab Teddy and sit down against the tree. It is a perfect shady spot. The grass is fluffy and soft here. It must still be early in the day because the dew is still glistening on the leaves and grass. The sun is peering through the leaves of the trees and it is still cool outside. I like this time of day, before it gets so hot my butt crack sweats. The breeze makes the leaves dance and rustle in the woods. It is so nice here and there is nothing to hurt me. I feel tired and pull Teddy close. I close my eyes and fall asleep.

The sun is hot and I open my eyes to the bright rays beating down on me. It is hot and must be late. I am not sure how long I was asleep but it must have been awhile because I don't feel tired anymore. I haven't slept without having a nightmare in, I am not sure how long. I stand up and look around. I am not sure where I am. I was so focused on getting away from Don's fists that I didn't pay attention to which way I ran. Gray prickles start to grow and my tummy is hurting. I take in a deep breath and remember that I have been all over these woods before. I know if I keep walking in one direction I am bound to pop out somewhere. Besides, I can't go home anyway. Not while he is there. I pick a direction and start walking. The grass is soft under my feet and I try to watch for sticks as I walk. I am hungry and hope I pop out somewhere soon.

I'm in a good mood. I know Don is not here and he doesn't care enough to come look for me. Being in the woods by myself makes me feel green. The breeze is blowing and I like the sound it makes. I start singing a song I learned at school about a Hawaiian fish. I don't remember how to say the words right so I make up my own and sing it. It makes me laugh. I walk on and still can't see any sign of a house or road. After what seems like forever I can hear a car, the road must be close. I walk a little faster and the trees open up. I jump across the ditch onto the dirt road. After looking around, I recognize that I am a little ways past my school. I keep walking and can feel my tummy start to hurt. I am ready to eat and hope Dorothy is home. Maybe she will cook for me. The thought makes my tummy angry and growly. Dorothy seems to like to cook for people or maybe it's only me she cooks for. I smile thinking about her food.

I start walking toward her house. The breeze feels nice and it makes the trees rustle. I start to hear gravel moving under tires and I move over into the ditch to get out of the way. The car passes me and the red brake lights come on. The dust makes me cough and as it settles I see the car. It stops in front of me and pulls off the side of the road. I don't recognize it and my heart picks up. I can feel my tummy churning. The car is small and white and the door creaks open slowly. I can't decide to stay or run. The trees are close and it would be easy to hide. I feel stuck to the grass. Out steps someone with jeans and a t-shirt on. Their hair is pulled back in a ponytail and is shiny in the sun. I still don't recognize them. The person takes off sunglasses and turns around toward me. I realize it is Ms. Benson, the principal. When I see her face, my heart feels purple and slows down a bit. I have spent a lot of time in her office and she is kind and cares. Even when I have meltdowns and hit her, she still seems to like me.

"Austin, what are you up too?" Her voice is happy and she starts walking toward me.

"Hi Ms. Benson! I pause and am not sure what I should say after that. I decide to tell the truth but leave out a couple parts. "I started playing in the woods behind the house. I wasn't paying attention and ended up lost and popped out here." I smile as I say it and keep my face happy.

"You are kind of far from your house for someone without shoes." She giggles and looks at my feet.

"Well, I kinda forgot them." I smile at her and she looks at me with these knowing eyes. She smiles back.

"Can I give you a ride home?" she asks

"How about a ride to my friend Dorothy's house? I'm going there for dinner." I am hungry and can't wait to see Dorothy's face. It makes me smile.

"Ok, you will have to show me the way." She turns and walks back to her car and I follow her. I have never had a ride with a principal before, and on a weekend. She is weird. It makes me laugh. I am having a good day after all. I walk to her car and it is dusty from the road and is close to the ground. It seems newer. I step in and it smells good and flowery inside. The car is clean with only a bag of papers and books in the back. I feel like I should say something but I am not sure what. I decide to ask her what she is doing today.

"So where are you going today?" I ask her.

"I was going to school to catch up on some things I need to do." She doesn't look at me when she answers and keeps her eyes on the road.

"Teachers work on the weekends?" How weird. It makes me laugh and she laughs with me. I look out the window. I see the school pass by and I think about the last week and I am excited to go back tomorrow. It is almost like Ms. Benson reads my mind.

"You ready for school tomorrow? We are starting reading groups so that will be exciting." This time she looks at me when she talks.

"I am ready for school, but no, reading groups sounds like slow torture." She laughs but I am totally serious. The thought makes my head hurt. I can't let Mrs. Roush see that I can't read. I can't even say the sight words they are always talking about. Last year, I always got kicked out of class with the angry eyes and hate-filled-fake-caring words. But if Mrs. Roush is teaching the group then it can't be too bad. She doesn't have the fake caring words and eyes. She really likes me and I can try my best with her. The thought makes me smile.

"That is Dorothy's house," I say as I point to the house. Ms. Benson slows down, pulls into Dorothy's driveway and stops.

"I will see you in the morning, Austin. I hope you have a nice dinner." She smiles at me and sticks her hand out for a high-five. I notice she did this slowly and I give her a high-five and smile. I get out of the car and start to walk to Dorothy's porch. I turn around and wave to Ms. Benson. She waves back but doesn't drive off. I am not sure what she is doing. She smiles at me and then waves to me to walk to the door. She must be waiting to see if Dorothy is home. It makes purple and green tickle my heart. I smile at her again and turn to walk to the door. I hope Dorothy is home and doesn't mind me stopping by. I don't really have anywhere else to go. Unless I go with Ms. Benson to school. I can't go home in case Don is still mad. If I wait long enough maybe he will be so drunk he will pass out so I won't have to deal with him. The thought of him makes me sigh and I try not to think about it. I walk up to the door and knock kinda hard, which I didn't mean to knock hard but I hope she is home.

I hear some movement and footsteps in the house and then the door opens. Her smile is big and it fills me up with warmth. It makes this morning seem like it was so long ago. I am going to ask to spend the night. I just need to think of a way for her to not call my mom. As I am thinking about how to ask and what to say her voice brings me back from my thoughts.

"Well, hi there Sugar! It is so nice to see you! Come in. Come in!" She opens the door all the way and motions for me to walk into the house. I turn and wave at Ms. Benson, then Dorothy waves at her too. When I step through the door, a wonderful smell fills my nostrils and my stomach growls quite loudly. I turn around to face Dorothy and she is standing with her hands on her hips with a serious look on her face. Seeing her looking that way makes gray pokeys in my tummy and it isn't because I am hungry.

"Austin, what in the world are you wearing? You look like Jake Darby! And why do you smell like pee and rotten bits?

You smell awful, doesn't your mom make you take a bath?"
Her tone is concerned and seems a bit frustrated at the same
time. Her eyes. Knowing eyes. I don't know what to say to her,
I didn't know I stink. I think of Ms. Benson and her car. Her
clean car. Oh no. She probably is bummed she let me in it. I
bet I stunk it up; the idea of her smelling me makes me feel
yellow. I wonder who Jake Darby is and think about how dirty
he must be.

"I woke up last night and I had an accident. I took the
clothes off but this morning these were all I could find and I
left the house in a hurry." I told her the truth but just left out
some parts. I like being able to talk to her. I hope she doesn't
want me to leave. I should ask her if she does. But then I would
have to go home. The thought makes me blue, I don't want to
ask but I do anyway.

"I am sorry, I can leave and try to clean up and come back."
I wait for her response hoping she says no.

"Oh honeybun of course not, but you are too nice of a
boy to be walking around smelling like an old boar hog." She
smiles at me. "Come on, I will see if I have any clothes lying
around and we can toss yours in the wash." She turns and walks
into the spare room and I follow her. I am so relieved that she
doesn't want me to go and I let out a breath. I must have been
holding it waiting for her response. She walks over to a closet
and opens the door. It is stacked and stuffed full of stuff, and
I have no idea how she would know where anything is at in
there. But she does, and next thing I know she is pulling out
some clothes and they still have tags on them. She likes to say

she buys these things for her grandkids, but I have a feeling she buys them for me.

"Here we go! I knew I had something in here, I tend to buy stuff for my grandsons and I forget they're in here." She turns and smiles at me. "I'm surprised to see you today." She waits for a response.

"Oh, I was just out playing and wanted to say hi," I respond and run my fingers through my hair.

"Hmm without shoes?" she pauses. "Oh, well, I ran into your mom and Don at the carry-out earlier today and they said they were going out of town for a break. I just assumed you were with them." She looks at me with concern and waits for me to say something. Mom left me. She doesn't even know where I am, how could she just leave me? I look at Dorothy and her face is serious and she is not going to move until I give her an answer. I don't know what to say and am not sure how to respond, so I change the subject to the yummy smell. Dorothy can't stand for someone to be hungry.

"I'm so hungry, what's that delicious smell?" I hold my tummy and look at her.

"Well I have a pork roast in and I'm going to make mashed potatoes to go with it. Actually, I should get started on the potatoes, dear, so why don't you get cleaned up? In the shower you go. Take these clothes with you, and put your clothes outside of the door and I'll get them in the wash." She hands me the clothes and starts to walk to the kitchen and I hear her voice again.

"And Austin, be sure to wash all of your bits using soap, and Teddy needs cleaned dear. I think he's been peed on more times than he likes, put him outside your door with the clothes."

I walk into the bathroom and put the clean clothes down on the counter. I take off the dirty ones and smell them. They are terrible. I can't believe I couldn't smell myself. I put them outside the door and hesitantly I put Teddy with them. He will be ok with Dorothy. I hop into the shower and start to clean up and in Dorothy's words, wash my bits. I can't believe my mom would leave town knowing I was out in the woods. Maybe she really doesn't care about me after all. I feel cold and try not to think about it. I bet Dorothy could tell I didn't know about them leaving and that is why she stopped asking questions. I need to find a way to ask her if I can stay the night. The thought makes me warm.

The house smells great and I am starving when I walk into the kitchen. Dorothy is setting out plates on the table and looks up at me and smiles. "There's my sweet boy." She is so kind to me.

"Have a seat and I'll make your plate. Also, I called your mother," she continues making my plate. But all the breath in me leaves and my heart starts racing.

"She said that they would not be back until tomorrow and that it is fine for you to stay with me." She hands me the plate and smiles. "You can sleep in the spare room and I will find clothes for you to wear to school in the morning." Dorothy sits down with her plate and starts eating, as if it is completely normal for me to be staying.

"I'd love to stay, thank you," I say as I start shoving food in my mouth. The roast is so juicy and tender and it is the best bite of food I have ever eaten. I can't wait to stay the night here. What a good day this turned out to be after a rocky start of course. I finish up the food on my plate and before I can even ask, Dorothy refills it with a smile. I gobble it all down and help Dorothy clean up the dishes and wipe the table. I am very tired and wonder what time it is. I feel like I am ready for bed, but then I remember I spent the day in the woods wandering around.

"Well dear, how about a movie and milkshake before bedtime?" Dorothy asks.

"Yes! I haven't had a milkshake in a really long time." The thought makes my mouth water.

"I make the best and they're full of love. The secret to make them perfect is to add a bit of sugar before you blend it up!" she smiles. "I laid out some jammies for you in the spare room, go put them on and I will start the shakes."

It is bedtime and my tummy is super full. The movie was great, I really liked how Ferdinand stayed kind the whole movie. Dorothy told me to brush my teeth, she had an extra toothbrush of course, and head to bed. When I walk into the bedroom, she has a book to read, and is waiting on me. I haven't had a story read to me since before my dad left. The thought reminds me of my mom, and it makes me feel blue. Mom used to read a book called "Go Dog Go" to me, it was my favorite and I can hear her voice in my head reading it. I am lost in the thought of her reading and Dorothy must have noticed. "Are you ok sweetheart?"

I don't know the answer. Am I ok? I miss my mom but yet she let me get hurt this morning. She just stood there and watched. I can picture her empty face and lost eyes. I try not to think about it. "I'm ok, I just haven't slept in a bed in a long time. My mom used to read me stories but she doesn't anymore. I hope I don't pee the bed." I didn't want her to know I pee the bed, but the words wouldn't stop. I really don't want to have an accident.

"Well, look here. I have a bed pad and a mattress cover just in case. And if you do have an accident it will be ok, and you'll come wake me up and I'll change your sheets and jammies, does that sound like a deal?" She smiles sweetly and I climb into bed next to a clean, good smelling, Teddy. Her voice is so fun to listen to, she changes it for the different characters in the book. We laugh at the book and she tucks me in and turns out the light. I pull Teddy close and snuggle into the fluffy pillows and soft warm blankets. I close my eyes and think about my day, even with the bad start, it was a nice day. I can't help but think about my mom. I hope she is ok. I try not to think about it. I start to doze off and with each breath, I allow myself to sink deeper into the bed and I am fast asleep.

CHAPTER 9

THE WARM RAYS OF THE MORNING SUN start to peek through the yellow curtains. I slowly open my eyes and look around the room, the smell of bacon and biscuits fills the air. I stretch out in the big bed and decide to just lay there a little longer, I could get used to this. I don't want to go home to sleep on the floor. I reach down and feel my jammies. I can't believe it, but I did not pee the bed. I smile and feel all warm, and it is not because I had an accident. I am not sure what time it is and the great thing is that it doesn't matter. I know that Dorothy will get me up and not let me miss school. I like to be cared for, it makes me feel something that I haven't felt in a long time.

The room is quite small and cozy. The dresser is white with a jewelry box on top with a few other things and a big mirror on the back of the dresser. I get up, walk over to the mirror, and look in it. I see me. My hair is shaggy and getting long, and I have some marks on my face and a small bruise, it is not too bad actually. One time, I was up kinda late when Mom and Don were gone, and I watched this movie called Harry Potter. At the end of the movie, Harry found an old mirror and the old wizard told him that when he looks into the mirror he will see what his heart desires or something like that. Harry saw his parents that died when he was a baby, he wanted his family back. I wonder if this mirror is like that one. I see a room that is clean, a boy who didn't have nightmares or wet the bed, and a bed that is safe. I don't see my dad, or my mom before my dad left, but I look again and I see Dorothy standing there with a smile.

"Good morning, sweetie. I was wondering if you were up. How did you sleep?" Dorothy asks.

"Great, and I didn't pee the bed or have bad dreams!" I sounded more excited than I intended to.

"That's wonderful! Breakfast is ready and I laid out some clothes for you in the bathroom to wear to school today." She turns and walks out the door.

"Can I skip school today and stay with you?" I know the answer but I have to try.

"Of course not! You have to go to school! Her voice was high-pitched and serious. It makes me laugh.

I take a quick look back into the mirror and see myself. I hope I can be strong today. I want to be better. I try not to think about it and walk to the bathroom to get ready. On the counter, there is a new Ironman t-shirt, underwear, a pair of jeans, socks and new shoes. Now, I may not be able to read but

I am not dumb, she did not have these hiding in her closet for grandsons. She must really like to shop and I like to be the one she shops for. The thought makes me smile and I get dressed. I brush my teeth and comb my hair. I don't know why but seeing the comb made me decide to comb it. My stomach growls and I head to the kitchen to eat breakfast.

"Well, don't you look handsome! It's amazing what a comb can do." She giggles and turns back to the stove to pull out the bacon. She puts the bacon on a plate next to the stove that has a paper towel on it. After pouring off some of the bacon grease into a coffee cup she turns back to me.

"How do you like your eggs?" Dorothy was already dressed and ready to leave, she must have gotten up early.

"I like them soupy, where I can dip my toast in the yellow stuff." The thought makes my tummy happy.

"Perfect! Fried it is!" She turns back to the stove and starts cracking eggs into the same skillet that had the bacon in it. After a few minutes, she hands me a yummy plate of food. "Here you go, full of love." It looks so good, eggs cooked perfect, bacon, biscuit and grits. I quickly gobble down every bite and feel incredibly stuffed. I didn't realize that while I was busy eating, Dorothy was only drinking coffee. Now that I think about it, I don't remember her eating breakfast before, I think she only cooks for me in the mornings. The thought makes me smile, and I put my dishes in the sink and thank her for the breakfast.

"It's time to head to school my dear, but I notice that you don't have your backpack with you. We can stop by your house and pick it up if you want to." Dorothy takes a sip of her coffee as she waits for my response. Gray tickles fill my tummy and I'm not sure why, but I don't want to go back home. What if he is home just waiting for payback from hitting him yesterday? His eyes flash in my mind, rage filled and drunk, ready to hurt. The image takes my breath away and my chest feels really heavy. I can't go home, not yet.

"Are you ok, Austin?" Her voice makes the image go away and the tickles disappear. I look up at her and there they are, knowing eyes. They see right through me and I freeze at her question. She looks at her watch and then back at me.

"Now that I see the time, I don't think we have time to go to your house first, we better gather our things and head to school." She gets up from the table and starts clearing the food and putting dishes into the dishwasher. I walk to the bathroom and wash my hands. I look in the mirror and see a shit, I can't be better, not when I am so worthless. The thought makes me want to cry but I hold it back and head to the car with Dorothy.

I can't go to the before school recess without an adult so I head to the office after waving at Dorothy. I wait with Mrs. Marsha until the bell rings to go to class. I really like her and tell her all about my night in the fluffy bed and the yummy breakfast I had. She laughs a lot and likes to talk to me. When the bell rings she gives me a high-five and says to have a good day, I smile and head down the hall to class. Mrs. Roush is waiting and has a big smile and kind eyes when I see her. She makes me fill up with purple and warmth. I walk up to her and she holds her hand out to give a high-five. I giggle a bit and slap her hand with mine and smile at her.. I walk into the classroom and head to my locker to put Teddy away. There are a lot of students just hanging out in the lockers talking and goofing around. I did not want to be in trouble so I put Teddy in my locker and walk back to my desk to wait for Mrs. Roush.

"Hi Austin!" Gavin pops up beside me and I jump sideways. My heart starts pounding and my ears get hot. "Look at the slime that I made with my mom last night, isn't it awesome?" Gavin smiles at me, he is so excited to show me. My body calms down and I smile with Gavin. I touch the slime and it is sticky, yet not really sticky, and kind of soft. He stretches it out, and starts playing with it as he walks to his desk. Mrs. Roush walks in after the last student and starts looking for something on her desk. Her desk is usually messy, but she seems to know where everything is on it. It is only minutes before Mrs. Roush asks Gavin to put away the slime. I can see why, it is distracting to me and I am not even the one playing with it.

Mrs. Roush settles the class and starts going over the day's schedule on the board. She stops at reading groups to explain that we will be going to different groups with different teachers. She starts talking about her expectations and I can only think about how she needs to be my reading group teacher. I cross my fingers and wait to hear my name, I can feel painful yellow growing and pushing in my chest. The thought of another teacher makes me feel weird. I can't just sit here, my body feels so jumpy. I raise my hand and show the bathroom signal. Mrs. Roush nods at me and I get up and walk toward the bathroom. I splash water on my face and take a deep breath, after a couple minutes I flush the toilet and walk back out to my desk.

She is announcing the groups when I sit down in my seat. I lay my head down on the wooden desk. It feels cool on my face and the smooth wood is relaxing to feel against my skin. I run my hand back and forth on the surface. I finally look up when I hear her start to announce her group.

"The following students will stay in this classroom with me, Frank, Macy…" Her voice trails off and I stop listening because she isn't going to say my name, I will be in the worst reading group, probably in the smallest room of the school. My old school had a tiny room for the dumb kids that couldn't read and it was smelly and stuffy, I had to turn my body sideways to fit past the book shelf and wall to get to the table.

"Ok the last group will meet outside of Mrs. Gentry's room, and that group is: Brayden, Mia, George, Tess, Nikki, and Austin." She looks at me and smiles when she says my name. I don't even know who Mrs. Gentry is or where her room is. I start to feel sick in my stomach and I want to go home, well, to Dorothy's house. The last reading teacher I had was nice enough but I always got kicked out of her group and then they just had me sit in the office during that time. She had kind, scared eyes. I didn't mean to scare her, I just couldn't read and wanted to get away from the group. I put my head back on my desk and the cold surface cools my cheek. My stomach is really pokey and I feel like I am about to puke. I can't do this, I can't go to reading group.

I can feel the darkness building. It hurts in my tummy. I hear talking around me but I don't know what they are saying. I close my eyes and I can see eyes, dark cold eyes. I don't like it and turn my head on my desk. I can't be better. The thought makes me feel yellow. I try to focus on my breathing. Maybe the reading teacher will be like Mrs. Roush and care. I hope so. The thought makes me feel better. The other teachers here are all nice and are still nice even after my meltdowns. I'm probably upset over nothing, she is going to be nice and she is going to like me. I bet she may even teach me to read. I want to read. As I am thinking about being able to read, I realize that the whole class is already at the carpet and Mrs. Roush is going over the calendar. I turn my head toward the class and listen to calendar time. I am glad Mrs. Roush lets me stay at my desk. Last year, I would have been dragged off to the office for not listening, or the teacher would bug me until I would just get up and leave.

I decide to join my class and get up and walk over to my carpet spot. Sophie is in my spot. I walk over toward her and she smiles, and moves for me to sit down. I like that the class is not scared of me yet. The last school, the students would scatter like ants running away when I sat on the carpet. I watch Mrs. Roush and she smiles at me as she is counting. I join in with the class and count along with the teacher. After a few minutes, I forget about reading group and we are singing our morning songs about the alphabet. When we are finished, all the darkness and hurt fills back up in my tummy, I know what is next.

"Class, Class. Line up at the door in line order and when dismissed you will go straight to your group." Mrs. Roush starts to walk to the front door with the other kids. My chest is really hurting, stabbing with every heartbeat. I need to get away. I need Teddy. I run to my locker, climb in it and hold

Teddy close. I pull up my legs and force myself to fit in the locker. My heart is thumping and I try to calm my body. I squeeze myself small to hide in the locker and hold Teddy next to my face. Maybe no one will notice that I am missing and I can stay here until reading groups are over. I hear footsteps and kids talking as they walk into the room. I freeze, hoping to not be found. Footsteps become louder and then I see shoes next to me. Shoot, I knew better. I should have run for it and found a better hiding place. But, I like this room and want to stay with Mrs. Roush.

"Austin, you are looking quite squished into that locker?" Mrs. Roush's voice reaches my ears. I peak at her and then tuck my head back into Teddy hiding my face. I decide to not say anything.

"I know it's hard to meet a new teacher but I think you'll like her, she's another first grade teacher and is just across the hall." She waits for a response but I still do not say anything. Last year at my old school, when I would not talk to my teacher she would huff and puff like the wolf from the pig story and then she would walk off and leave me alone. I am hoping that Mrs. Roush will leave me be and then after reading groups are over I will go back to my seat. I push myself into the corner of the locker, it is really squishy.

"Sweetheart, it's not a choice to stay here in your locker, the locker is not a very good teacher and you're too good of a kid to not be learning. So please come out and I will walk with you to your reading group. I know you'll do great if you just give it a try." She holds out her hand and I look in her eyes. I'm not sure what made me do it but I moved Teddy, reached out, and put my hand in hers. Her voice is so nice and she makes me feel like she thinks I can do anything. I look into her eyes and there is kindness and love, not the fake kind but the real stuff. It makes my tummy pokes go away, I get up with her, and we walk toward the door.

I don't say a word and watch my feet as we walk. It isn't very many steps until Mrs. Roush opens the door to a classroom and we walk in. It is plain, not much on the walls except for a few boring posters, it is cold and office-like. The desks are in the shape of a U and the teacher desk is behind it. The floor is messy and papers are piled up in random places. The classroom does not seem like a classroom and is not very colorful. At first I do not see a teacher, but some moving around catches my eye. The kids are already sitting around a table in the back of the classroom. The students all turn to face us and the teacher stands up to walk toward us. The look on her face makes her look like a witch. My heart starts to sink and I haven't even met her yet.

She is short and has on high heels that click with every step she takes. Her hair is fake white blonde and short, like Gavin's haircut, and she has a pointy nose with a pair of glasses resting on the tip. As she walks closer to me she peers at me with a stern, kind of blank look on her face. The look of her makes the gray prickles start to grow. Her clothes are dress up clothes and she seems like she means business. She finally stops in front of us and lets out a sigh and her eyes roll to the side as she looks at Mrs. Roush. Teachers must think that kids can't see very well or something, like I can't see her face. The thought makes me feel sick, she sees the shit I am and knows I'm a bad kid. She has not met me but her mind is already made up. I am such a worthless student. I look to the floor and let out a sigh. The gray starts to turn into the darkness and I try to keep it from growing. I step behind Mrs. Roush and squeeze her hand.

"Hmmm, well I didn't think you were coming today." Dark eyes. She is cold and hate-filled already. She doesn't want me here and it is obvious, she doesn't even try to fake care. The gray starts to turn to darkness and I squeeze Mrs. Roush's hand tighter and step closer to her. I want her to not leave me here.

"Is there a problem already Mrs. Roush?" Already. What is that supposed to mean? The darkness gets tighter in my chest. I continue to squeeze Mrs. Roush's hand and look back to the floor. Please don't leave me here. Please don't leave me here.

"No problems, Mrs. Gentry, we were just looking for something before walking over." Mrs. Roush smiles and then bends down to look at me. "Austin, it's ok and you will learn from this group. I will see you in half an hour, that is only one episode of Doc Mcstuffins." She lets go of my hand, I try to hold on, but know I need to let go. She smiles at me, stands back up and walks back out of the classroom. Her words did make me feel a little less dark. It will be fast. I am lost in my thoughts when I hear my name in a grumpy gruff voice.

"Austin…. Austin! Go take a seat, we have wasted enough time getting started." She doesn't even look at me when she is talking and turns to walk back to the table. My tummy hurts and I can feel my heart thumping in my ears. I walk over and sit down with the other kids. My body is hot and I put my head on the desk to feel the cool surface on my face. I take in a deep breath and try to push back the sick that is growing in my stomach. "Get up, you can't just put your head down, what are you thinking?" Her words are sharp and full of irritation. I look at her and there they are, cold and dark-filled eyes glaring back at me. "You are holding up the entire class for the second time."

I put my head up and take in another breath. I can do this. I can do this. I am feeling warm, this room is so hot. I feel like my stomach is on fire and the gray stabs at the flames. I think I am going to puke. I put my hand on my face and without thinking, I put my head back onto the table. It is cold on my cheek. The cold makes the fire not hurt so much. I run my hand along the table to feel the surface. It is smooth except for a couple dirty spots. I try to focus on something else, like my night with Dorothy to help calm the gray stabs in my chest. As I am picturing the movie and milkshakes, the teacher's words fill my ears again.

"Get up! What do you think you're doing? I've already asked you this once! This is not naptime! You need to pay attention and follow along." Mrs. Gentry's sharp words make the darkness grow in my chest. I start to feel hot and a fire starts building inside. I don't pick my head up and continue to keep my head on the cool table. I need to stay in control. I don't want to have a meltdown. I take in a breath and try to cool the fire. As I am focusing on staying calm, I hear more of the teacher's piercing words, like fuel to the flame inside it flashes higher. And in slow motion, I see the teacher stand up in front of me. No. No.

"Don't touch me! Don't hurt me!" I yell out before I can stop the words. The darkness consumes me. I can't breathe as the teacher's hand touches my shoulder. I see dirty, grubby hands. The stench fills my nostrils and all I can smell is cigarettes and old beer. "Don't Touch Me!" I scream it again. My voice is loud and I need to get away from here. I shove the chairs to the side to get away from the hands and crawl under the table.

"What are you doing? Get out of there now!" The words are angry and I start to lift the table up with my feet. I don't respond to her. As I am lifting the table up and letting it slam, the darkness starts to back down. I like the feel of the table hitting the floor. Out of the corner of my eye, I see legs and a hand reaching for me.

"NO! Don't touch me!! Get away from me!!" The words come out of my mouth before I can think of anything else. I can't breathe, my heart is rushing. I need to escape, I have to get away from him. The hand grabs for me, but I run between the chairs and push them behind me to keep him away. It feels like a hammer is pounding in my ears. I run as fast as my legs can carry me. I can hear words echoing behind me and there are voices in the hall. I am not sure what they are saying, but I keep moving. I run toward the lockers in the back of the classroom. Like Spider-man, I climb up the lockers in a few quick leaps. I jump onto the area that separates the lockers from the other side of the classroom where the reading group area is. I push some boxes to the side and make myself small between them. Maybe no one will find me here.

"What in the world are you doing? Get down here now! This is not how a student acts in my reading group! I am going to go call the principal and you can go to the office!" Her voice starts to trail off as her footsteps walk away from me but I can still hear Mrs. Gentry's words.

"How am I supposed to teach with a student like that, he can just go and they can deal with him." Her words make my heart blue, she is right. I am a bad kid and don't belong here. The thought makes tears start to fall from my eyes. I want to go back to Dorothy's house. I am lost in my thoughts and forget where I am, when a squeak of the door brings me back to the room. I can hear voices talking.

"He needs to be removed from my room so I can teach, he is on top of the wall over there." Her words are angry.

"Do you know what happened?" Ms. Benson's voice sounds calm.

"Yes, he doesn't want to work and had a fit to get out of it and now I can't teach the group with his behavior in here. I don't know what you want me to do with that!" Mrs. Gentry's words are followed by fast footsteps. I hear a chair scooting on the floor and she starts teaching the reading group again. I take in a breath. I can't help but think that she doesn't like me, I didn't mean to be bad. I hate this. I am such a shit. I feel the darkness grab me again, I am the bad kid in class again. The thought makes my heart race, I kick the box that is next to me and it falls to the floor and art supplies fly everywhere. I will show her how to deal with "it," and I grab a pile of posters that are sitting on top of another box. I look at them and then start throwing them as far as I can.

My face feels hot and blue and my knees are itchy. I look down and see Ms. Benson. Now she knows, the bad kid that I am. I am a shit. I look into her eyes, they are still kind, they are not angry. I can't hold back the tears and they fall down my face. I can feel their warmth move down and fall onto my arms that are wrapped around my knees. I hear some words but I don't know what they are saying. There are some scissors in a clear container. I take off the lid and start cutting the edge of a box with them. The box is thick and it is hard to cut it. As I am forcing the scissors through the brown cardboard, my mind wanders back to Mommy. I hope she is ok. The thought about Mommy makes gray spikes grow, the box reminds me of my closet, it is dusty up here too. I can smell the stink and his drunk voice pierces my ears. I plug my ears with my fingers. I can still hear his voice but not as much. Mommy. Where is she? I suddenly hear movement next to me. Him. I try to move away. Boxes fall over toward him. Oh no. "Leave me alone!" "Leave me alone!" I try to make myself small. I keep my fingers in my ears. Please don't hurt me. Please don't hurt me. The thought makes the darkness grow.

I can feel something on my back. It feels good. I take in a breath and then another. The darkness starts to turn to gray and I take my fingers out of my ears. Slowly, I look over to what is touching me and it is a hand. It is not dirty or stinky. It is Ms. Benson. She is slowly rubbing my back with her fingers.

Her words fill my ears. I am hesitant to look at her eyes, I don't want her to be angry at me.

"It's not safe up here, can you come with me to another place that's safe? We can go to my office or Ms. Jennie's office." Her words are calm and caring. I look at her and her eyes are still kind. She doesn't look angry at me. Maybe she doesn't see the bad kid in me.

I can't find my words, they seem to be lost. I am not sure what to do. I want to run and hide, but my hand reaches out and she takes it. I like to hold her hand. I climb down with her. She doesn't say another word to me, only smiles. She leads me to the door closest to us and unlocks it. She pushes it open and waits for me to walk through and then she follows. We start walking together, I am still holding her hand. After a few steps, a door opens and a teacher walks out. I have seen her around but I don't know her name.

"Well hi Austin! So good to see you today! Are you giving high-fives or fist bumps?" She sticks her hand out and waits, smiling. I look at her and she has happy eyes. I smile and shake my head no. I don't know her but she seems nice. We keep walking and Ms. Benson tells me that the teacher is a third grade teacher in my hallway. I smile at her and hope she can be my teacher in third grade. My words are still lost. We make our way to the office and Mrs. Marsha looks up at us. "There's my favorite boy!" Her smile is contagious and I can't help but laugh at her. "Did you hear that he had a great night last night at his friend's house, Ms. Benson?"

"I didn't, can you tell me about it?" Ms. Benson smiles at me as we walk into her office. She sits down and waits for me to start talking. I just look at her, waiting. I know I am in trouble and she is probably going to kick me out of school. The thought makes me gray and I hope she calls Dorothy instead of Don. I feel sick and put my head down on the table. I don't like to be in trouble. The cool surface is kinda sticky and grosses me out so I sit back up. My eyes meet Ms. Benson's and she is just staring at me, kind and interested. I wonder what she is thinking. Probably what consequences she can give me. The thought makes my heart drop.

"Your friend, the one you stayed with last night, was it Dorothy? I dropped you off at her house, right?" Ms. Benson smiles at me.

My face is sticky and I feel gross all over. "Yeah, I got to stay at her house and we watched a movie and made milkshakes. And I slept in a bed!" Oh no. I didn't mean to say the last part and I need to change the subject. "What's sticky on here?" I ask, pointing to the table.

Ms. Benson looks at me with knowing eyes. "I have no idea but that's nasty, do you want to wipe your face? It really is hard to tell." She laughs and reaches for a drawer. She pulls out some wipes and starts to clean the table off. I smile at her and walk into her bathroom and grab a paper towel and clean off my face. I look in the mirror, but I feel something strange. I don't really see a worthless little shit, I see a boy with clean clothes and hair. I smile at myself, and I am not sure the feeling I have, but it is green and feels warm.

I walk back out to the table and Ms. Benson starts talking to me again. "So you slept in a bed last night, how was that?" she leans onto the table waiting for an answer.

"It was so fluffy and warm, and I didn't pee the bed!" I said too much again. It's so easy to talk to her and I want to tell her things, but I really can't say so much. The thought makes gray bubbles in my tummy, Don would really hurt us if he knew.

"That sounds like a perfect bed to snuggle in. You don't have a bed at your house?" her face turns serious and she is staring at me again. I need to pick my words. I don't want Don to hurt us more.

"I did at my old house, it was a cool Avengers one, but it hasn't been put back up at Don's house yet." I smile at her and try not to look weird. That is the truth, I just left some parts out, so it is not completely lying.

"I see, well hopefully you will get it back soon," knowing eyes again, they feel like they can see through me. "How did you feel in Mrs. Gentry's room?" Ms. Benson asks, changing the subject.

That is not what I expected her to say. She is weird too. And now she is still staring at me. I touch the table and it is not sticky anymore. I look back at her and she smiles at me. If I don't answer her she is not going to stop looking at me. "Gray," I answer quickly.

"Gray? Hmm, well what does gray feel like in your body?" She just keeps looking at me.

"Well, sometimes it is pokey in my tummy and a lot of the time it feels like prickles inside me." I look down and feel funny. I have never told anyone that, but no one has ever asked.

"Oh, and how do you feel when you think of going back to Mrs. Roush's room?" She keeps staring, but now she is leaning on the table with her head on her hand.

"Purple, and it is warm." I smile and sit up when I say this. I really like Mrs. Roush and I think she likes me.

"Austin, you did not make very smart choices in Mrs. Gentry's room, what could you have done differently?" She smiles at me.

"I don't know." I look down.

"Well, you could have asked for a break and came down here or to Ms. Jennie's room. Or you could have tried deep breaths, or chair pulls when you started to get upset." Ms. Benson takes in a breath and smiles at me. "You have to use your calm down tools, you cannot throw chairs or yell at teachers." She looks at the clock and sits back in her chair. "Ok, well since your recess is over, why don't I walk you back to Mrs. Roush's room?" She stands up and heads toward the door.

I follow her and feel a little lost. "Ms. Benson?" I wait for her answer and walk faster to catch up. She looks over at me and makes a noise that I think means that I can ask her my question.

"Am I in trouble? What is going to happen to me?" The gray prickles build up and poke at my chest as I wait for her answer.

"Well…we talked about it and now you know how I would like you to handle this if it happens again. So if you find yourself upset again, you are not going to push chairs or kick the table or climb walls, is that a deal?" She looks serious when she says this.

"I will ask for a break." I respond quickly, take in a deep breath and smile to myself. She doesn't see me as a little shit, maybe I am Ironman. The thought makes me feel green and purple all over. I can't help but smile as I watch my feet walk on the shiny floor toward my hallway. When we turn the corner to the other hall, the smiley teacher from earlier is standing by her door. She looks at me with fun eyes and smiles. She doesn't say anything but her smile makes me smile back at her. At the end of the hallway my class is walking in from recess and they go into the back door of the classroom. I don't see Mrs. Roush, I hope she isn't mad at me about what happened. I start to feel gray bubbles in my tummy and take in a deep breath as I reach for the door. It creaks as it opens up and it seems like slow motion as I walk through to the classroom. I look around, hoping to not see angry eyes.

I stop and stand near the whiteboard. Some students are at their desks, some are putting coats away, and some are goofing off. As my eyes scan the room, they find Mrs. Roush. She looks at me, but she does not have angry eyes or frustrated ones. She is kind and her face fills with a smile when she sees me. The purple grows and pops the gray bubbles. I can't help but smile back at her as she starts walking toward me. I hear someone step next to me and when I look, I see Ms. Benson and the door shutting behind. I turn back to Mrs. Roush and her eyes are so kind. I feel weird inside and the feeling is new, one I don't feel very much. I like the feeling and it blooms inside me.

I don't know what happened. Mrs. Roush walks and stops close to me. I think she was about to say something, but I did not give her the chance. I throw myself around her and hug her. The weird feeling that I have fills me and I pour it into the hug. A big hug. I am not sure why I did it, but I try to put so many words into the hug. It is the first time I remember hugging a teacher. She wraps her arms around me and I feel a warmth that I haven't felt in a long time. She smells good, like home, safe, like flowers and springtime. I could stay in her hug all day. When she releases me, I feel like I could do anything, maybe I am not a bad kid. Maybe I can be strong. The thought makes me smile as I walk over to my desk and sit down for class.

CHAPTER 10

THE DISMISSAL BELL RINGS AND THE REST
of the class heads outside to meet their families. I look around
and realize that I am not sure where I am going after school.
Usually, I would walk home but maybe I should go to Dorothy's
house instead. I start to gather my stuff and mess around in my
desk. Maybe if I take longer to leave, Dorothy will be home.
I start heading to the classroom door, and hear voices in the
hallway. I think it is Mrs. Gentry's voice because it sounds cold
and hate filled. Her words are sharp and angry. She seems like
she is rushed or out of breath from talking so fast.

"I don't know why I have to deal with a student who acts
like that, it is a waste of my time and he just wanted to ruin my
reading time. Now the other students who want to learn can't.
And he knew exactly what he was doing and did it on purpose
just to get out of working. You know he just went to the office
and probably played in the counselor's office. Well, I will tell

you now that if it happens again he will not be welcome in my room, kids like him should just go to a different place and then other kids can learn without disruption. Someone needs to have a place for them so we don't have to deal with disruptive students," her voice is angry and cold.

It makes me turn blue. I didn't mean to be such a shit. I don't want to go back to her room anymore. I stop listening and walk out of the door. She is standing there and looks down at me with her pointy witch-like nose. She makes a grunting noise and rolls her eyes. Her face is angry. The teacher she is talking to just looks at me with disgust and then looks the other way. I think she teaches at the other end of the hall across from the smiley third grade teacher. I look down and quickly walk past them. I head to the doors and start to run. I need to get away from here. I am such a shit. Red flames start to ignite as Mrs. Gentry's words echo in my head. I see her eyes and then they turn into his eyes. I can smell him. I run faster and can feel the ground move beneath my feet. Suddenly, I run into something. I hit hard and fall backward onto the ground.

I look up and can feel my heart beating in my chest. I see a smile and a hand reaching for me. "Don't Touch Me!" I yell and scoot my body backward. Ms. Jennie takes a step back and her words are soft and kind. "Are you ok, Austin? I did not see you running, I am sorry I ran into you." Her eyes are kind and I start to breathe deeply. I don't have any words and I just look at her. She waits and her eyes are calm. I get up and all I can think to say is bye and I run past her toward Dorothy's house. I hope she is home. If I go to my house he will be there. I don't want to see him, but I do need to protect my mom. Mommy. I don't know if she is ok or not. The thoughts keep rushing in my head and the darkness builds inside. I am sweating and the sun is really hot and beating down on me. Sweat is rolling into my eyes and my chest is hurting from breathing. I keep running and the gravel road slips beneath my shoes. I lose my balance, falling hands and face first onto the road sliding to a stop.

I just lay still and a dust puff surrounds me. The gravel is hard and dry on my face. Dirt and dust fill my eyes as the tears fall. I stretch out my arm moving the rocks and dirt in its path. My muscles hurt and my hands are stinging. I let out a breath that I think I was holding in. I am so stupid. Such a shit. I start to cry and let it out. No one is around to see me anyway. I see my mom's scared face in my mind. I hear Mrs. Gentry's voice and it turns into his voice, dark and cold. The thoughts make me feel gray and I need to get away from them. I roll over onto my back and sit up. I wipe the tears from my face and my hands are covered in dirt and blood. The sun stings. Leaning forward, I put my hands over my eyes and hold my head up. Lost in my thoughts, I can't think straight. I don't hear the gravel shifting under the tires of a truck that is driving toward me.

The shifting gravel moves and pops beneath the tires. The truck lets out a loud squeak from the brakes slowing down. My heart starts to race and I feel the darkness forming throughout my body. I can't get myself to look up. My head is heavy in my hands and I keep hiding my face. My body is thumping and I can hear the beat in my ears. It is him. It is his truck. I need to be small. Maybe it is not his, I hope that it is not his truck. It sounds like his truck. I try to breathe but the air is stuck in my throat. I think I am going to puke. I hear the sound of the car door shut and it echoes in my head. It hurts. I feel a shadow in front of me and it blocks the sun from my eyes. A soft voice and kind words find my ears. Looking up, I see a smile with Dorothy's caring eyes.

"Oh sweet boy, are you ok? You are a hot mess, just look at you! Come on, come on, let's go get you cleaned up, now." Her words push the gray and darkness away. She reaches for my arm to help me up and I can't hold back anymore. I start crying and melt into her chest. I don't have words but let the tears fall down my face. She rests her head on top of mine and offers comfort in her touch and words. "It's ok Austin, I'm here to help, let's get in the car and head to my house, ok? You can tell me about your day, before you fell, anyway." She starts to walk me toward her car. She opens the door for me and I climb in and buckle myself. She walks around the front of the car and gets in. We start to drive and she doesn't say anything else. I am thankful that she came along and cared enough to stop for me. I don't understand why I heard his truck in my ears. Sometimes my mind seems in a different place than the rest of me. I try to not think about it.

We pull into her driveway and I take in a deep breath. I climb out of her car and I freeze. I can't get my feet to move and stare at the ground. Mommy. I wonder if she is home. I hope she is ok. I picture her face empty and blank sitting in the corner of the kitchen. I can hear his breathing, deep and growling slowly. The darkness starts to vine up my throat. A hand lands on my shoulder and I can feel each finger as they close around me. I jump forward and drop my shoulder to get away from it. I look back, expecting to see his ugly face, but it is Dorothy looking at me with knowing eyes. Caring, knowing eyes. She puts her hand down and we walk into her house. She takes me to the bathroom and asks me to sit on the sink. I climb up while she walks over the closet and gets out a washcloth. She turns and smiles at me. Her smile is warm. She runs water over the cloth and starts to clean my face up. It stings and I flinch but hold still as much as I can. When she is done with my face, she cleans my hands and elbows and puts on some bandages. I don't remember the last time someone put a bandage on me, or helped me clean up. I like it. The thought makes me smile.

"Ok, sweet boy you need to clean up your knees. But you'll need to take off your pants, so I will step out. Here is the cloth and bandages, I'll be in the kitchen making you an after school snack." She smiles again and walks out of the bathroom, shutting the door behind her.

I jump off the counter and take off my pants. There is blood all the way down my leg and I wipe it up and stick a bandage on it. Just as I am about to get dressed again, I hear the doorbell ring followed by hard pounding on the door. Instantly, my heart jumps and it feels like lightning bolts run down my arms and legs. I freeze and listen. I can hear Dorothy's footsteps walking to the door. I finish pulling up my pants. The door pushes along the floor as she opens it. I can hear her voice saying something but I can't hear what it is. Then another voice. His voice. It is him at the door. The darkness consumes me.

I can't move and I feel like I am falling. I can't go home with him. I don't want to go with him. But I see my mommy's face and she needs me. I don't have a choice. I have to help her.

"Where's Austin? He needs to be home, and has no business coming here after school." He sounds angry and his words make me feel small. His voice sounds drunk, and is scary. I hope he doesn't hurt Dorothy. I should walk out there before he has the chance to hurt her too. I start to move but I stop when I hear her response.

"Of course he has business here, you ditched him last night and it was fine for him to be here then! And I will always help him when he needs it. You have no business coming to my door talking to me like that, Don. Now, if you are asking me if Austin is here, then yes he is. He fell on his way home and needed some bandages and to be cleaned up." Her voice was different. I have never heard her sound like that before. I felt the darkness but I also felt green around it. I still did not move from the bathroom.

"Fine, I need him, so tell him to meet me at the truck, it's time to go home." His voice sounds angry and grumbly but it is softer. He changes his tone with her. I knew Dorothy could be scary. I hear his footsteps on the porch and then a truck door slam. I let out my breath and step out of the bathroom.

Dorothy's eyes meet mine and they are very straight, not angry but not happy either. I am not sure what they are. She finally smiles at me. "Oh hon, your parents are waiting outside and it sounds like they're wanting you home. I bet your mom missed you!" She smiles again, but it isn't convincing.

I try to hide the gray and darkness that is forming in my body from her. I don't want her to worry about me. "I don't want to go home." The words are out of my mouth before I realize it wasn't just a thought in my head. I look quickly to the floor and start walking to the door. When I start to open it, Dorothy's words fill my ears. "Austin, I'll be right here if you need anything, ok?" Her eyes look scared and very serious.

"I'll be ok, and thank you for your help and the ride." I smile when I say this then quickly walk out of the door without looking back.

The truck rumbles in the driveway and I can see him sitting there, head down. I don't see my mom and the darkness swirls. I freeze and don't want to get in the truck. My breath is slow and I don't know what to do. He looks up at me. Hate. Dark. He starts to wave at me to get in the truck. I try to get my feet to move but they are stuck. His eyes turn angry and he opens the truck door. It is like slow motion as he walks toward me. As I am watching him, he puts his hand in the air and waves. Confused, I look behind me to see Dorothy standing on the porch watching. It makes me smile and feel green. Don reaches me and takes his hand and puts it on my back. "Go, now," as he says this, he takes his thumb and shoves it into my back, hard. Pushing me to the truck, he starts to walk as well. I am sure he is trying to hide this from Dorothy, which I think she could get scary if she needed to.

I hurry to the truck and open the door. Blue beer cans fall to the ground. I just look at them. "Pick it up," his words are gruff. I toss the cans back into the truck and climb in. The floor is covered in cans and it smells like smoke and dirt. I don't say anything, I don't want to make him angrier. As I am looking at the floor, I see bags that are in the middle close to his legs. They are held together with a rubber band and they have some weird looking white stuff in them. I wonder if it is something for baking or even some kind of fertilizer for plants. Next to them there is a small box with the lid half off with weird stuff in it. There is a stick looking thing that is wrapped in what reminds me of those nasty sandwiches that gas stations have in the heater shelf. I can see a spoon, and a glass tube thing. I want to ask him, but my instinct is to not ask. I have seen him smoke this chunky parsley looking stuff and when I asked about it he slapped me in the face and told me to mind my own damn business. I just look away and watch the trees go by as he drives toward our house.

Drugs. Nasty drugs. That has to be what the stuff on the floor is. Maybe this is why he is so mean. I hope Mommy is not eating the drugs too. The thought makes me feel sick and I try to not think about it. Don flips the stick and a beeping noise comes on. The truck slows down and we start to turn toward the house. I hope to see my mom waiting for us, but I don't see her anywhere. Gray stabs start to form. I take a breath and look at Don. His eyes are dark and sunk in. He looks dirty and hairy like he hasn't showered or shaved in a while. I decide to ask him where Mom is and I have to talk myself into using my words.

"Don, is mom at home?" my voice is shaky. I wait for a response and it seems like it takes forever.

"Yes, that bitch is home. She done passed out on the kitchen floor," his voice sounds angry. He puts the truck in park and opens his door to get out of the truck. When he steps out, he stumbles and almost falls, then turns and grabs the box of stuff from the floor. He walks weirdly to the house. When the screen door closes behind him, I open the truck door. More cans fall to the ground and roll under the truck. My tummy starts to feel sick and the gray explodes in me. I want to go in, but I am wanting to run away. I know Don is angry but he said Mommy is passed out. I need to check on her. I walk up to the porch and open the screen door, letting it slam shut behind me. My eyes quickly find her. There is Mom, sitting up at least, on the floor. She looks awful. Darkness surrounds her eyes. She seems empty. Looking at her fills me with blue and red, it swirls and fills me up. I walk up to her and sit down. I put my hand on her shoulder.

"Mommy...are you ok?" my voice sounds like a baby. She moves her head toward me and touches my face. The feel of her hand on me makes the red and blue shrink some.

"Oh... my boy... I am fine." She smiles at me but it is so weak. She drops her hand to the floor and she just sits there, staring at the floor. Footsteps come into the kitchen behind me. Before I can move, I feel a hard kick to my back. I scramble to get out of the way as his words echo through the house.

"Get the fuck away from the fridge door!" He reaches for the door and forcefully opens it. Food falls to the floor and he kicks it out of the way, squirting mustard. He grabs the blue cans out of the fridge and slams it back shut. He turns toward my mom and he has a look of disgust on his face. He stares at her. Cold dark eyes. He looks scary. He looks down at her as he sits one beer down on the counter and opens the other. He pulls the can up to his face and chugs it gone. He takes the empty can and squishes it in his hand and then launches it at my mom. The can hits her on the shoulder. My mom just sits there. She doesn't say anything or move. Don just starts laughing. It is a creepy laugh. I am stuck and want to run but I can't get my body to move. I start to scooch myself away when he stops laughing and starts screaming.

"Fuck! You need to get up. How much of that shit did you shoot up? Dumb bitch." He reaches down and grabs her shirt. He lifts her up and slams her against the counter. "Now, get your shit together and start cooking!" He starts to laugh again and drinks the beer as he walks into the living room. Mom stands there and leans onto the counter. She seems lost and weak. I find my strength and stand up. I walk over to her and put my hand on her arm. "Austin, go to your room." She doesn't even look at me and her words hurt. I want to help. Her words pierce through me and I drop my hand away from her. I don't have words. I am worthless. I can't help her. I let out a breath and walk to my room. I look around at the dirt and piled up boxes. I want a bed. I think about my night at Dorothy's and it makes me feel warm. Oh no, I left Teddy at her house this morning. I start to feel gray and yellow. I need him. I have to go back to get him. I walk out to the living room. Mom is messing around in the kitchen and Don is watching T.V. He has a beer in his hand and a couple empty ones on the floor. I just walk out the front door without notice. They don't care about me, I don't even know why he came to get me.

The sun is cooler and it is starting to get late. I walk quickly and head to the shortcut through the woods. I can't help but think about what that stuff was on the truck floor. Is that why my mommy has been empty? The thought hurts. I can hear sticks break under my feet and decide to run. I don't want to make Don upset if I am gone too long. I see her house and I am out of breath. I stop to take a little break to catch it before I get there. I hear a noise next to me and my heart jumps. I turn to see what it is. A deer. It just looks at me and walks off. Must be nice to be free and not worry about stuff except eating grass and not getting hit by a car. Oh, and hunting season of course. I start laughing, maybe being a deer would not be that great.

I knock on the back door and Dorothy answers it with a smile. "I knew you would be coming back!" she said excitedly as she turns and walks back into the kitchen. I follow her and smell something delicious. She has Teddy sitting at the table waiting on me. I walk over and pick him up. He makes me feel safe. I think I will really need him tonight. I hug him tight and start to walk back to the door. I don't want to make Don mad if he sees I am gone. He probably hasn't noticed yet. Maybe he will drink all his beer and pass out, then I won't have to deal with him when I do get back. Dorothy's voice stops me.

"Where are you going so fast? I made dinner and it is ready. Here is your plate, and help yourself to some fresh sweet tea in the fridge." She does not give me a chance to say no as she slides the plate in front of me. It made me smile. I turn and pull out a chair at the table. A few more minutes shouldn't make a difference. It would be rude to turn down food that she has ready for me. I am hungry. My tummy feels angry. Chicken that looks like it was baked with gravy and I think, stuffing. Green beans on the side. Mmmm. My stomach growls and I don't hesitate and start to eat the food. She is such a good cook. "You are a great cook. Thank you so much," I tell her with a mouth full of food.

"Love my dear, that's the secret ingredient, well and extra butter of course." She laughs and sits down with a plate of food. "Why did Don want you home today? He doesn't usually pick you up does he?" She asks this as she pours two glasses of tea.

"No idea, he didn't tell me." I keep eating. "But I don't want to make him mad so I can't stay long, they don't know that I'm here. Didn't even notice I left!"

"No, let's not upset him, he already seemed on edge when he was here." Her face seems different when she says this. We sit and finish our food without talking. Dorothy seems to be lost in her thoughts. I feel that way a lot too. I wonder what she is worrying about. I take my plate to the sink and thank her again as I walk toward the door.

"Austin, I will be here for the rest of the night and do not have plans to go anywhere. I will see you in the morning on your way to school then?" Knowing eyes. I should just tell her about the ride home, but I need to protect my mom. I just smile at her. I hold Teddy close and head out the door toward home. I decide to make it fast again and run. The sun is going down and the sky is turning orange and purple. There is a breeze blowing through the trees making a calm rustling sound. I like it out here. Maybe I should just stay here tonight, but it is starting to get cold and the leaves are starting to turn colors. It is pretty this time of year. I try to stay focused and feel like I need to hurry home. I don't like the feeling and gray bubbles form.

I reach the front porch and my heart drops and I am frozen to the spot. His voice fills my head and the darkness forms. The voice is angry and scary. I can't get my body to move. Mommy. Oh no. I need to help her, but I am a pussy and keep standing there. I can't hear anything except my breath filling my lungs and then pushing out. My heart is racing and I want to run away but then I hear my mommy. Her screams escape from under the door. I have to move. I have to protect her. I need to be Ironman. I take in a breath and calm my heart. Then another and shield myself from the outside. I am Ironman. Teddy drops to the ground. I run to the side of the trailer and climb up to the window. I want to see what is happening before I barge through the door. I quietly push it open and pull myself through and onto the floor.

"No! Nooo!" Mom's voice is followed by some thumping noises.

"You dumb bitch, you're the reason I have to drink. Why is that guy texting you? Are you a slut now too?" His voice is fierce.

"I am in his class at school!!" She is crying and sounds desperate.

I walk softly down the hall to see what is going on. Looking into the kitchen Mom is on the floor and has her head resting in her hands. Don walks heavily into the living room and I make myself small to hide from him. He picks up the box from the truck and goes back into the kitchen. After digging through the box, he has some of the white stuff and is doing something with it. Next thing I know, he is taking a shot, like the one I get at the doctor, and jabbs it into his arm. He stands there for a short time and then he reaches down and tangles his slimy fingers in my mom's hair. She starts to cry out as he lifts her up from the ground by her hair. She grabs his hand and tries to break free but can't. I feel sick watching him hurt her, but I don't dare go out there. Not yet. He starts laughing at her and then bends down and whispers something in her ear.

"No I didn't. Stop it! Stop it! I love you!" Mom's words are full of tears and her face looks scared. He then shoves her against the counter and holds her there by her hair. Her head is pulled back forcing her to look at the ceiling. He continues to whisper words onto her neck, I can't hear what he is saying. With his other hand he reaches down and pulls off her jeans. As her pants fall to the floor, my breath stops. I drop my eyes. I can't watch this. But I am stuck. I look back at my mom and she is trying to stop him. He still has her hair and head pulled back, and his face is buried in her neck. As she struggles to get away, Don takes off his belt and drops his jeans to the floor. I know that people do weird stuff, but I don't think my mommy wants him touching her. I bet the darkness is in her too. He pushes her farther onto the counter by her hair. She starts to scream as he starts pushing himself onto her, hard. She is kicking and manages to get a hand against his face to push him away. This makes him mad and he makes a weird grunt and then grabs her by the throat. He keeps shoving onto her. She is grasping at his hand, trying to pull it away from her neck. He keeps shoving into her and her face is starting to turn purple. She can't breathe.

I have to do something. I take in a deep breath. I am Ironman. I try to shield myself and I run as hard as I can and ram into him. He stumbles sideways but doesn't move very far. He is still on her and I back up and with all my might kick him right in his nuts, but from the back. And as soon as my foot falls to the floor, I wind up and do it again. And again. I start to feel a fire build in me. I hate him and I keep kicking until he falls over away from Mom. She falls to the floor and curls into a ball. Mom hides herself and starts crying. I look at her and I am full of red and fire. I turn to Don who is starting to get up. He is grabbing his crotch and looks at me. Hate filled eyes. I don't look away and I try to match him with the hate that is in me. I walk up to him and with every kick I say a word: "Leave. My. Mom. Alone. Bastard!" I kick him wherever my foot lands. With the last kick I fall backward and start to cry.

I crawl over to my mom and hope to comfort her. "Mommy, are you ok?" My voice is weak and out of breath. She doesn't respond. I need her back. I hope she will leave with me. "Mommy, leave with me, come on get up." I pull on her arm and she flinches and moves away from me. "Mom, come on please." As I am trying to get her to listen to me, Don gets to his feet and walks down the hallway. His footsteps echo. I can hear him hitting the wall with his fist. I start to shake my mom and beg her to get up and leave with me. She ignores me. Finally, she sits up and looks at me. Her eye is black and her face is dark and sunken looking. I look into her eyes and try again, "Mommy, please listen to me, come with me, get away from here." I let the tears fall as I watch her stand up and lean onto the counter.

Don's footsteps bounce off the walls and fill my ears. It happens so fast. He comes at me and grabs me by the throat. He holds me up as he punches me in the stomach. I try to get free. I am so stupid. Mommy. I try to catch her eyes but she just stands there in a daze. Don finally throws me down. I hit the floor and try to crawl away. I look back at him as I try to catch my breath. Then he starts to yell, but it doesn't make sense. He sounds like he is panicked and starts pacing around the kitchen. He is sweaty and his words are hard to understand. He sounds funny, like he forgot how to talk.

"Fuck, leave me, well fuck that." He grabs his head and I notice something in his hand. My heart stops. The darkness chokes me and I can't breathe. A gun. He has a gun. I try to make myself small. Maybe he will forget about me. He walks over to my mom and kisses her cheek then grabs her face. He points the gun to the side of her head. "You cannot leave here, I will kill you." His voice sounds different. He turns to me. I try to push myself back on the floor but it is too sticky and I can't move much. He lets go of my mom's face and starts to walk toward me. I am not Ironman and I am so stupid. I try to be invisible and make myself small. In slow motion he reaches for me and I try to shield myself. I close my eyes and try to picture something else. I am sitting on the couch and my dad is smiling at me. The thought makes me warm, but the darkness is too much. Red takes over me as he picks me up again. I am dangling by my shirt. He still has the gun pointed to Mommy's head. I try to punch him but I can't reach him. He starts laughing and his eyes look crazy. He doesn't look normal and it is scary.

"You little shit! I can just shoot you and then be done with it!" He seems serious and I can't breathe. He turns to my mom and with a quick movement launches me across the room. My head rings as I hit the table and fall to the floor. My ribs are on fire and I think I hurt my head. I try to climb under the table and hide but he grabs my foot and pulls me back. "I want you where you can watch this." He turns to my mom and starts talking again. "Well, I am done playing house so you can decide who you want to be with, so make a choice, but if it is him then I can get rid of your little bastard son." He points the gun to me. I have never felt this way before and I just close my eyes. I can't watch anymore. I am going to die. I feel full of gray and then I picture my dad's face. If I die, I can be with my dad again. The thought makes it not so scary, and I take in a breath. Maybe I would be better off if he does shoot me. I am lost in thought when I hear movement and open my eyes.

Mom walks toward him and grabs his face and kisses him. It is a long disgusting kiss, but the gun slowly moves away from me and points to the floor. I want to run but I feel like a rock. Mom grabs his hand and then the other one. She moves the gun onto the counter. Don is just looking at her. Then I think he begins to cry because there are streaks of stuff on his face. He looks like a little kid standing there lost. Mom doesn't say a word. She doesn't look at me. She just pulls his hands and surprisingly he walks with her. He wraps her arm around his back and they disappear down the hallway. I can see the shadow of the bedroom door closing and hear the movement that I think is the door locking. It is dark and silent in the kitchen. I don't know what to do. I almost died. He almost shot me, and she kissed him. She chose him over me. I am done.

I lay down on the floor and feel the surface. It is smooth and dirty at the same time. I hurt all over and my body is sweaty. I move my arms down toward my legs and feel a wet puddle. I am covered in pee. I pissed myself again and it is all over. I can't do this anymore. I hate him. I hate her. She doesn't love me anymore. I love her and want her to be safe but I can't, I just can't. I am no hero, and I need my mommy. My mommy is gone. Gone like daddy. I need to get out of here. I take in a deep breath and stand up. Looking around everything is dark and I have no idea the time. I start to have short breaths and my chest is hurting. I don't know what to do. Teddy. I need Teddy. I walk into the living room and my feet run into beer cans and they slide across the floor. The door creaks open and slams shut behind me. I don't care if they get up. I don't care anymore. I find Teddy and hold him close. As I am squeezing him, I close my eyes and picture a gun pointing at me and my mom standing there doing nothing. Tears fall down my face and I let them fall.

I can't be here anymore. I jump off the porch and run down the driveway, the gravel slides under my feet. It is cool outside and the stars are shining brightly in the dark sky. I stop running when I get to the road that leads to Dorothy's house. I step off the road and walk to the edge of the woods. I sit down and lean against the tree. The sounds of the whippoorwill bird echoes through the trees. It is relaxing. I let the sounds fill me up and I try to breath out the darkness in me. The pain shoots through my body and I start to get cold and shiver. The shivers hurt me. My side is very painful and it hurts to breathe. I stand up and grab Teddy. I start to walk and try to be gentle with my steps. I walk and I can't help but think about my mom. She picked him over me. She loves him more. I need to get away, the thoughts make the darkness choke me. Run, it is all I can do. So I run until I can't feel the pain anymore.

CHAPTER 11

THE SUN WARMS MY FACE AND IS TWIN-
kling through the curtains. I pull the blankets over my head
and try to go back to sleep. My head hurts. It feels like a tiny
hammer pounding my brain. I roll over and a pain shoots
through my side. I haven't hurt like this before. It hurts to
breathe and rolling over is painful. I don't want to go to school.
I hope that Dorothy doesn't make me, but I know better. She
doesn't know what happened last night. I told her that Don
and Mom got into a fight and I couldn't sleep. She looked at
me with those knowing eyes, and I almost told her everything.
My words were lost and seemed to be hard to put together
when she answered the door last night. She had a smile on her
face but she also looked worried. I watched her lock the door
and then she checked it twice to be sure. She didn't push too
many questions on me and let me get to bed quickly.

I can hear Dorothy moving around in the living room or the kitchen, I can't tell really. I pull the blankets off my head and get up. I feel like Optimus Prime ran me over. I wince as I stretch and walk over to the mirror. I think about yesterday morning and how I thought this mirror was magical, but now it only shows a worthless, weak shit. I look away quickly. I look terrible but I don't care anymore. If my mom doesn't care then I don't either. I hope my mommy is ok. I feel gray start poking me in the stomach and then I hear a voice behind me and I jump away. The darkness fills my head and I back away falling onto the floor. I can feel my heart beating and I look up and only see Dorothy. I try to calm my body down but I feel like running away.

"Good morning," I say, trying to hide the truth.

"Is it now?" She pauses before saying anything else. "Austin what happened to you last night? I don't believe you and I think you are not safe and something bad happened last night. So just tell me so I can help you." Her voice sounds different and very serious. I just stare at her. I don't know what to say. I do need help. I am tired of it. My mom won't keep me safe but I have a feeling Dorothy will. I feel like my words are stuck. I have so much to say but can't say anything. I look to the floor and stay silent. She finally starts talking again, "Well, I guess when you are ready to talk, I will be ready to listen. Breakfast is ready and after you eat you need a shower before school. I can't have you smelling like this, not while you are staying here." She turns and walks out of the room. I grab Teddy and follow her. We eat breakfast without talking. I don't feel like talking yet. She made sausage gravy and biscuits and it is the best I have tasted.

"Thank you for breakfast, I am going to get in the shower now," I tell her as I put my plate in the sink.

"Ok dear, I will get you a change of clothes and put them in the bedroom."

I can't help but wonder if she has a whole dresser of clothes for me. I smile and head to the shower. The hot water feels amazing on my ribs. I look at my side and it is purple and the bruise is huge like a football. It hurts to the touch and still hurts to breathe. It looks awful and it feels like my stomach is broken. I close my eyes while I rinse off. I see her face. Gone and lost. I can picture him choking her and then a gun pointed to my face. I open my eyes quickly. My breath catches in my throat and I swallow hard. I try to push the picture out of my mind. I turn off the water and get out. I wrap a towel around my waist and walk toward the bedroom.

"Oh my sweet boy! What happened to you? Look at that bruise! You can't tell me that you are safe at home! What happened to you?" Her voice sounds panicked and she has tears in her eyes. She moves toward me quickly and I am not sure what she is doing. As she reaches for me the darkness takes over. "Don't touch me!" I see him reaching for me and I run to the bedroom and shut the door. I sit on the bed and try to calm my body. I don't want to yell at Dorothy, I don't understand why I am like this. Such a shit. I put my face in my hands and start crying. I feel Dorothy sit next to me and the bed sinks down.

"I am sorry Austin, I shouldn't have reacted that way. But I am scared for you, and want you to be in a safe place." Her voice was calm and caring.

"He hits me a lot. When he is drunk, he hits my mommy. He yells. And is scary. And he stinks too. I hate him." The words fall out before I can think to stop them. I let the tears fall. Strangely, I start feeling something. I am not sure what it is and I feel like I want to keep talking, but I keep crying.

"Austin, it is time to get dressed and get ready for school." Dorothy's voice is serious and when I glance at her she is crying.

"Ok," I respond as I stand up and pick up my clothes. Dorothy walks out of the room and disappears. I carefully get dressed so that I don't hurt more. She is right, I want to be safe too. I need to tell people the monster he is. As the thoughts about losing my mom fill my head I can see the gun pointing to my face. My breath catches and heart pounds. If I tell everything, he could kill me or my mom. Dorothy's words fill my ears and it is time to leave. I take a last glance in the mirror and let out a sigh. This is a bad day. I hope I can make it through school. I walk out to the car and climb in. We drive in silence all the way to school. The drive seems like it takes forever to go down the dusty dirt road. It is early and the sun is glistening off the leaves that are starting to show their colors. I like this time of year when it is getting cooler outside. I see the school coming closer and my body fills with gray stabs and yellow bubbles. I don't want to go.

Dorothy pulls the car up to the front of the school and gets out. She walks around and waits for me but I can't get my body to move. She opens the door and continues to wait and just looks at me. Finally, she starts to talk and I don't look at her. "Time to get out, I bet Mrs. Marsha is ready to see you."

I look over at her and she seems relaxed. She smiles and looks at me with her knowing eyes, but this time she actually does know some of what happened. I keep sitting there and do not show any sign of moving. My words are gone too. My mind is going crazy and I am not sure what to think about everything happening. I shouldn't have told her but I felt like I needed to. I hope my mom is ok. The thought makes the gray build even more. Lost in my thoughts, I didn't notice Ms. Jennie and Ms. Benson walk out to the car.

"Good morning Ironman!" Ms. Jennie says as she smiles at me.

"Hi Austin! I am glad to see you this morning, are you ready to come in with us?" Ms. Benson is perky and seems excited to see me. I keep sitting there. I don't think I can do this today. I should run and get away from here. When I start to move my body to run, Ms. Jennie steps to the side and blocks my escape path. It is like she read my mind. These teachers are annoying. I start to feel red and need to get away. I look around and I don't think I can get past the three of them. "I don't want to go to school today," I say to them but look at the sidewalk.

"Where are you going to go then?" Ms. Benson asks. This is a good question. I can't go home. I don't have anywhere to go unless Dorothy lets me stay at her house. What am I going to do at the end of the day? I have nowhere to go. I start to panic. My breathing is fast and my eyes are burning. Where am I going to sleep? The darkness builds inside, I do not like not knowing what is going to happen after school. I pull my knees up to my chest and wrap my arms around them and make myself small, my mind is wild. I close my eyes and picture Mommy and the gun. I quickly open them and look at Ms. Benson. She seems to be watching me closely. Knowing eyes.

"Ms. Jennie, do you still have cartoons in your office? Maybe a cup of hot chocolate and some relaxing time in your office would be a good morning plan for Austin." Ms. Benson looks at Ms. Jennie and waits for a response.

"Oh yes, I have yummy hot cocoa and marshmallows for the top, and I happen to have some cartoon channels too, maybe we can find your favorite?" she asks me and waits for a response. "And I bet Teddy would like to hang out with his friends in my room with you."

"Goodness, I think I am going to head in and start making hot water for us because now I want cocoa too. So don't take too long because the water won't stay hot for long." Ms. Benson claps her hands together and then turns and walks into the school.

I do like cocoa and I haven't had any in a really long time. I guess they are not going to leave me alone if I keep sitting here. "Ok, I guess I can come in for cartoons and cocoa. You are not going to leave me alone if I stay here anyway." I smile and get out of the car.

Ms. Jennie agrees with me. They start to laugh. It makes me smile. Dorothy says bye to me and tells me to have a good day. I walk in with Ms. Jennie and she leads me to her office. Ms. Benson walks in with three cups filled with hot water. She sets them down on the counter and smiles at me. "I will be right back with the cocoa powder and marshmallows." She turns and walks out of the room. I walk over and sit in the big comfy rocking chair and put my stuff next to it. I unzip my backpack and pull out Teddy. I hold him close and start to rock in the chair. I am tired. I let out a sigh and look at Ms. Jennie who is sitting next to me in the other rocking chair.

"Well, do you want me to turn on cartoons? Or do you want some quiet time?" She pauses and waits for my response.

"Do you have Paw Patrol?" I smile. I don't think I can sit in quiet, that would just be weird. She gets up and grabs a remote, after a few buttons she has Paw Patrol on. I hold Teddy close and keep rocking. After a few minutes Ms. Benson walks in and finishes making the cocoa and hands it to me. She takes a drink of her cocoa and smiles at me. "I am so glad you decided to come to school today, I enjoy having you here." She smiles and walks out of the door. I look back at the T.V. and take a drink of my cocoa. It is warm and makes my tummy happy. I think about the last time I had cocoa. It was a long time ago. My daddy made it for me in my Mickey Mouse cocoa cup he bought me. He used to put whipped cream on top and it would get on my nose. The thought makes me laugh.

"My daddy used to make me cocoa. I would get the cream on my nose and we would laugh." I smile at Ms. Jennie thinking about it.

"That sounds fun, tell me about your dad." She looks so kind and interested.

"Well, he had a great smile and we laughed a lot. I miss him. He left me, I wish he didn't have to leave." The thought makes me blue and I look down.

"Where did your dad go?" Ms. Jennie waits patiently. I am not sure what to say to her, but I want to talk.

"Mommy said his car was going too fast and the snow was bad. She said he passed away and now lives with Jesus. I remember going to the doctor and they told Mom they lost him. I keep hoping they will find him again, but I don't think he is coming back." I keep looking at the floor. I have never told anyone this before.

"Oh Austin, it sounds like your dad died, and when someone dies they can't be found and they can't come back from that. It is really hard to have someone close to you die." Her voice is soft and her eyes are caring and kind.

"Well, I guess that makes sense. I knew he wouldn't leave me. I just want him back. I need him back. Mommy needs him too." I start to cry and I don't hold it back. My mind quickly goes to my mommy. His stench fills my nose and I can see his eyes. I close my eyes and try to think of something else but it doesn't work. I can hear her words telling him no, and his voice forcing himself on her. "I hate him." I open my eyes and look at Ms. Jennie. The look on her face shows that she is confused.

"Not my dad. I hate Don, my new dad. You know he makes me call him dad, even though he isn't?" I look at her and wait. I am not sure if I should keep talking or not.

"Hate is a strong word to use. Does he do something that makes you feel that way?" She takes a sip of her drink, and sits back in her chair. She looks interested and relaxed.

"Yes." I wait and drink some more cocoa. It is starting to cool off and is the perfect temperature. I keep drinking it and get to the bottom. I pull the cup down and still have some on my lip. It makes me laugh and I wipe it off with my sleeve. Ms. Jennie laughs with me and it makes me smile. I like talking to her.

"Tell me about what Don does that makes you hate him." She pauses and reaches over to pick up a container of putty. She pulls it out of the container and hands it to me. It feels nice in my hands. It is hard and soft at the same time. I start to pull it and roll it. I like the feeling of it on my hands. It is smooth and slick. I stretch it out and squish it back together. I like it.

"He stinks. And is dirty. He gets drunk a lot. He always has angry eyes when he looks at me. He's scary." I watch the putty stretch out and start to toss it around. It hits the floor and bounces back. "He hits me and Mommy all the time. Like every day. Unless I'm at Dorothy's. Sometimes they forget about me and that's nice because I can sit in the living room." It feels good to talk and I throw the putty against the wall and it bounces onto the counter and back to the floor.

"That doesn't sound good. Does he ever leave marks on you?" She watches me pick up the putty and stretch it out again.

"Yeah, all the time. All the bruises I get are from him. Punches, kicks, and he throws me a lot." I pick up my shirt and show her my ribs. The bruise is big. I look at her. I have never told the truth before and it makes me feel green and yellow. I want to tell her more. Her eyes look like they have tears in them, but she stays calm. She does care about me.

"Oh Austin, that's not ok. What else happens at home?" She holds the tears back and waits for my response.

"Well, yesterday he picked me up from Dorothy's house and I saw drugs on the floor of his truck. He put a shot in his arm. It was gross. His words were all messed up and he hurt my mommy, bad. I tried to protect her but he hurt me. I did kick him in the nuts a lot and he didn't have pants on so you know that hurt. My mom just watched him hurt me then she grabbed his hand and took him to the bedroom. I ran away to Dorothy's." I stop talking to catch my breath.

I throw the putty again, except this time I throw it hard and my body starts to turn gray and the bubbles are all over. I miss my mommy. I hope she is ok. Then I picture the gun. I should tell her about the gun. I pick up the putty and stretch it and make it look like a gun in my hand. "And before they went to the bedroom…" I take the putty gun and point it to my head and pretend to shoot. I make a shooting noise and then throw the putty again. I chase it this time and grab it and throw it again against the wall behind Ms. Jennie. It flies back and hits her. I pause. Oh no. I didn't mean to. I run back over and jump into the rocking chair. I try to make myself small and pull Teddy close to me. What did I do? I should not have said anything. I am such a shit.

"Oh goodness, that putty really bounces doesn't it." She bends down and picks it up. "Austin, thanks for talking with me, do you want some more hot chocolate? She stands up and looks at me while she puts the putty back into the container.

"That would be great." I sit up in the chair and start rocking it. She tells me she will go make the cocoa and will be back. She walks out of the door and leaves it open. I can see her walk past

Mrs. Marsha and turn into Ms. Benson's office. I start to watch the cartoon, and keep rocking in the chair. I like this chair. It feels nice. I keep rocking and I feel like I could fall asleep. A commercial comes on the T.V. and distracts me. I look around the room and realize that she has been gone a long time. I don't want to be in here anymore and want to go to class. Mrs. Roush is probably wondering where I am. I pick up Teddy and stretch my back and legs. It hurts a lot and I wince. Teddy and I walk out to Mrs. Marsha's desk. She smiles sweetly at me.

"Hi Austin! Good to see you today! Are you giving snuggle loves today?" She says this as she holds out an arm waiting to see if I am going to give her a hug or not. She does give the best hugs. I walk over to her and lean into her embrace. She gives me a side hug and smiles. It makes me smile too.

"I want to go to class now. Can I head to Mrs. Roush's room?" I step away from her as I wait for her response.

"Ms. Jennie had to make a phone call and she might be a while. I think Mrs. Roush will be happy to see you. Grab your stuff and you can head that way." She smiles and turns back to answer the phone.

"I only have Teddy." I say as I turn back into Ms. Jennie's office.

I pick up Teddy and keep holding him close. I head down the long hallway toward class. The sun is gleaming through the windows and it makes bright yellow rectangles on the smooth floor. I watch my feet as they hit the tiles. I remember how my feet looked when my mom was dragging me through the hospital. I feel like she has not been happy since that day. The day when the doctors told her that they lost my dad. I think about her face and how gone she is, empty. I can't believe she didn't help me. She stood there while he had a gun to my face and her face. I can't go home. I just can't. I start to feel the darkness tighten inside me. I am not paying attention to much except my feet when I turn the corner of the hall. I feel myself hit someone and I stumble backward and hit the wall before catching my balance. The darkness consumes me and I look up to see his face.

"Watch where you're going you dummy!" The student's face looks angry and his eyes are dark. I close my eyes. I try to get the darkness to back down but his eyes flash in my mind and between them are a pointed nose and a gun barrel. I need to get away. I scramble to my feet and run as fast as I can. I can hear his words echo in my head. He is going to kill me. My heart is racing and I don't stop until I get to Mrs. Roush's classroom door. I pull it open as fast as I can and run through the other kids and push past the line at the back and climb into my locker. I hide my face and grab a backpack from the locker next to mine and hold it over my head.

"Austin are you ok?" It's a kid's voice and then I feel a hand touch my arm. I throw the backpack at him. 'Don't touch me, get away from me," my voice is loud and squeaky.

"Gavin please line up at the door. Class, class, please quickly line up at the door." Mrs. Roush's voice is calm. "Austin, are you ok my dear?" No, no I am not. I need to get away from here. I jump out of the locker and make a run for it. I head to the back door but it won't open. I turn and quickly go for the front door, but the class is blocking it. I turn and I don't know where to go. I need to get away. "Leave me alone!" I yell it loud. I push desks out of my way and pick up and toss a chair. Mrs. Roush walks to the class line and they leave. I don't know where they go, but I am not going with them.

I head for the back table and I climb under it. I start lifting the table up with my feet and letting it fall onto the floor. I like the feeling of the table hitting the floor. It starts to make the darkness back off me. The floor is cool and feels good on my back. I close my eyes and try to go to my happy place. I see Dorothy and she is making us milkshakes. I take in a deep breath and can smell popcorn. The darkness starts to let me go. I hear something. I freeze and it grows back up my throat. I look over and see legs. I am not sure who it is and I make myself small. They start to walk toward me. And then I hear a voice. It is gruff and cold. Mrs. Gentry. Why is she here? The thought makes me feel red. I can't deal with her.

"I see you are at it again. The whole class had to leave... I would like to think you would want to be learning rather than rolling on the floor having a fit about whatever you don't want to be doing right now. You need to get off the floor and go to the office so the rest of the kids can come back to their room." Her voice sounds like nails on a chalkboard. I take my feet and with all my strength I launch the table toward her. The table crashes to the floor and the items on the table go flying. She moves back quickly and is about to say something, but I don't give her a chance. I grab the tub of counting cubes and start throwing them at her. She is jumping all over trying to avoid

them. Finally, I hit her with one on the shoulder and she pauses long enough for me to hit her again in her witch nose. "Go
away, I hate you." I let the words come out.

"You are being such a rat. Stop throwing things! What is
your issue?" Her words are flustered and angry.

"You are a worthless bitch and I want you to go away!" I say
this as I grab the rest of the tub of cubes and launch it at her.
She turns and walks off and out the door. I jump up and take
off as fast as I can run and burst through the door, running into
Mrs. Roush. She falls back but catches herself on the door handle and I take off down the hallway. I jump into the closet and
hide behind the cleaning supplies and brooms. I hope I didn't
hurt Mrs. Roush. I start to rock my body back and forth quickly. I like the feeling of rocking. I need to calm myself down. I
start to cry and tears fall to the floor. I hurt her. I am no better
than him. I am such a shit. I bury my face in my hands. I hear
voices in the hallway. I hope they don't find me.

"Why were you in the classroom and what did you say to
him?" Mrs. Roush's voice sounds rushed.

"He needs to get it together and stop acting like this. I
was trying to help and he threw things at me and called me a
bitch." Mrs. Gentry's words are harsh.

"You had no reason to go near him and obviously you're
not helpful so go back to your classroom and leave my student
alone." Mrs. Roush is serious and sounds protective. It makes
me feel green. I hope I didn't hurt her. I take in a breath and
the dusty closet makes me cough. It really is smelly in here, and
sticky. Gross. The light switches on and I can see Mrs. Roush's

face. She looks at me with calm knowing eyes. And she climbs into the closet beside me.

"Austin, I'm sorry that I didn't get back to you fast enough. I had to take the rest of the class to a different room. It seems like you're having a rough day today." Mrs. Roush smiles at me. "Are you ok sweetheart?" She kneels down in front of me.

I look at her and I am not sure what to say. I am not ok and I want to hide. Class is where I thought I should be, but now I am not so sure. I decide to tell her that and take in a breath. "No, no I am not ok and I can't be here right now. A kid called me dummy and then I fell and then that witch wouldn't leave me alone. She really looks like a witch, you know." I hide my face when I say this. Mrs. Roush laughs, and holds out her hand for me to take. Her laugh is kind and her smile makes me feel better. I take her hand and stand up off the floor. We walk out of the closet together and she keeps a tight hold on my hand. I look and see Mrs. Gentry standing at the other end of the hallway by her classroom. I turn my eyes away from her quickly. Mrs. Roush turns the other direction as well.

She walks us quickly down the main hallway to the office and checks her mailbox. We say hi to another teacher in the hallway and then walk past the library and check the playground for something but she doesn't say what we are looking for. Then we start to walk back to the main hallway and toward the classroom. "Well the class needs to come back in from gym class, but I think you left it a mess. What do you say to us getting it picked up?" She doesn't look at me and keeps walking while she asks me this. I feel like this is a question that I'm not meant to answer.

We walk into her room and it is definitely a mess, and I threw blocks everywhere. We pick up her room and I help her turn the table back over. I gather the cubes and put them back in the tub and get the chairs and desks back in place. I walk back to the locker and put the backpack back into the locker and grab Teddy. I walk over to her desk and she is checking her email.

"I think I picked it all up. I am sorry for running into you when I pushed the door open." I squeeze Teddy and wait for her to look at me.

"It's ok dear, but I want you to work on noticing when you need a break, before you throw tables and cubes at teachers. Now, it's time for class. Where do you feel safe in this school?" She pauses and looks serious.

"Well. In here, most of the time. And in the office with Ms. Benson or Ms. Jennie. I really like Mrs. Marsha too." I think about her hug this morning and it makes me smile.

"Ok, well. Where do you need to be to be successful? I want you to really think about this. You've had a rough day so far, but it doesn't have to stay that way. I can send work down and you can be in the office or if you think you can handle it in class, you are welcome to stay here." She stands up and puts her hands on her hips.

"I'm tired. I think I would do best in a quiet place. Can I go to the office?" I am tired and I don't know if I can be around other kids today.

"Of course," she says and walks over to her desk and gathers a stack of work and hands it to me. I carry the work and Teddy and we walk down the hallway toward the office. Mrs. Roush stops at the gym doors to get the rest of the class and I keep walking to the office. As I pass the gym doors, I wave at Gavin, and he smiles back at me. I hope I didn't scare him earlier and he will still be my friend. I could use a friend and I like him. He makes me laugh. I head into the office and Ms. Benson is waiting on me. She gives me a serious look. I haven't seen that look from her before. It makes the gray bubble.

"Austin, I'm disappointed in your behavior choices. We talked about this before and you really need to try to pay attention to how your body is feeling and take breaks and let us help you. You were not in a good place to go back to the classroom. You could have hurt someone, or hurt yourself. We care about you and I want you to be the best you that you can be. Now, I understand that you had a bad night and have been through a lot. But you still have to be safe at school." Her face looks less serious now, and I shake my head yes. She is right, I can do better. I hand her my pile of work and she hands me one handout and points to her table. I walk over and sit down. I look over the worksheet, it is reading. I can't read. I can't do this. I ask to go to the bathroom and walk away from the table.

Mrs. Marsha smiles as I walk by and I stop to talk to her. She is talkative and starts to tell me about her son and his new bike. This was a great way to avoid that reading worksheet. I'm listening and laughing at her story when two ladies walk into the office followed by a police officer. I stop laughing and stop moving. I see the name tags hanging from their necks. I know who they are, but why do they have a police officer with them? I can't breathe and my knees start to ache. Mrs. Marsha looks at me and her face becomes very serious. She gets up and walks over to the counter to talk to them. I make a run for the bathroom. I can hide in here for a while and avoid them. I know that they called them and now they are here to take me. How can I protect my mom if I am not home? But she doesn't care about me. If she did she would not have let him point a gun at me.

I sit down on the boxes of paper that are stored in the shower and pull the curtain shut. I should tell them everything, but what if he kills her and it would be my fault. The thought makes the darkness swirl and I put my head into my hands. I know what I need to do, but I am not sure if I am strong enough. I am not Ironman because I am weak and a pussy. I start to cry and hear voices and footsteps outside of the bathroom. I freeze, but I know that they know I am in here. There is a knock at the door and Ms. Jennie's voice follows.

"Austin, it's Ms. Jennie. Can you come out please? It's ok, the ladies are here to help you. You deserve to be safe and happy. You deserve to not get hurt. They can help you and help your mom." Her voice is soft and caring.

"They can help my mommy too?" That would be great if it is true. Maybe they can make her leave him. I like the idea of them helping her but I have never heard of them helping moms before. I decide that I can talk to them, and I will ask Ms. Jennie to sit with me. It can't be too scary and if she is with me, then they can't take me away. But why is there a cop here too? That is a first for me, but I have never been honest and actually told someone what happens to me. I get up and unlock the door. Ms. Jennie smiles at me and we walk back to the front office. She guides me into her office and I find myself looking at the police officer and the ladies. She left before I could ask her to stay. The door slowly shuts behind me and I'm by myself. I look at their eyes and can't help but let the darkness take over. I fall to the floor and make myself small.

CHAPTER 12

THE QUESTIONS KEEP COMING, I DON'T respond. The darkness has me and I can't escape. As their words pile into my ears it fuels it. The darkness is controlling and I am stuck. I try to look at the workers but I can't focus on their words. I close my eyes and her face is there. Lonely, dark, and hurt face. My mom is gone and all that is left is her shell. Maybe they can help her. I hear her screams and his eyes glaring at me. I try to think of something else, but the gun is there. His anger-filled eyes are peering over the barrel. I can't get the image out of my mind. I try to hit my head with my hand but it is still there. Suddenly I hear a click and then feel something hit me on the side. I open my eyes and run to the other side of the room. Looking back, I see the door is open and Ms. Jennie is standing there. My body feels like the gun fired and hit me. She came back for me. I start to rock my body back and forth.

I look at her and my heart slows down a bit. She hands me Teddy and I hold him close to me. I breathe in slowly. I reach down and I feel the tile floor. It is cold and smooth on my hand. I smell the air and it is stuffy and damp. The darkness releases me and retreats to gray simmers in my chest and tummy. I bury my head into Teddy and start to cry. I am not sure what the questions are or what to say to them. I take in a breath and I stand up slowly. I peek around Teddy and pull up my shirt. The bruise is huge on one side and the other side is smaller. I touch it. It hurts. This should answer some of their questions. I have to find words. I shield myself and I need to be strong

"He hurts me. He stinks and is nasty. Sometimes he slaps me and other times he kicks me. Last night he threw me into a table. I was trying to help Mommy. He hurts her too. I try to keep her safe but he's strong. Then after I hit the table, he held a gun to my mom's head then to my head. He had drugs and gave himself a shot in his arm. He's drunk all the time and really hurt my mommy last night. He was naked hurting her, and he will hurt me and my mom again." I sit back down and my body feels lost, light, and weak.

I start to rock back and forth on the floor and wait for them to respond. I keep Teddy close. Ms. Jennie sits next to me. I watch her sit next to me, but then I watch her reach her hand out to put it on my back. Her hand changes to his hand, and the nasty fills my nose.

"Don't touch me!" I move away from her and I can still see his eyes looking at me. The two workers write notes and then the police officer walks closer to me. He is tall with brown eyes but they are not dark. They look kind and he seems strong but not a strong that would hurt people. He doesn't have a uniform, but does have a badge clipped to what looks like a belt. He also has a gun. As he walks toward me the darkness sparks again. I hold my breath and freeze. He stops. I look up at him. He smells good. He kneels down in front of me. He smells like fresh air and good stuff.

"Austin, I know this is weird and you don't know me, but I need to take a picture of your bruises. Can you show them to me again?" He was serious and I didn't want to make him angry. He looks calm but I bet he can be scary when he needs to be. I look up at him and he takes a picture of my face from two different angles. Then I stand up and pull my shirt up. He takes a lot of pictures of my ribs, side and my back. After what seems like forever he stops and walks to the door. He turns to me and nods, but I am not sure if it was a bye or a thank you. He opens the door and leaves. I have never had a policeman in an interview before. The gray continues to spark and poke my tummy. I kind of feel sick. I want to go home. I can't go home. Don will hurt me, he could even kill me.

If he finds out I told, he will kill me and my mom. I try not to think about it. I look at the ladies and they smile back at me. They are fake smiles. They are not telling me something. Their eyes are blank and I can't tell if they are kind or mad. They stand up and start walking to the door after the police officer. The blonde one turns toward Ms. Jennie as the other one opens the door.

"Do you have a couple minutes to talk to us before we leave?" She waits for a response. Ms. Jennie turns to me and smiles.

"I will be right back Austin, here's the putty if you'd like to use it." Her eyes are sad and she hesitates to leave. The blonde worker looks back at me as Ms. Jennie heads to the door.

"Austin, thank you for talking with us and we'll see you later." She pushes the door completely open and then walks out of it. She stands next to the police officer and the other worker. Ms. Jennie joins them and Ms. Benson walks out and waves everyone to come into her office. They all follow her in and Ms. Jennie is the last to disappear out of my sight. I stand still. I am not sure what to do. I can feel the gray vine up inside me. It feels like it is wrapping around my ribs and spreading them apart. I can't be here anymore. I walk over to Mrs. Marsha and she smiles at me. I just stand next to her. I lost my words and I feel like she knows this. She extends her arm out and I step into her. She holds me tight and I melt into her touch. I start to cry and it feels like the gray vines are falling out of my eyes.

She continues to hold me and I slow my crying down. I can hear voices and a door opening. It is coming from Ms. Benson's office.

"Thank you and we'll be back shortly with temporary guardianship paperwork and we will be picking him up from school. Don't release him to anyone else." It is a woman's voice, but not Ms. Jennie. They are coming for me. I am getting taken away. Mommy. Who is going to watch out for her? Where am I going to go? I pull away from Mrs. Marsha and I grab Teddy. I have to get out of here and fast. I look at the workers and then look to the door. I can make it. I need to get away. I have to hide. I bolt past the desk as fast as I can. As I run around the corner of the office, toward the school entrance, I can hear my name echo throughout the school. I don't stop. I run as fast as I can. The gray turns to darkness and wraps itself around my throat and it is choking me. I can't stop.

I jump off the road and run through the ditch until I reach the woods. I find the biggest tree I can and duck behind it. The huge maple tree hides me while I try to catch my breath. My rib really hurts and the pain shoots through my lungs. I look back and see people running all over looking for me. I take off again. I can't stay still. I can't go with them. I can hear voices and one seems close to me. I push myself faster and my feet barely hit the ground before lifting off again. It seems like a long time before I can see a white house with the red Impatiens on the porch. I slow down and look behind me. I don't see anyone. I take off again for Dorothy's house. She will know what to do. I reach her steps and I jump over them and make a fist. I pound on the door as fast and hard as I can. She needs to be home. She has to be. I don't have anywhere else to go. My heart is beating fast and I feel sick. I run over to the edge of the porch and throw up. I try to catch my breath and I hear the door open behind me.

I turn around and I see her face. Sweet Dorothy standing there with her hands on her hips. She looks confused and concerned.

"Good Lord Austin! What are you doing here! You can't just leave school, they are probably looking for you." Her voice is surprised.

"I am. I…I." I run to the edge and throw up again.

"Oh, Well…you are sick! Come in now, I will get you some ginger ale." She turns and walks into the house. I have to tell her. I am sure they will come here. Ms. Benson dropped me off here once.

"Dorothy, they are coming for me. Please don't let them take me away. Please! I want to stay with you, don't let them take me." I am desperate and I stare at her and wait for her response.

"What are you talking about? Who would be coming for…" The doorbell rings before she can finish her sentence. I jump and start to cry.

"They are here for me. Please. Please don't let them take me." I let the tears fall and the darkness squeezes my insides.

"Oh Austin, I am not sure what is happening, but I will not let anything happen to you. Come along now." She turns and walks toward the front door. I disappear into the bathroom and peek through the crack of the door, I don't want to be seen. I can't breathe. I feel like I could throw up again. In slow motion she reaches for the door handle, turns it, and there stands the police officer looking very serious. Dorothy did not give him a chance to talk first and he looks like he is surprised to see her.

"Oh, well…Look at you! You have grown into a handsome young man now haven't you! Jeffery, it has been years! What brings you to my house and who is that behind you? Come in, come in." Dorothy smiles and moves to the side to welcome him into the house.

"I didn't expect to see your face behind the door." He laughs and walks into the living room followed by the case workers. "Looks the same here as it did when I was a kid. As much as I would like to catch up, I'm here about a situation." He sits down on the couch and watches as Dorothy walks over to the chair.

"Can I get you some tea? Or something to eat?" She eyes up the case workers as she is asking.

"No thank you. Have you seen a boy named Austin?" His tone of voice changes back to the serious one he had at school.

"What do you want with Austin? Has he gotten himself into trouble at school?" Dorothy looks at him with knowing eyes.

"No ma'am. But we saw him run this direction from school and we need him to come with us." He glances around the house as he is talking.

"Well now, I am guessing these ladies are social workers then. I have been reporting stuff for months and finally you can do something about it. That boy is not safe in that house and I'm so thankful he is speaking up about it." She leans back into the chair and looks at the workers with a strange look I haven't seen before.

"Dorothy, we need to know if he's here and if he is we need him to come with us for a safe placement. I'm aware of your reports and we appreciate you looking out for people. But Austin needs to come with us." The blonde lady shifts in her seat as she talks to Dorothy. She seems uncomfortable.

"Yes. We're addressing the issue and he'll be in a safe foster placement." The other worker sounds nervous. I can see why. Dorothy's body language changes and she is looking kind of scary. She sits up in her chair and shifts her body toward the workers.

"Austin is not going anywhere. He is here and he will stay here." Her tone of voice is deeper and quite serious.

"Now Dorothy, you know that's not how this works." Jeffery sits a little taller, and seems like he has gray in his tummy too. I can see what makes him sit up. Dorothy looks like she is ready to fight.

"You're not trained for foster care. He'll come with us and if you want to take him in you will have to go through the proper process to do so. We have to follow protocol." The case worker sounds snippy and stands up. The energy in the room changes and it makes gray spark and poke at my tummy. Dorothy stands up with her and puts her hands on her hips. She takes a step toward the worker and leans forward. Jeffery and the blonde stand up as well.

"Now you listen here, and listen closely." She is now pointing a finger at all three of them. It makes them take a step back. She takes a breath.

"You can forget protocol when it comes to Austin and him leaving this house. While you were out following your process, I've been looking out for him for months. He has been through enough and he needs to be somewhere where he's loved and safe." Dorothy's words are getting louder as she talks and it builds to a loud growl.

"And if you think you're going to take him out of this house then you must be a special kind of stupid.... Now if you excuse me, Austin and I have to go get some shopping done for his new bedroom. So you can go back to your office and start the process of making this his placement and you can tell your supervisor down there that I said to tell her hello and to stop by and visit me sometime." Dorothy waves her arm toward the front door. The two workers look at the police officer and seem like they expect him to do something.

"Well, you heard her. She can get the paperwork filled out. But Dorothy, he needs a health check by a pediatrician. This will need to be done today. Can you take him or would you like me to?" He waits for her response and runs his hands through his hair.

"Of course I can take him, where do you want him to go? And what do I need to know about what is happening with Don?" Dorothy's voice is starting to return to normal, but her hands are still on her hips and her eyes are very serious.

"The clinic is fine, these ladies will call ahead and talk to them. And Austin can have no contact with Don or his mother until further notice. These ladies will file the paperwork to make it official, and should have it shortly. You probably won't have to worry too much about Don for a while." He smiles and looks at the workers. "We will be on our way and if you need anything, here's my card. Tell Zach I said hello next time you talk to him." Jeffery walks over and hugs Dorothy and then turns toward the door.

"You two were always close friends growing up, I'll let him know you stopped by. Thank you Jeffery and I'll call if anything comes up. Now, which one of you is going to be his case worker?" She still has her hands on her hips and scary serious eyes. She looks like the witch from the Harry Potter movies that is scary but cares about everyone.

"We're not sure who will be on the case. We'll be in touch once we have more information for you." They walk out of the door followed by the policeman.

"Oh, I'm sure, I'll be in touch. Have a good day and I'll need the proper paperwork by tomorrow so I can give it to the school and thank you for all you do." Dorothy shuts the door and walks back to the living room as if it was just another day.

I get to stay here. Dorothy said I need to be somewhere I'm loved. Does she really love me? I'm not sure what I feel about this. What about my mommy? I don't know what is going to happen to her. Who is going to protect her? I can feel the gray build up and I am not sure what to do. I feel stuck in the bathroom and I can't move. I slowly lean against the counter and slide down to the floor. I pull Teddy into my lap and I hold him close to me. Will I see my mommy again? What if she leaves me like Daddy and I won't see her anymore. I bury my head into Teddy and try to make the thoughts stop. I am full of colors. I feel gray, red and blue. I'm lost. I let the tears fall. I feel something touch me. It is soft. My heart jumps and I move away. Dorothy is standing in the doorway.

Her touch is soft and caring yet it hurts and makes the darkness grow. I look at her and keep crying. "I want to go home," I tell her this but I don't mean it.

"I know you do. But home is not safe for you. Austin, you're safe here and you deserve to have someone take care of you. I hope your mom makes some changes in her life so she can take care of you, but while she is struggling, you're safe here." Her voice is light and kind. She sits down on the floor next to me.

I sniff and wipe my nose on my arm. I stop crying and look at Dorothy. "Do you think they can help my mommy?" I ask her.

"Oh... well your mom will get help if she wants to get help. She needs to make the choice to get better. We can just pray she makes the right decisions and in the time it takes her to, you have me." She slowly reaches over and takes my hand into hers and squeezes it. I lean into her and she holds me. I feel purple grow and push over the other colors. They swirl and mix and I am not sure what is happening. Dorothy stands up and I stand with her. She walks out to the living room and turns to me with a big smile.

"Well, I guess since you're home early, we need to go shopping. I want to turn my extra room into your room, so we need to go find you some things to make it your own. So what do you say we get that check-up over with then hit the stores in town?" She picks up her purse off the sofa table and heads to the door without waiting for my response.

I take in a breath and start to walk behind her. I don't want a check up, I can't remember ever seeing a doctor. I hope it doesn't hurt. I try to not think about it. I guess shopping could be fun, I haven't been to a store in a really long time. I don't remember the last time I picked out something for myself. The thought makes me smile and I catch up to Dorothy. When I open the car door she smiles at me and pats the seat. I feel my heart get bigger and I like the feeling, but it is different inside me. It makes gray grow but my big heart pushes the gray away. I hop into the seat and buckle up, I can't help but smile. Maybe I can be Ironman. Maybe I can be strong for Mommy while she gets better. She will get better. My heart tells me she will. I let out my breath and watch the trees blow by the window while we drive. Dorothy seems lost in thought and I start to get excited about shopping. Maybe it will all work out, me being at Dorothy's and Mom getting help. My head is full of maybes and it starts to hurt. I close my eyes and focus on breathing. I can rest for a few minutes, it is at least a 20 minute drive to the clinic. I lean my head on the window and fall asleep.

CHAPTER 13

The air is thick, cold and very damp. The walls are rough and water is oozing down the sides. I can hear the water dripping and the sound is bouncing around the walls. The cave is deep and keeps going. I try to find my way out. I don't know how I got here. I take a right turn, a slope, and it is slippery. I fall and start to slide. I see something at the bottom, a light, a red light. I yell for my mom and my words echo through the rocks. Her words echo back to me. They are yelling my name and asking for help. I am coming Mom! I try to get up but I keep sliding. When I hit the bottom I am on a ledge. It is very high. I try not to move because I might fall. Austin! Austin! Help me! The echo is coming from behind me now. I turn to see where she is. A gun. The gun is pointed at my face. I feel a push on my chest and my feet stumble and I fall backward. Falling, falling. I try to grab the rock wall but it is too slippery and then I hit. I am gone.

I JERK AND MY EYES OPEN QUICKLY. I AM breathing heavy and look around the room. I am not sure where I am and I feel around me. My fingers find Teddy and I pull him close to me. My eyes adjust to the dark room and I remember that I am in bed at Dorothy's house. It has been a long day. I am not sure what time it is and I roll over to get comfortable again. I feel the bed and it is wet. Oh no. I peed the bed again, I peed Dorothy's bed. I kick off the covers and feel them. They are dry. I slowly sit up on the bed's edge. I support my rib as I stand up. The doctor did an x-ray and said I have fractured ribs and deep tissue bruising. It is starting to heal. She also said that I was handsome, even with a black eye. I don't want to wake up Dorothy so I pull off the sheet and the mattress pad. I walk over and leave them by the door. I walk back toward the bed and run into the side table. It makes a loud noise and instantly a light comes on outside of the room. I can hear footsteps quickly moving toward me.

"Austin, are you ok?" Her voice is groggy and soft. She walks into my room and looks at the pile of sheets next to the door.

"I'm ok. I'm sorry I woke you up, I didn't turn on the lights and I ran into the side table." I smile at her. I hope she is not mad about the bed.

"Did you have an accident? I told you I want you to wake me if you do so I can help." She starts walking towards the closet without waiting for an answer. "Here," she says, handing me clean clothes. "Now go change your clothes and I will change the bed." She walks over to the bed and starts putting on the sheets.

I like that she takes care of me. I smile as I change my clothes. She has the bed made by the time I walk back to the room. She tucks me in and tucks Teddy in next to me. She tells me goodnight and turns out the light. As she leaves the room I can feel purple grow in me. I am really glad I met her. I roll over and snuggle into my pillows. It doesn't take long before I fall back asleep.

The sun pushes through the curtains and it makes the walls turn red. The red light reflects off the pictures and brightens my new blankets. I was so excited when I found them on our shopping trip. I didn't know they made Ironman blankets with matching pillow cases. I smile when I think about the trip. We couldn't find Ironman curtains and after the third store, Dorothy stopped at a store I have never been before. It was full of fabric of all sorts of colors and they all felt different. She searched and searched and then pulled out a big roll. She had the biggest smile when she turned around to show me. It was some fabric that had Ironman on it. She said it was perfect for curtains and asked what I thought. I loved it of course. She said she could sew the fabric into curtains for me. I never had anyone make something for me before. I smile thinking about it and roll over to hug Teddy.

I have been waking up in this bed for a couple weeks. It has been wonderful with fluffy pillows and warm blankets. I don't want to go back to not having a bed. I can lose everything else but the bed I want to keep. I have school today and the thought makes me sigh. It has been hard. It has been a good week, but the darkness has been bigger. The gray is always bubbling. It has been very hard to control my "outbursts." I haven't seen my mommy since I have been staying here. I try not to think about it. I hope she is safe. I picture her eyes looking at the gun. I need to get up and think about something else. I climb out of bed and think of what day it is, and suddenly I realize my birthday is tomorrow. I wonder if Dorothy knows about my birthday. I haven't had a party since before my daddy left me. Maybe I should ask her about it, but I don't want to bother her with more stuff. I decide to not mention it.

"Good morning, Sugar." Dorothy smiles at me from her chair. She is in her robe and drinking her coffee. "Are you ready for breakfast? I have cinnamon rolls in the oven." She takes another drink of her coffee.

"That sounds really good! Do I have to go to school today? I am feeling like…" I pause and try to think of the word.

"Are you sick?" She looks concerned.

"Well, I just feel like I need to not go to school today." I smile at her as I say this.

"Oh…well, you need to go to school today. Did you forget what day it is?" She walks over to the oven to check on the rolls.

"Why? What is happening today?" I try to remember and gray starts to stab my ribs.

"You have a visit with your mom today. Ms. Bethany will be picking you up from school and taking you to see your mom. She'll stay with you and it is at her office. Bethany said that your mom has been really trying to get better since Don was arrested." She pulls the rolls out of the oven and starts to put icing all over them.

I get to see my mom today. I am not sure what I think about this. I haven't seen her since the night of the gun. The thought makes the gray explode inside me but I also feel, what is the word, excited about or maybe nervous. Ms. Jennie has been working with me to name my colors. I also have had to talk to this other lady about stuff. We usually play and she has the best toys. She has been helping name my colors too. Mrs. Michelle is her name. She sits on the floor with me and we laugh a lot. I am lost in my thoughts as I eat the delicious cinnamon roll with extra icing. It is warm and tingly on my tongue, they are my favorite. Dorothy's words bring me back from my mind.

"It's time for you to get in the shower."

"But I had one yesterday!" I look at her.

"Yes, and your bits get gunky everyday, and you had an accident last night and need to wash off the pee." Her eyes are serious. I decide not to argue with her, I tried a couple days ago over not doing my homework. Let's just say it didn't go well for me, and I completed my homework. I didn't like what Dorothy called a routine at first, but now I know what to expect my day to look like. I get picked up from school and get a snack, then she helps me with homework. Then she cooks dinner while I can play or watch cartoons. I have to say I have not been hungry since I have lived here, it makes me feel green, well safe I mean. I think that is the word we came up with when I feel green. I take my plate to the sink and head to the shower. I am not sure about seeing my mom. I wonder if she wants to see me. I think about her face and eyes. Will she still look empty, will she even care how I have been?

I do always feel better and ready for the day after a morning shower. I get dressed and walk out to the living room with my backpack. I have some questions for Dorothy and I am not sure if she will know the answers or not. She is dressed and ready to go. We walk out to the car, the weather is cool and crisp. Halloween is in a few weeks and the leaves have all fallen to the ground. I love to step on the crunchy ones, sometimes I will chase them in the wind to crunch them. This past weekend, Dorothy raked them all up in a pile in her backyard and we jumped into them. I smile thinking about it, it was so much fun. I jump into the car and shut the door.

"Dorothy, how long is Don going to be arrested? What happens when he is not arrested anymore? And if he goes home, will Mommy still be allowed to live there?" I am talking fast and have so many questions about things. "What time is my visit? And will I have to have visits with Don too?" I can smell his stench and hear his voice at the thought of having to visit him. The thought makes me stop talking and I look out the window.

"Well, sweet boy. I don't know the answers to your questions. I would hope that you never have to see him again, and I would hope and pray that your mom can leave him and get better for you. But adults make their own choices and we can't control what they do. We will just have to be positive and see what time will tell us. But I do know your visit is at 10 a.m. today." She smiles as she pulls in front of the school.

"Have a great day today, and I hope your mom is better for you. I can't wait to hear about it when I pick you up." She smiles at me. "Can I have a goodbye hug?"

I lean over and let her hug me. It has taken a few goodbyes to get used to the hugs, but now I look forward to them.

"Bye, have a good day." I climb out of the car and head into the school.

The kids are all hurrying to class so they are not late. I don't have to stay in the office anymore because Dorothy doesn't bring me early. I do start my day in the office and eat my breakfast with someone. Sometimes it is Ms. Jennie, or Mrs. Marsha, and once in a while I can eat with Ms. Benson if she is not busy. I walk into the office and it is busting with kids checking in and a few parents talking to both Ms. Benson and Mrs. Marsha. I make my way through the crowd and walk into Ms. Jennie's office, but she is not there either. I take off my backpack and sit down Teddy on the rocking chair. I turn on the T.V and the channel is still on cartoons from yesterday. I settle into my favorite chair and pull out the fuzzy soft blanket she has. I will relax until the office settles down then I will go talk to Mrs. Marsha. Spiderman comes on and it is an episode that I have already seen but I don't mind.

"Well good morning Austin! I was wondering if you'd be here. I see you're all settled." Ms. Jennie smiles a big smile. She has kind eyes that are always happy to see me. "How are you this morning?"

"I'm ok. I haven't checked in with Mrs. Marsha yet, she was pretty busy when I walked in." I don't want to be marked absent. She turns and walks out to the office. I bet she is telling Mrs. Marsha and getting my breakfast. I pull Teddy over to me and go back to watching my show. I feel funny inside and I am not sure what it is. I try to rock more in the chair to calm the feelings. Gray is swirling in my tummy and making me feel sick. I wonder what my mom will look like, maybe she will be happy and smiling. I picture her laughing and holding me. It makes me feel warm and I really hope to see her laugh again. I am distracted by Ms. Jennie bringing in my breakfast. I am never really hungry to eat breakfast at school, but they always bring it to me. I eat as much as I can so I don't waste. I heard a teacher once say "always feed the bears" which I am not sure what that meant but it makes me laugh.

Ms. Jennie sits down at her desk and opens her computer. After a couple minutes she starts to talk to me again.

"So, Ironman what specials do you have today?" She sits back and waits for my response.

"Well, I guess I have a visit with my mom today. I haven't seen her since I have been at Dorothy's house." I let out a sigh.

"Today is the first visit? How are you feeling about that?" she asks as she picks up some putty and tosses it to me.

"I'm not sure, I want to see her but I don't want her to ignore me. I'm feeling full of gray and it is making my tummy pokey and sick."

"Gray? What feeling comes to mind when you think of gray? Here's the feelings chart." She points to a poster on the wall. I don't want to answer her right now, right now I want to just go back to watching my show. I don't want to mess with her counseling stuff this early in the morning.

"I can't do your counseling stuff right now, Ms. Jennie." I turn back to the T.V. and hold Teddy close. I know she won't get mad about this and will understand.

"Ok then, if you want to talk about then you know where to find me. It's time for reading groups to start anyway. Why don't you head over? Stop in after and I can walk you back to class. See you in a bit." She smiles at me and hands me my reading group stuff, the look on her face makes me laugh. I stand up and grab my things.

I am so glad that I have a new reading group now, it was really hard to be in Mrs. Gentry's group. I think about the last time I was in her room. It was the day after I called her a bitch and she was so mean to me. I walked into her room and her eyes were so hate filled. They looked like Don's and just looking at her made the darkness grow. She told me that I held back the whole group because I wouldn't work. I don't remember what else she said that day, but I did ask for a break because I felt myself about to blow up. She said no and then I threw my book at her face followed by the box of pencils. She tried to grab me which made me run under the table and kick it over to block her from touching me. Ms. Benson came and she was not happy with me, but I told her I tried to ask for a break and she wouldn't let me. Mrs. Gentry told her that she said no to me, and then I think Ms. Benson was more upset with her than me. Either way, she told me I didn't have to go to that reading group anymore, and she would teach my reading group. Now, it is just me in Ms. Benson's group.

I try to get out of reading as much as I can, so I toss my stuff in a chair by her table in her office and head to the bathroom. If reading groups are starting, that means it is nine, and soon it will be time for my mom's visit. I thought I would feel better about seeing her but I only feel gray. It starts to climb into my chest and catches in my throat. I take in a breath to try and calm it, but it keeps growing. I shut the bathroom door and put my head in my hands. Maybe I should just run and get away from here. Then I wouldn't have to go on a visit. But then I wouldn't get to see my mom. Mom. I wonder if she has tried to get better. I am not sure she would get better for me. I look into the mirror and feel so lost. Looking at myself, I am clean and my bruises have healed. I have not had to fight for or take care of my mom in what seems like a long time. I don't know what is going to happen. As my mind is racing, a knock on the door makes me jump. My breath leaves me and my heart pounds in my chest.

"Austin, I know you don't want to practice reading, but the bathroom is not a place to hide, I have to use it! Please come out." It is Mrs. Marsha and she sounds like she is in a rush.

I open the door and smile at her. I walk back to Ms. Benson's room and she is waiting on me. I sit down and look at her. "I just can't today," I tell her as I let out a sigh.

"Oh now, I know that you can. Listen, I know that reading is hard for you, I know this. But I also know that you're able to learn and if you'd just try you could be reading in a short time. So, will you please let me help you? I believe that you can do this." She looks so serious. Her eyes are caring and they make me feel like she is telling the truth. I really like that she does care about me. I haven't made it easy for her to do, especially this past week. I have kind of been a shit. But my body feels all crazy inside, and sometimes I can't help it. I take in a deep breath and let it out a little too loudly.

"I guess I can. But you need to make this quick, before I change my mind." I laugh at her and she smiles. She grabs the decoding sheets and starts in. I want to show her that I can try harder and decide to do my best. The decoding sheet is hard for me but she is so patient and kind. She keeps encouraging me and after a few tries I am able to read the words. I feel purple inside. Purple...I like this feeling. She hands me the story that goes with the decoding page. She opens the book and reads the small words and then points to the big word. I take in a breath and decide I can try this. I look at the word and start to sound it out "aaa...nnn...ttt....aaaaannnn.....tttt.....ANT!" I look at her and she smiles at me a really big smile.

"Yes, it is ant, great job! See what happens when you try! You can do anything if you believe in yourself and try!" She gives me a huge high-five and I'm so excited. That's the first word I have read. I look at Ms. Benson and she seems just as excited as I am. I am not sure what prompted me but in my excitement, I wrap my arms around her and give her the biggest hug. She leans back a bit and seems surprised, but hugs me back. When I release the hug, I look at her and she is smiling at me. I don't say anything, I can't find the words. But I am so thankful she helps me. Maybe I can read, maybe I can be better. Ironman can read. My thoughts are whirling when Ms. Benson starts talking to me.

"Ok, well we have the rest of the book to read, so keep going." With her help I am able to read the big words in the book. I want to read it to Mrs. Marsha too and ask Ms. Benson if I can. I walk to her desk and show her the book.

"Can you read this with me? You have to read the small words and I read the big ones." I wait for her response.

"Of course!" Mrs. Marsha holds the book and starts to read the words. I read the big words and it seems easier for me this time. She gives me a big hug after the last page. I am getting used to her hugs and they don't make the darkness spark anymore.

"I'm so proud of you!" She is smiling and has happy eyes.

I start to walk back to Ms. Benson's office when I see Ms. Bethany walk in. It must be time for the visit. Gray explodes in my chest and throat, and immediately my heart starts running and pain fills my head. I try to calm myself and focus on breathing, but it is not helping. I decide to keep walking and I put the book on the table and then go into Ms. Benson's bathroom. I lock the door and look in the mirror, I am such a shit. I can't even be brave enough to go see my mom. I take in a breath and try to calm my racing heart. I hear a knock at the door and Ms. Benson's voice follows.

"Austin, it's time for your visit. Come out please, I bet your mom will be happy to see you. Open the door or I can unlock it."

Well poop. I guess I better unlock it if she has a key anyway. I splash some water on my face and dab it with a paper towel. I unlock the door and open it. Ms. Bethany is waiting. I step out of the bathroom and look at her. She is short and has brownish blonde hair. She has kind eyes and smiles a lot when she talks. I really like her. She is my case worker and works with Mom too. She said she would try to help my mom make good choices. She smiles at me.

"Are you ready to go, Austin?" She waves her hand toward the door.

"No, but let's go." I walk past her and head to the front doors. I don't stop in case the darkness makes me change my mind. I wait for Ms. Bethany at her car. It is white and a big car; seems new. I remember the first time I was in it, it smelled like it had never been used. It was spotless inside, not even dust.

"Ok, climb in and we'll get going." She walks around the car and clicks the car to unlock it.

The building is brick and looks a little worn and dirty. My insides feel like they are going to jump out. Ms. Bethany gets out of the car. I think about not moving and locking the door on her, but that would not be a good choice. I unbuckle and slowly get out of the car. I can't find any words to say and follow Ms. Bethany inside. It smells clean and looks nicer inside than it does on the outside. We walk into a small room with three doors, she goes straight and it opens into a room with chairs and some toys. The carpet is brownish tan and the walls are white with a few posters on them.

I walk over to a poster and it has a black line around it and a picture of some mountains in the middle. It has one word on the bottom. I try to read it. BB..eee...lllll..iiiii..ee...vvvvv. eeee.....BBee..lll...iii..vvveee...Be be..ll..ee..iiive ....hmmm....I will have to ask for help on this one. I look over to Ms. Bethany and she is talking to a lady behind the desk. She is really big and has a hat on. She kind of reminds me of a toad. The thought makes me giggle. I walk to a table that has Legos on it and start playing with them.

"Austin, we're a few minutes early so we will hang out here for your mom." She sits down behind me.

"What does that poster say?" I ask as I point to the mountain poster.

"Well, lets see. It says Believe." She smiles back at me and I turn back to play with the Legos. Believe. That is a good word. I believe the visit will go well. I believe that my mom can make better choices. I like that poster. I take in a deep breath and my chest starts to relax and feel better. I can't wait to see my mom, I hope I can hug her and she hugs me back. I close my eyes and picture her hugs, the ones she gave me before my dad left. I mean died. Ms. Jennie has been helping me with my dad's death. Mrs. Michelle helps me too. I can picture Mom wrapping her arms around me and kissing my cheek.

The sound of the door distracts me and I turn to see who it is. My heart skips, but it is a guy I don't know. He has a little girl with him. She looks dirty, and she looks like she has gray inside her too. She looks at me. Her eyes are heavy. I know. I know she gets hit, I can see it in her eyes. I smile at her and she walks over and starts to play Legos with me. I lost my words and I am not sure what to say to her. She has a bruise on her ear. She smells funny too. Looking at her makes me feel sad. I hope she is getting help. I decide to ask her.

"Hi, are you here to get help too?" I smile at her

"I don't really know. I was at school and that guy asked me a lot of questions and now I am here." She doesn't look at me when she talks and keeps moving the Legos around.

"That happened to me too, except I ran away before they took me to their car. But it is good, and I'm doing ok. I'm here to visit with my mom." I smile at her but she keeps quiet and lets out a sigh. I can see the gray and darkness swirling in her. I hope things get better for her. I understand how she is feeling and it is not good. Looking at her makes me glad that I have Dorothy. I don't know where I would be sleeping without her. Maybe Dorothy can give her a place to stay too. Then I would have to share my bed and I don't like that idea. I realize that we have been waiting for a long time. I look around and my eyes meet Ms. Bethany's. She smiles but her eyes are fake happy. I know. I can see it on her face. My mom is not coming.

My heart drops and it feels heavy. My eyes start to burn and I take in a breath. I don't feel gray but I feel blue, sad. I am sad that she didn't come. She doesn't care about me. I walk over to Ms. Bethany and she sticks her arm out. I lean into her and she hugs me tight. I try to hold it back and be strong, but I can't and tears run down my face. I need to go home. I don't want to be here anymore.

"Can I go home now? I'm feeling sick," I stay leaning on her and I don't have to try to make my voice sound sick.

"I will call Dorothy and see if she is home. Austin, I'm sorry. I'll call your mom too and see what happened. Maybe her car broke down or something. Lets go." She stands up and walks to the front desk.

I look back at the little girl. I hope her mommy does better than mine. I head to the door and see the poster. Believe. That is a hard word to do. I watch the floor move as I walk out to the car. I hear the click and it unlocks. I climb in and the gray hits me. She didn't come. More tears fall and when Ms. Bethany climbs in, I turn away from her. I have nothing to say. The leather seats are cool and smooth on my hands. I rub my face on the seat. I like the way it feels on my cheek. I hope Dorothy answers and I can go home. I just can't today. I just can't. I let out a sigh and watch the trees go by out the window.

CHAPTER 14

I AM NOT GETTING OUT OF THIS BED. I
have decided. I won't move. I don't care who tries, I am not
doing it. I just can't. I don't know how long I have been in
here, but I haven't left since I was dropped off. Dorothy tried
to talk to me after I was dropped off, but I ignored her. I came
into this room and stayed. She made me lunch but I couldn't
eat it. My tummy was too sick and pokey. Mommy. I hope she
is ok. Maybe I should sneak out and go to the house to check
on her. The thought makes the darkness grow. I know I can't
go over there. He might be there and I don't want to see him.
He would hurt me. His eyes flash in my mind. Stop it. He is
not here. I roll over in the bed and pull the covers around me
tighter, holding Teddy closer.

"Austin, can I come in?" Dorothy knocks on the door.
I don't answer. Maybe she will leave me alone. But I know
better. I hide my head under the covers. They are soft on my

face. They smell like dryer sheets. I am getting hot. I can't breathe under here. I try to wait it out, but I can't. I pull the covers off of me and the cool air hits my face. It is refreshing. Dorothy is standing in the doorway. She is waiting too. I try to not look at her, but she smiles at me. Her smile is contagious. I close my eyes to keep myself from smiling back at her. I feel the bed lower as she sits on the edge. There is a tug on the blankets and I can't help but open my eyes. She smiles at me again.

"I think it's time for you to get out of bed."

"No, I don't think so." I roll over

"Austin, you can't stay in bed all day. Besides, it's almost time to get dinner started. I was thinking you can make dessert for us." Dorothy waits for a response.

"I don't know how to cook. No." I try to be stubborn but it is really hard with Dorothy. I would like to make dessert.

"Ok, well if you want to sit in here and mope then go for it, meanwhile I'll be in the kitchen making baked Mac-n-Cheese with chicken tenders. I guess we won't have chocolate puddin' pie if no one makes it." She gets up and walks out of the room without waiting for me to say anything.

Yummy, I love Mac-n-Cheese. My stomach growls. I didn't eat lunch and I can tell. I haven't felt hunger since I have been at Dorothy's house. I don't like the feeling and it makes my tummy angry. I would like to make a pie, and Dorothy could show me how. My mouth starts to water and I get out of bed. I use the bathroom and wash up before heading to the kitchen. Dorothy has music on and is dancing. It makes me smile. I have never heard the song before. It's different. She turns and sees me standing by the table.

"Sing with me." She starts to sing the words, in a low growly voice. She bends over a bit and slides her feet side to side. Her butt is stuck out and her hips are wiggling all over.

"I said yeah, yeah, yeah, yeah, yeah, well you could shake it, Mony Mony." She smiles and then mumbles something before I could understand her again. "Don't stop cookin' cause I feel all right now. Don't stop now, come on Mony, Mony Mony!" She starts laughing at me and then slides over a small box and a crust that is already made. She keeps dancing and makes her way to the fridge to open the door. She grabs the milk jug and slides it over to me. I stop it from falling off the table. Then she dances her way to the cupboard and grabs a big bowl then pulls a whisk out of a drawer. She is funny, I never pictured her as a dancer. I can't help but want to join in with her, but I just watch her for a few minutes and laugh. Then the song goes off and she pauses her phone.

"Ready to make a pie? You need to dump that box into that bowl. Then add 2 ½ cups of milk into it. Use that whisk to beat it for 5 minutes and pour it into the crust. We will make whipped cream for the top after it chills. Ok well, get started." She pulls out these weird looking cups and slides them over to me. She turns back to her phone and plays the next song. I feel like I have heard it before and I can't hold it back anymore and start dancing with her. I don't really know how to dance but her smile and the music makes my body wiggle. I move my feet all over and shake my butt. I smile at her and she turns back to the stove and stirs whatever is cooking. She starts singing with the music and the words to the song. She pulls out the spoon that she was stirring with and uses it like a microphone.

"Just take those old records off the shelf, I'll sit and listen to 'em by myself. Today's music ain't got the same soul, I like that old time rock and roll." She keeps dancing as she is mixing cheese into a pot on the stove. She looks at me and I am dancing too, she yells over the music. "Get going on the pie!"

I pick up the cups she gave me and I can see that one is 1 cup and the other is 1/2. I get the milk mixed in and start beating the pudding. It smells yummy and it makes my tummy happy. I think about my mom. I miss her. She used to like to dance. I focus on the pudding and try to think of something else. I keep mixing and mixing until my hands hurt. I think it is ready and dump it into the crust and spread it out. Dorothy puts it into the fridge and then puts the Mac-n-Cheese into the oven. She takes out chicken tenders and she shows me how to bread them. She uses crunched up chips and then she starts to fry them. My tummy starts growling. I am super hungry.

Dinner is delicious and I think it tastes even better because I helped. I crunch into the tenders and dip them in Ranch.. The Mac-n-Cheese is the best I have ever tasted. I enjoy each bite. While I take a drink of my water, I hear a loud bang on the door. It makes me jump and spill my water. Dorothy jumps too. We look at each other, and the gray bubbles up inside me. I don't like this. For a few minutes we don't hear anything else. Dorothy goes back to eating her food, but she takes one bite and the banging starts again. This time it is on the back door. The pounding is fast, hard knocks, almost like it is a kick instead. Someone is trying to get in. My heart matches the pounding on the door. Dorothy starts to stand up, but I don't want her to open it.

"DON'T!" I yell at her. "Don't answer it. It's him, I know it's him. He is here to hurt us." I can't breathe and my chest is hurting. I look at her and her eyes look like she has some gray in her too. She starts to push in her chair, and more pounding happens. She looks at the door. This time it sounds like they are hitting the wall. I just hope the doors are locked. We need to get away. My body is thumping and I can see my heart beating in my eyes. I want to run but he is outside, we need to hide. I need to get Dorothy to hide with me. "We should hide somewhere." I stand up as I tell her this. I need to protect her. My ears are burning. I squeeze my fists tight. I stare at Dorothy waiting for her response. She turns to look at me, her face is serious.

"It may not be him dear, it will be ok." She smiles a fake smile at me. "I do not answer the back door, so let's go into the living room and see if they come to the front of the house." She walks around the table and puts her hand on my shoulder. "It will be ok, come along." As she walks to the living room I follow her. My body is ready to hide, and I am fighting the urge to run to the bedroom closet, or the sewing room. That room is a mess and there are lots of things to hide behind. I stand behind the chair in the living room and Dorothy walks over to the couch. It gets quiet and I wonder if he left. Dorothy sits down and waits, I join her on the couch. My heart is slowing down and I take in a few deep breaths. I start to feel my body relax. Dorothy puts her arm on my arm and pats my hand.

Suddenly, his voice fills my ears. Nasty. Beer and smoke and nasty. I close my eyes and there he is, dark angry eyes. I can smell his stench, it is in here. I stand up and instantly darkness consumes me. I run into my room, grab Teddy, and climb into the closet behind the hanging clothes. I make myself small and wrap my hands around my knees. I am not sure what to do. I squeeze Teddy close. I hear someone come into the room. My breathing stops. Please don't find me. The clothes move to the side and Dorothy looks down at me. "You're safe, Austin. It's only me." She holds her hand out for me to grab. I take it and she helps me up. We walk back out to the living room, I am not sure why because hiding seems like the best choice. He pounds harder and starts to jiggle the door handle. He is angry and is yelling. Dorothy stops walking when he jiggles the door handle and his words are very loud and angry.

"Open the fucking door, I know she's in there. Come out! Come out! I know you're here with your bastard son. Fuck, open this door or I will kick it in." He is drunk, I can hear it in his voice.

"Dorothy, please we need to hide, he is drunk and scary." I pull on her arm. She looks at me and her eyes look angry and scary. I have never seen her eyes look like that before.

"Austin you listen to me and listen closely, I'll keep you safe and you need to trust me ok? I'm not going to hide from him. I want you to go into your room and close the door please. I will be calling Jeffery and the police, but in the time it takes for them to get here, you stay in your room but don't hide, we are stronger than him and he can't hurt us. I just don't want you to hear that kind of language."

She turns and walks into her bedroom. I walk toward my room and stop in the doorway. Am I stronger than him? What did she mean by that? Don is still pounding and screaming and is now hitting the window. I hear Dorothy talking and then she comes out of her room. I can't stay in here and let her get hurt. I need to be Ironman. I take in a breath and try to shield myself. I step into the living room. I can be strong with Dorothy. She is standing in front of the door. She has a long gun. Like ones you go hunting with. Her face is serious and she looks like she is ready for a fight. I stop behind the chair. I think that Dorothy is strong, but I am staying here.

She walks over to the door and starts to open the locks. My heart is racing and I can't breathe. Don is about to break the window and is still screaming. I should go help her. I don't want her to get hurt. My chest is tight and my heart can't beat any faster. I sit on the floor. It is cold but the carpet feels soft and clean. I peek around the chair and look toward the door. He is going to get in through the window. I bet that is why she is going to open the door. Dorothy starts to talk as she cracks the door open. The darkness has me. I need to be Ironman and keep her safe, but I am too scared. I try to move but I am stuck to the floor.

"DON! Don, you listen here, I am not going to allow you to come to my home acting like a bubbling idiot. Get off my porch before I have to show you that this is NOT a gun free zone. Off NOW!" Her voice is low and firm. She sounds scary. I don't think Dorothy needs anyone to look out for her.

"Fuck, where is she? You think that gun scares me! Get out of my way! His voice makes the darkness choke me. I hear loud footsteps and then BOOM. A gunshot. She shot him! Oh shit. She shot him. I can't believe it. I don't know if I should stay in here or go outside to help.

"Fucking crazy bitch! You almost shot me!" Don's voice changes, now he has gray in him.

"The next one I won't miss, now get off my porch. Oh look, perfect timing," Dorothy's voice sounded lighter.

"You called the police? Fuck." Don's voice sounds more distant. I bet he finally got off the porch. I don't need to be Ironman, I just need to be strong like Dorothy. The thought makes me laugh, I knew she could get scary if she needed to.

"That bitch tried to shoot me! Fucking tried to shoot me!" He is back to sounding drunk.

"Well, Don, if she did try then she would not have missed." Officer Jeffery's voice was low and serious. I bet he is right, but I thought she shot him too.

"Jeffery, thank you for coming and I am sorry to have to bother you. I am going to go back inside, I do not want him back on my property again because next time I won't miss," Dorothy laughs. I can hear her footsteps on the porch, she did not wait for a response. She opens the screen door and it slams shut behind her as she walks back into the living room.

I run over to the window, move the curtains to the side and look out. Don is in handcuffs. He is talking to the police officer. He looks upset and gross. His clothes are dirty and worn. Jeffery puts his hand on Don's head and pushes him into the police car. Looking at him keeps the gray rolling inside me, but it is not as big as it has been. I look at Dorothy. She is sitting on her chair and seems like she is a bit lost in thought. She smiles at me and I run over to her. I wrap her in a big hug. I have so much to say but struggle to get the words out. I am glad she is ok and I am glad she didn't let him hurt me. After a minute, I let go of her and build up the words.

"Thank you for not letting him hurt me." I smile at her.

"Oh...well... honey, he will never hurt you again as long as I can help it. Now, if I remember correctly, we have whipped cream to make for that pie of yours." She stands up and smiles at me again. She walks to her bedroom and I think puts away the gun. I head to the kitchen and wait for her. The look on Don's face when he was getting put into the police car appears in my mind. If he was looking for my mom, then she is not at his house. Where is she? I hope she is ok. Where was she earlier if she wasn't with him? Maybe Ms. Bethany was right and she didn't have a ride to the visit. I am lost in my thoughts when Dorothy distracts me by opening the fridge. She pulls out a carton of something and walks over to this machine on the counter.

"Why do you think my mom missed the visit today? And I thought Don was in jail, how did he get out?" The thought that he could have hurt Dorothy makes me feel blue. I wait for her to answer, but she turns on the doohickey that she dumped the carton into. The noise is loud and I walk over to see what it is doing and stand next to Dorothy. She starts dumping in white powdery stuff and it makes a poof in the air. After a couple minutes she turns off the doohickey and hands me the whisk part of it to lick. It is delicious. It is smooth and cool on my tongue. Makes my tummy happy.

"What is that thing?" I point to the machine.

"A mixer, it makes the magic happen." Dorothy starts to dump the whipped cream into a big bowl. She still hasn't answered my questions. We walk into the living room and we decide on a movie. As I am eating, I think of the day and realize tomorrow is my birthday. I haven't had a party before, and I start to ask Dorothy about it. I stop, she looks tired and I don't want to add to her stress. Instead I ask her about my mom again.

"If Don was looking for my mom, then where do you think my mom is?" I pause and wait.

"Don was bailed out of jail. That's why he was out. That means someone paid to get him out of jail until he goes to court. But now he will be back in jail. As far as your mom, Ms. Bethany said she was staying with another friend while she works on her choices." She goes back to eating her pie. "Oh, and I have Ironman party invitations for you to give out to your class tomorrow." She looks at me like I know what she is talking about. She knows about my birthday, and bought me invitations. She said party; she is throwing me a party. I am not sure what to say. My chest inflates with purple.

"A party?" I smile while I am saying the word.

"Well, yes. You can't have a birthday without a party now can you?" She laughs and takes another bite of her pie.

"I guess so, but birthdays don't happen for me." I look at the floor and the thought reminds me of a memory that I have.

It was sunny and sticky hot outside. I remember waking up to my dad throwing balloons around my bedroom. He was singing the birthday song and dancing around. I see his face and smile. His smile would make spots on his cheeks. He had a round face with brown eyes. They were soft and always kind. It was just a few days before he died. Mom made us chocolate waffles for breakfast that day. Later, we had a party in the backyard with sprinklers and water balloons. A neighbor friend came over and we played for hours. Then my dad brought out a cake, it was a Thomas the Train cake. It had candles on top. I don't remember what my presents were but it was a ton of fun. I smile at the warm thoughts. Dorothy's words bring me back from my thoughts.

"Are you ok?" She looks concerned.

"Yes, just thinking I guess. How did you know it was my birthday?" I smile at her.

"Well, I know everything," she laughs. "We will have your party on Saturday."

"Can we have one of those things you beat with a stick to get candy?" I smile and wait for her response.

"Oh, well we can see if they have one in town, but right now, it is your bedtime. So go brush your teeth and get your jammies on." She stands up and takes my pie plate then heads to the kitchen. I am too tired to argue, even though I don't want to go to bed this early. I snuggle into the fluffy warm blankets and Dorothy comes in to read a story. The story is so fun, and we laugh a lot during it. It is about a farting dog and anything with the word fart in it is funny. I was even able to read some of the smaller words and she helped me read a few others. She turns out the light and the room goes dark except the moonlight peeking in the window.

A window cracks and the glass shatters across the floor and slides to my foot. His eyes are hate filled, dark, angry. I run. The floor pulls me closer to him no matter how fast I go. My feet start to hurt as they pound the floor. I can't get away. I can't breathe. I can't run anymore. I stop and hear his voice behind me. "She's dead, your mom was weak and now she's dead, come here and you can join her." The voice is low and growly. I turn around slowly and there is a gun and then a loud crack and darkness. I fall and keep falling. The wall is slick and smooth. I can't stop myself. I try to scream but nothing comes out. I see the bottom. It is close and then I hit...I jerk up and look around. Where am I? What is going on? I reach for the side table and knock off the lamp onto the floor.

I can't see and try to get up but the covers are all tangled around me. I need to get free. I kick and kick until they start to fly off. I fall onto the floor and I hear some commotion coming from the living room. Him. He is here. I quickly feel my way to the closet and climb in. He doesn't know where I am or what room. My eyes are thumping as my heart races and I don't have Teddy. Oh no, I should go get him but I can't get myself to move. The light switches on and I stop breathing. I don't move. I can't. Mommy. Where is she? I start to cry but I hold it back. I am cold. Wet. Full of the dark pain. The closet door slides open and I scream. He is going to kill me, my eyes fill with red. I start to fight. I kick and punch. I feel my leg hit something and then my fist hits. I push past him and make a run for the front door.

The lock is stuck and I can't get the door to open. Back door, I quickly make my way there and hear a voice yelling my name. I can't stop. I pull the lock and then the other. The door makes a loud noise as I push it open. The screen door slaps on the hinges and I step through it. My foot hits something on the porch. I lose my balance and fly off the back steps. My body slams onto the cold wet ground. I feel the grass under my fingers. It is damp and smooth. My face cools at its touch. I let go of my tears and my eyes fill with them. I want my mommy. I need her to get better. I hear the screen door open behind me. Soft footsteps move down the stairs. I know it is not him. I don't look at her. I hit her. I hurt her. I am such a worthless shit. What if she sends me away? She may not want me here now that she has seen the real me. I am not strong, a pussy, that is what I am. Pussies cry and I can't hold back the tears.

Dorothy's feet stop in front of me. She doesn't say anything and I can't look at her. I hope I didn't hurt her too much, I didn't mean to. I curl up into a ball and stay on the ground. I start to rock my body back and forth, sometimes it calms my body. I feel Dorothy's hands wrap around me. I let her, but it isn't a hug. She scoops me into her arms and squeezes me close. I search for my words and attempt to get them out. Dorothy interrupts me.

"Shhh. It's ok. You are safe, I have you," her voice is low and soft.

She holds me close and walks back inside. She doesn't turn on lights and doesn't put me down. I don't move and let her keep me in her arms. She sits down in the big comfy chair. I thought she would put me down to have a talk about what happened, so I start to move. She tightens her embrace. The chair forms around my back and cradles me as Dorothy rocks back and forth. I think my head wants me to get up, but everywhere else in my body doesn't want to move. I am not sure how I feel about this, but she keeps her hold on me. The movement and feel of her touch brings the tears back into my eyes. I don't hold them in and they flow down my face. I take in a breath and try to calm my body. I relax into her arms and her hold loosens. She doesn't say anything but does start to hum a song. My mind gets lost listening to her, my tears dry up, and I fall into the rhythm of the chair. My tears stop and my eyes get heavy. I try to keep myself awake, but my eyes close and I fall asleep with a song in my ears.

CHAPTER 15

I HEAR THE ALARM CLOCK SINGING MUSIC in the next room. I roll over and find Teddy. He has been much cleaner since living with Dorothy, I think he likes it better. I smell him and he is fresh like flowers. It is my birthday today. I close my eyes and remember the last fun birthday I had. Balloons all over and my dad's smile. The thought makes me feel warm. Once Mom met Don, I didn't get much of a birthday. I remember my fifth birthday, Mom did make me a cake for dinner. We were about to cut into it when Don started screaming about using his grocery money for a stupid cake. He walked into the kitchen and threw the cake against the wall. It still tasted good. Dorothy's voice floats into the room. I remember last night. I hurt her. She didn't seem mad, but what if she is today? If she tells Ms. Bethany I might have to live somewhere else. The thought makes my tummy hurt, or maybe I am hungry.

I jump in the shower and get cleaned up for school. I really like taking a shower, the hot water helps wake me up in the mornings. I practice writing my name in the smoky stuff on the mirror when I get out. I want to write my letters better. I am excited about going to school today. Ms. Benson said she has a new book to read with me. I am actually looking forward to hearing it. I laugh at the thought. I smell breakfast. My tummy growls. I get dressed and walk into the living room. Thinking about the school day and if Gavin will be there, I wasn't paying attention to much. I look up and stop after a couple steps. Above the entrance to the kitchen, there is a colorful banner hanging.

I try to read the words. I see the letter H and start to sound it out. I think it says Happy Birthday. It makes me smile and I feel a warm purple explosion inside me and my smile grows. There are balloons tied to the kitchen chairs and in the middle of the table, a huge chocolate cake with candles. Around the cake there are brightly colored presents of all sizes. I feel my heart freeze. I am not sure what to say. I feel a heavy feeling in my chest and when my eyes find Dorothy's I have tears falling down my cheeks. Her smile is huge and she walks over toward me.

"Oh, dear, don't cry over this! I could take them back if you want me to?" She embraces me in a huge hug. I don't move, I feel like my feet are stone. I can't believe she did this for me. Even after what I did to her last night. She lets me go and walks back to the stove. After grabbing a plate, she turns around with a plate full of food.

"Don't just stand there! I made a perfect breakfast for the perfect boy on his birthday!" She walks to the table and sets the plate down, then looks at me again.

"Austin, happy birthday. You are loved and this is what I do for the people I love. Now, stop standing there looking all crazy and get over here and eat this food before it gets cold." Her tone sounds more serious and she stomps over to her cup of coffee. I start laughing and my body seems to relax. Her words fill me up and I run over to her and give her a hug. My insides are full of a feeling that I don't feel very much. I don't let her go and hold tight onto her. I want her to know what I want to say to her but I can't find the words. When I let her go, I look at her and the words came out.

"I love you, thank you so much." I wipe my face and get to my breakfast before it gets cold. It looks amazing. Strawberry french toast, with big chunks of strawberries, bacon, and scrambled eggs with cheese. I shovel the food into my mouth and it is the best breakfast ever. I am really enjoying the food and I look up at Dorothy. She is still sitting across from me at the table drinking her coffee. I stop chewing when I see her eyes. They have tears in them, but her eyes look like a happy sad. I swallow and she smiles at me. I am not sure what she is thinking, or why she doesn't eat breakfast, but I don't try to. I finish my breakfast and my stomach is completely stuffed.

"You are looking like Jake Darby with that strawberry syrup all over your face, go get yourself washed up and we will have time for you to open a gift before school." She laughs at me and takes my plate off the table. I hurry to the bathroom to clean up. I wonder what I am getting, I can't wait...maybe she will let me skip school today and I can stay home with her. Right. I laugh as I walk back to the kitchen. She is waiting on me with a fresh cup of coffee and a smile. I walk over and run my fingers along the colorful wrapping paper on the packages. It is smooth except for the seams and I can feel the tape holding it together.

"Well, are you going to just pet the gifts or are you going to pick one to open?" She sips her coffee and looks at me over her cup.

I smile and look back at the gifts, I grab the big one, it looks like a box. I pick it up and pull it toward me. The paper rips easily. I tear it to pieces, I pull off the rest of the wrapping and hold up the perfect gift. I smile and can't hold it back. It is the best Ironman action figure I have ever seen. It has blast gear and is the tallest action figure ever! I open the box and it seems like it takes forever, I pull at the plastic but it won't open.

"Here, honey, I have some scissors." She reaches out for the toy and I hand it to her. My heart is pounding and I can hardly wait. She hands me the Ironman and then takes out the accessories for it. I put the ammo in the blaster and shoot it across the room. It shoots far. I run over and grab it and take Ironman to the living room and start playing with it. It even makes noises when I push the buttons. I am flying him through the air when I see Dorothy walk into the room.

"Well dear it is time for school, grab your things and let's get going." She walks over to the coffee table and picks up her keys. A part of me is trying to have a fit, I can feel it building.

I take in a breath and hold it back. I can't lose it, and need to calm myself. I have to go to school, It is going to be ok. It will be a good day. I have been trying a coping skill that Ms. Jennie talked to me about, sometimes it works and sometimes it is hard. She called it no more "stinkin thinkin". I take in a breath and say it again, it is going to be a great day. I hope it is anyway. I look back at my toy and I think of my birthday last year at school.

I was late for school. I overslept and my mom wasn't home. I remember being scared when I woke up alone. I hurried to the school in the same clothes that I wore the day before. The school was close to our house and I could see it from my window. When I rushed into the office, I dropped my eyes to my feet. I did that often because the look in the office ladies' eyes were never kind and they made the gray burst. The office was dark and smelled funny. It was not like the office at my new school. The office ladies stopped talking when they saw me. I looked up, hate filled eyes rolling at me. One walked over and glared at me over the counter before talking to me. I looked back at the floor.

"Well, you are late, here is your slip, and breakfast is over." Her cold voice went through me. I didn't even look back at her when I took the late slip and left the room. Then I walked into my classroom and the teacher sighed and said, "Where is your helper? You are not supposed to be here at this time." She didn't even look at me. She hated me, and her eyes were always angry and cold. Then later that day, she made a point to tell the class that it was time for birthday treats. She knew I didn't have anything to hand out. She waited for my response. I threw a desk and ran from the room. I can still hear the crash in my ears as the desk slid across the floor. I am so thankful I don't have to go to that school anymore.

Dorothy's words bring me from my mind and I stand up and walk over to her. I keep the Ironman toy in my hand. I unzip my backpack and gently tuck him into the bag. I grab Teddy and walk outside behind Dorothy. She seems in a hurry today. Now that I think about it, she seems like she is thinking a lot today, and she is taking her purse with some printed papers in her hand. She doesn't normally have things with her when we leave for school. What is she doing? The thought makes prickles pop in my chest. The sun is cooler and the dew is still relaxing on the grass. The days are not as hot and summer is over. I really like the fall time. I hurry to catch up to Dorothy and jump in the car. I want to ask her about treats, and about where she is going, but I don't want to be annoying. She did so much for me already. More than my mom. Mommy, I hope she is ok. I will invite her to my birthday party if Ms. Bethany will let her come.

I see the school and a lot of kids are heading to the doors. Dorothy pulls the car over and I unbuckle my seatbelt and start to open the door when her words stop me.

"I will drop by after lunch to bring you something, have a wonderful day, and work to keep your body calm." She reaches over, pulls me to her, and hugs me. I love her hugs. I close my eyes and relax in her embrace.

It is going to be a good day. I jump out of the car and wave as she pulls away. I make my way through the crowd of kids and head to the office to check in. I know I don't have to check in anymore, but I want to show Mrs. Marsha my Ironman toy. The office is busy with adults and kids. I walk around them to stand by Mrs. Marsha's desk. She is talking to another person, but smiles at me when she sees me. It seems like it is taking forever for Mrs. Marsha to be able to talk to me. I want to interrupt but I know that would not work out for me, so I take in a breath and wait. Finally, the last parent leaves and she spins her chair toward me and has a big smile on her face.

"I hear it is someone's birthday today! Happy birthday, Austin!" She holds up her hand for a high-five. I smile at her and I feel warm inside. I give her a high-five and start telling her all about my morning and how it is the best birthday ever. I pull out my Ironman toy and show her how it works. She even hit the button and the blaster shot out and hit Ms. Benson as she was walking by. Mrs. Marsha laughs and her laugh makes me start laughing. Ms. Benson looks at us with a fake mad face then she starts laughing too. I laugh so hard I can't catch my breath. I try to stop and reload the blaster and launch again, but at Mrs. Marsha. She catches it and tries to catch her breath too.

"Oh Austin, you are too funny, give me some love bugs and you need to head to class." She opens her arms and I run into them. She squeezes me and when she lets me go I gather my things and start to walk to class. I hear the late bell ring and echo in the hallways, I am late. Shoot. I start to feel my heart jump, I don't want to be late today. I walk faster and then break into a run. I run quickly, trying not to fall or hit anyone. I move to the side and fly past Ms. Jennie and hope she doesn't stop me.

"MORNING, I'M LATE!!" My voice bounces in the hall, but I don't stop and turn the corner toward my room. I can see Mrs. Roush holding the door open for the class to come in. I don't slow down until I reach the line. My chest hurts and I am out of breath. I lean on the wall and relax a minute.

"Goodness, Austin. You didn't need to run that fast!" She laughs. "And it is your birthday today, Happy birthday!" She smiles a big smile and has happy eyes. I smile back at her and want to show her my toy but she starts talking to the class. I will have to later. I hang up my stuff in the locker and remember the invitations to pass out. Pulling them out of my backpack makes me excited to hand them out. I carry them to my desk and there is a birthday chair cover on my seat and a crown on my desk. It makes me smile. Gavin runs over and helps me put my crown on and he tells me happy birthday. I start to hand him my invitation, but Mrs. Roush interrupts us.

"Austin, wait until recess and I will help you pass out your invitations. Right now we need to get our day started." She smiles and walks back to the front of the room. Gavin turns back to me and keeps talking while I sit down, Mrs. Roush turns around and gives us the teacher-waiting-for-you-to-stop-talking look, and Gavin quickly goes to his seat. I look around and I feel like I am the most important person in the room. This birthday crown is the best and it makes me feel purple and green inside. I smile and look at Mrs. Roush. She is talking and going over the calendar but I can't hear the words she is saying. I can only think about my birthday invitations and handing them out.

I count the invitations and sort them on my desk. I make smaller piles and then stack them back up. I recount and move them around my desk. I wonder if all these invitations will actually come to my party. The thought makes me smile. I want a piñata. Maybe that is where Dorothy is going this morning. She seemed so serious and was definitely going somewhere. She said she was going to drop off something, I bet it will be birthday treats. I suddenly feel a hand on my shoulder and I jump sideways away from it, almost falling to the floor. My crown falls off and rolls under the desk next to mine. I look up and I can see the thumps of my heart in my eyes. It is only Mrs. Roush. She kneels down next to me and holds out her hand to put it on my shoulder.

I hate that I am still so jumpy. I put my head on my desk and look at her.

"Sorry about startling you, I dismissed the class for reading groups and you seemed lost in thought." She pauses and seems to be waiting for a response. I smile at her.

"I guess I was thinking about my birthday party and what will happen at it. I haven't had a party in a really long time." I smile at the thought.

"Well, it is time for you to head to the office for reading groups." She walks me to the door. "See you after recess."

"Ok." I turn and skip off to the office. Ms. Benson was waiting for me in her room. I sit down and she spins her chair around and rolls over to the table.

"Happy Birthday! I brought you something." She smiles at me as she slides over a wrapped gift. It is small and very thin. I look at her and her eyes are happy. I tear open the paper and hold up a book. It has the Avengers on the front of it. I look up at her and she starts talking.

"I wanted you to have a book to read and we can practice together." She leans back in her chair and looks at me over her hands.

"Can you read it to me?" I hand her the book and smile. She gives me a high-five and leans on the table placing the book in front of us both. I lean in and look at the pictures. It makes purple bloom inside. She starts reading but I can't hear the words. I look at her and then quickly wrap my arms around her in a hug. I can't find the words to say, but I hope she understands. She pauses in her reading and then continues with the book. She finishes the story and then slides it over to me.

"Ok, now it is your turn, I will help you." She smiles at me and seems to read my mind. "I know you can read this, it is at your level and I can help you." She puts her finger under the first word on the first page.

I take in a deep breath and I look at the words. I can feel the gray starting to boil and grow. I can do this, I can do this. I try to stay positive and use the positive talk stuff that I have been told to use. I go ahead and give the word a try. The, hmm.. t, h, e says the t, h, e says the, every letter makes a sound and t,h,e says the. I remember that song. I start reading the words and they seem to come out. I keep going. And I smile because the words are coming out of my mouth, I pause and look at Ms. Benson.

"See! I told you that you could do it!" Her smile is huge. Her eyes look watery as she leans over and wraps her arm around me in a side hug. I can feel the gray disappear in her embrace. I turn back to the book and start reading again. I pause at a word and Ms. Benson reads it, then I keep going. I finish it, I can't believe it but I do finish it. I needed some help but I did it. I feel green and purple pop up all over. I can't help but smile. I think Mom will be so excited to hear me read to her. The thought is not a happy thought for very long. When will I see her again? It is my birthday and she isn't even here to tell me happy birthday. I let out a deep breath and hand the book to Ms. Benson, but she hands it back to me.

"Take it home, it is yours. I am so proud of you! You have been working so hard." She gives me a high-five. I hold the book close and smile at her. We stand up and head toward the classroom. As we pass Mrs. Marsha, I hear Ms. Benson start talking to her.

"Mrs. Marsha, Austin just read a book to me and he only needed a little help!! Isn't that great?" She pauses for a response.

"Oh my goodness! That is the best news! You are such a hard worker!!" She reaches out and gives me a high-five.

I did read it! I can read. The thought makes me smile and happy. I look up at Ms. Benson and she smiles back at me. She looks like she is about to say something but stops. She asks me to head back to class and I start walking there. The sun is brightly shining through the hallway window making yellow squares on the floor. I stop in the middle of the first yellow square. I hunch down and jump as high as I can and land in the next yellow square. I laugh and leap again to the next one. Just as I am about to make the third jump, I hear a cold voice and feel someone touch me. I pull away and fall against the wall.

Cold dark eyes. Mrs. Gentry is glaring down at me. I feel the gray pull at my ribs and try to take in a breath to keep it controlled. I stand up straight and walk past her. I ignore her words and keep walking. I am not sure what she is saying and I don't care. Her voice keeps echoing in the hall and I see him. His nose, his eyes. His stench fills my nostrils. I try to think of something else. I see the hall, I see the floor, the back door. I am safe at school. He is not here. He is not here. I turn to my hallway and see Mrs. Roush outside the classroom door waiting for the other students. I run toward her. The gray fills me and I look back to see if someone is chasing me. When I turn back I try to stop but slide onto the floor at her feet. As I am trying to stand up, I hear Mrs. Gentry's voice behind me.

"He just ignored me and ran all the way down the hall after jumping through the other hallway!" She is short of breath and her voice is high pitched. I don't look at her. Mrs. Roush helps me up and gives her a simple reply.

"Thank you for letting me know." She turns and walks into the classroom with me by her side. She doesn't look back or say anything else to her. She walks through the classroom to the locker area and helps kids put on their jackets and line up for recess. She doesn't say anything to me about Mrs. Gentry's comments. I feel the gray fizzle but I know I am not in trouble with Mrs. Roush. I sit down at my desk and put my face on the cold surface. It is smooth and cold on my cheek. I take in a breath and the gray disappears. Sitting back up, I stack up my invitations and count them again, then spread them out on my desk. I need to wait for Mrs. Roush to come back in to make sure it is ok for me to pass them out. I hope I have some extra to invite my mommy. I hope she is safe. It is my birthday and she is not around to have cake or even tell me happy birthday. I feel blue and tears start to build in my eyes. Her face appears in my mind. Empty and lost. I can picture him on her and her screams. Mrs. Roush's voice pulls me from the thoughts.

"Ok. First, you need to walk in the halls so you do not get hurt or hurt someone else, ok?" She is smiling at me.

"Ok, I will." I pick up my pile of invitations.

"I will help you, let's put them in the Wednesday envelopes to go home to parents. Students will lose them if they are left on their desk." She turns and walks to the back of the room. I hold open the envelope and she drops in the invitation. We talk and laugh while we stuff the envelopes and then finish the last one. I have some left over and count them. Seven extra. I look over at Mrs. Roush and hand her an invitation.

"Well thank you! I will have to see what I have going on this weekend before I can say if I can come." She smiles and sits at her desk. "You have about eight minutes of recess left if you want to go give anyone else an invitation, then we have library after." She bends down and puts the invitation into her bag, or purse, I am not sure which because it is huge. I turn and head to the door without saying anything, I don't want to waste time. The hallway is empty except for a couple teachers from the end of the hall. One is the nice one that smiles at me a lot. I did learn her name and I think it is Mrs. Kelly. I stop in front of her and hand her an invitation and smile at her. She thanks me and I walk down the main hall toward the office.

There are a couple parents in the office checking kids out. Mrs. Marsha is on the phone and I don't see Ms. Benson. The parent tries to ask Mrs. Marsha about signing out the student, but she is on the phone. I walk over and show her the sign out sheet and go sit at the desk. Mrs. Marsha gets off the phone.

"Thank you for helping out, Austin. What can I do for you?" She is typing on her computer and seems really busy.

"Here. It is my birthday party invitation at Dorothy's house." I smile and walk the invitation to her.

"Oh how fun! I will see if I can make it! Thank you." She holds her arm out for a hug and I melt into it.

"Can I leave this one for Ms. Benson and Ms. Jennie?" I hold out two more invitations.

"Of course, put them in their mailboxes." She stands up and walks over to the boxes on the wall. "There, they will find them when they are not busy. Head back to class now." She sits back down and smiles again as she answers the phone.

I walk back out and head to the library. My class is already here and I take my seat. The seats here are tall and comfortable. I put my head down on the desk and feel the surface with my hands. I am not sure what the teacher is saying. It would be fun if my teachers would come to my party. I hope Dorothy can find a piñata in town. I wonder where she was headed this morning. She seemed so serious and like she was on a mission. She is someone that I think will not stop until things work out the way she sees best. I hope she remembers to bring birthday treats for after lunch. I sigh and close my eyes for a second. I am very tired.

Balloons. Red, gold, and silver ones. There are big ones and small ones. And some that are not even blown up yet. I hear her laughing and walk into the other room. It is Dorothy and she is at the table laughing. I look over and I see my mom but she is sick and Don is yelling in her face but I can't hear his words. I run to her. Mom! Mommy! He takes his hand backward and slaps me in the face.

I fall backward to the floor and wake up in a jerk. I am wet. Oh no. No, no. I peed myself and I am in the library. I fill up with yellow. Everyone is looking at me. I jump up and run. I don't stop even when the teacher tries to stop me. I push past some students in the hallway. I am such a shit. What was I thinking, falling asleep in class? I rush into the office and stop at Mrs. Marsha's desk.

I am trying to catch my breath and she is on the phone. I lean over and I am covered in pee. As I am waiting, Ms. Jennie's door opens and she walks out. I look at her and I start to cry. I let the tears fall and walk over to her.

"What is going on Austin?" I don't respond and look down. "Oh, oh, I see. Come on now. Let's get you changed." She walks to the back of the office and starts digging through some boxes. I wait for her and she hands me a change of clothes. I head to the bathroom and change. Looking in the mirror, I splash water on my face. My heart slows down and I look back at myself. Mommy. Ugh. I can't think about that right now. I change my thoughts to my birthday party. Piñata, ice cream and chocolate cake waiting on me.

I walk out of the bathroom and Ms. Jennie takes me to lunch. It is Mac-n-Cheese day, my favorite. I think the lunch lady gives me extra and she is really nice to me. I sit down next to Gavin, he is saving me a seat. No one says anything about the library and we eat and talk about my party. I tell them about a piñata and that it is an Ironman party. We giggle and laugh at Nikki's hulk impression and then we go outside to recess. I am too busy playing a game that Marley made up to think about anything else. She keeps changing the rules and it is very frustrating. Gavin and I decide to go play something else and walk out to the soccer field. We join a kick-catch game and play with some kids from Mrs. Gentry's class. I don't know their names but I am glad I did not get stuck in that class. The bell rings and we run to the line spot. I race Gavin there but he is faster and beats me.

As we are standing in line, I remember what Dorothy said this morning. She would bring me something after lunch. I wonder if she is here yet. I try to look into the doors but there are too many students in the way. What is taking so long? I step out of line and run to the doors, the girl holding the door pushes me away and I push her back and tell her to stop. Finally, the classroom door opens and Mrs. Roush walks out and Dorothy is right behind her. I feel my heart relax and I let out my breath that I must have been holding. I don't wait for them to walk to me, and push past the bossy girl at the door. I run up to Dorothy and give her a hug. I am so happy to see her.

She hugs me back and we walk back into the classroom before anyone else does.

"There are the cupcakes I brought for your class, and I also picked up some juice boxes for added sugar." She points to the box on the table. They are chocolate cupcakes with red and gold frosting and a ring on top that looks like Ironman's head. They are perfect and look delicious.

"I love them! Will you help me pass out napkins?" I start to walk to the back sink but she starts talking with the teacher again.

I keep walking past the table but notice Dorothy's bag she had this morning. Sticking out of the outside pocket is a blue envelope and I can see the last half of my name on the outside of it. I look back at Dorothy and she is still talking and seems distracted. It does have my name on it, so I can take it. I reach out and pick it up and read my name again. I recognize the handwriting, but it can't be. I feel my chest tighten and my ears get hot. I turn the envelope over and tear it open. It is kind of loud but no one notices. I slide out the card. It has a dog on the front with some balloons on it. Dorothy gave me a card this morning, so why would she give me two cards, maybe it is from...no it can't be.

I open the card and it has some words in it. I try to read them. Happy Birthday and then other words. I skip over them because no one reads the cards anyway. I look at the name written in pencil at the bottom. I sound out the first word. Llll, oooo, vvvv, eee Loovvee, love. The first word is love. Then I recognize the writing again. It says, Love Mom. That is it. Love Mom. My heart starts beating fast. This card is from Mommy. But how? How did Dorothy get it? I look back at the word, Mom. I see her face smile, the kind of smile that makes her eyes squishy. I miss her. I look at Dorothy and I feel red forming in my eyes. How did she get this?

CHAPTER 16

MY HEART BEATS QUICKLY AND I TAKE IN
a breath. I look around the room and the kids are talking and
moving around. Mrs. Roush is distracted by Dorothy and I
need to talk to her. I close the card and quickly walk over to
her, I feel my eyes burning and my chest is hurting. I need to
not let my anger monster take over. I try to use some calm
down tools that Ms. Jennie has been teaching me. I close my
eyes and picture my happy place. My bed, warm, cozy with
Teddy and the smell of bacon filling the room. I open my eyes
and both Mrs. Roush and Dorothy are staring down at me.

"How did you get this? Have you been talking to my mom?
Dorothy! How did you get this?" I pause but I need the answer.
"Why didn't you tell me?" I try to hold back tears but the anger
in my eyes turns to tears and I let them fall. I pause and wipe
the tears off my cheek and I wait for her response. She takes a
step closer to me and kneels down. I start to pull away but I

stay as she puts her hands on my shoulders. She takes a hand and wipes away the tears as they fall.

"Austin, I am so sorry dear. I wanted to give this to you after school so we could talk about what has been happening with your mom, but since you found it I will answer your questions." She takes in a breath and then stands up and walks over to the back table. She sits down and pats the other chair. I hesitate and feel like I should run, but I fight the urge and walk over next to her.

"Your mom asked me to give it to you. Yes, I have spoken with her and we can talk more about this after school." She looks at me with kindness in her eyes. I still have so much to say but I can't find the words. I start to get up, but she stops me. Knowing eyes. "We will talk about everything, I promise, but school is not the place. She is safe and making the choices she needs to to get visits back with you. Now enjoy your cupcakes with your class and we will talk more after school. Everything is going to be ok."

I take in a deep breath and nod my head at her. She will tell me. I know she will. I can still feel my heart beating and want to know more, but I know she won't tell me right now. I walk back to get napkins and start to hand them out. Dorothy walks over and tells me that she needs to run a couple errands before school is out. She gives me a hug and leaves the classroom. She waves as she walks out of the room. I go back to passing out napkins but I am struggling to focus. Where is my mommy? Is she really getting better or is she just telling Dorothy that she is? I am not sure what to believe. I am lost in my thoughts when I hear Mrs. Roush's voice say my name. I look at her and she waves me over to the table. Mrs. Roush picks up the cupcakes and holds them while I pass them out to each student. I hand out the last cupcake and sit down with mine. The class sings to me and I smile, they seem so excited. I put my crown back on and take a bite of the cupcake. Then everyone else starts digging into the cupcakes and icing is everywhere. It is loud. The class is laughing and talking. It is a nice break in the day. I finish up my juice and sit back down at my desk.

Looking around the room, everything seems like slow motion. Everyone is talking but I can't hear their words. My mind is not here and my heart is feeling lost. I should be excited and ready to talk to my friends, but all I want to think about is that card. Mom. My mom. Her face shows up in my mind again. Hurt, screaming. He is shoving into her and has his hands around her neck. I feel the darkness wrap around me. Dorothy has been talking to her and didn't tell me, why wouldn't she tell me? I take deep breaths but it does not help. I am hot. I itch all over. I feel every inch of my shirt on me and it feels like it is burning me. I scratch at it. I can't, I just can't. I take off the birthday crown and put it on my desk. The darkness tightens on my throat and I can't breathe. I need to help her. I can't. I put my face on my desk and feel the smooth surface with my hand. I feel so lost. Lost like my mom. I can feel the class walking around the room and see them line up. I must have missed the direction.

Mrs. Roush puts her hand on my shoulder. I look up at her and she is looking at me with knowing eyes. I stand up and line up with the class. It is time for gym. I do like gym class. We walk into the gym and start stretching. Mr. Harris divides the class into teams and we start running an obstacle course. Both teams go at the same time. I line up with my team and wait my turn. The darkness still has me and I am trying to keep control. I can feel my heartbeat in my eyes and ears. I move up to the start of the course. When the whistle blows, I jump sideways, I wasn't paying attention. I start to run and jump through the hoops, Micheal is running next to me and we both turn the corner. He trips me and I fall to the floor. My arm slams into the cone and I slide to a stop. I look over and he is on the floor too. I stand up. He jumps up and starts yelling at me. I am not sure what he says but I hear stupid mixed in the words, then he pushes me. His hands feel like fire and his stench singes my nose. Cigarettes and beer. Nasty and dirt.

I feel another push and I need to get away. I need to be Ironman. I hear my mom's scream in my head, it hurts. I have to protect her. I shield myself and make a fist. I start hitting him. I hate him. "Get away from me! Get away from her!" I keep hitting and start to kick. I am hot and my chest hurts. I feel him grab me and the darkness chokes as he pulls me backward. "Don't touch me, Don't touch me! I need my mom. Mommy! Don't hurt me." I have to get away, I hit him. He won't let me go. I put all my strength into a kick and miss. I grab his arm and pinch really hard then scratch him. Finally, he puts me down and I run to the corner of the room. I am trapped. I wrap my arms around my knees and make myself small. I rock back and forth on the floor. I try to take in a breath but the darkness blocks it. I am such a worthless shit. A stupid pussy. How could I think I could be better?

I feel someone next to me and they hand me Teddy. I hold him close and start to cry. I keep rocking myself. "I miss my mom," I say while burying my face into Teddy. Ms. Jennie puts her hand on my back.

"I bet you do." She is so calm, especially since I just hit her. She starts to rub my back and I lean on her and let myself cry.

"He hurt her a lot. I don't know if she is safe or hurt. She didn't come to my visit and somehow Dorothy gave me a birthday card from her." The more I talk, the more I say, and the more I want to tell her.

"He hurt you a lot too, but you're safe now. I hope your mom makes the choices to be with you," She doesn't look at me and has a calming voice.

"Dorothy has been talking to her but she didn't tell me. It makes me feel red." My voice sounds small.

"I can understand why it would, but what is red?" I knew she would ask me this. We have been trying to name my feelings.

"Angry, and hurt. She should have told me." I sigh

"Maybe she had reasons not to, Dorothy cares about you and wants what is best. She doesn't want you to get hurt again." She is probably right. I know Dorothy cares about me. I look over at Ms. Jennie and her hair is a mess. I instantly feel blue, I mean sad. I hurt her again. I put my face back into Teddy.

"I'm sorry." I don't know what else to say and I know that sorry is not enough, but I did try to keep calm most of the day.

"I know you are. It has been a hard day today. I am going to set a timer and you can take a break, then we will work on some classwork before you head back to class." She stands up and lets out a grunt, pretending she can't stand up. It makes me laugh.

The time goes by fast and Ms. Jennie walks me back to the classroom. It is close to the end of the day, and I join the class at the carpet. Gavin nudges me and smiles. We listen to the story and gather our stuff to go home. I hope Dorothy doesn't wait to tell me what is going on with my mom. I need to hurry and get to the car and ask her. The class lines up and it is taking forever. I start to wiggle my feet trying to stay calm and wait. I like the feel of the floor sliding under my feet. Finally, Mrs. Roush says her goodbye song and starts walking students out the door. I can't wait anymore and take off running past everyone. When I get outside, I see Dorothy standing by the fence waiting on me. She is talking to another lady and I stop in front of her.

"It is time to go now, I have a lot of questions for you." I hope she hears the urgency in my voice. I wait for her to say something but she just holds up a finger. She is wanting me to wait to talk! I can't wait. I let out a sigh and stare at her. I can feel my heartbeat move faster, and I poke at her arm.

"Ok, sweetheart let's go." She smiles at me and looks back at the other lady. "Have a great day, Jayme, see you on Saturday." She turns and starts walking toward the car.

"Who was that?" I look at Dorothy and wait to hear. She said she will see her Saturday and that is my party day.

"That is Gavin's mom, she is bringing him to your birthday party." She takes my backpack and holds it while I climb in the car. She walks around and opens the door. Before I have a chance to ask about my mom, she starts talking.

"Your principal called me about your behavior. Sounds like you had a rough day today and you hit a student and the counselor. Austin, I know you have a lot going on, but I still expect you to make good choices and work hard to keep yourself calm." She looks over at me and I can see the seriousness in her eyes. I look at the floor, I don't want to see her disappointed in me. I let out a sigh and I know she is waiting for me to say something.

"I know, I am sorry." I really am sorry. I need to do better. I can be strong like Ironman and keep my anger in control. She starts the car and I can feel the gravel shift under the tires as we drive home. I watch the trees go by and notice that most of them have lost the leaves. Dorothy's voice pulls my attention back to her.

"Your mom, well, she is staying with a friend of hers. I contacted her after she missed your visit. I have been giving her rides to her appointments. I want to help her. She really wants to make things right. And she has not had contact with Don. She says she has not taken drugs or been drinking since you have been living with me." She doesn't look at me and keeps her eyes on the road. She seems so serious. I am not sure what to say. Maybe Mom is trying to do better. Can she be better? I can't find the words to say, and I am not sure how I feel about this. Maybe she still cares about me. The thought makes me feel purple, it is swirling inside. Mom can do better, but what if she moves back with Don.

I can't find any words to say to Dorothy, and I look back out the window. I would love to have my mommy back, but I would want the mom I had before my dad left. Died, before he died. Ms. Jennie said I need to understand that my dad didn't choose to leave me, that it wasn't his choice. I let out a sigh and feel Dorothy pat my arm. I look at her and she doesn't notice. Turning my eyes back to the window I see Dorothy's house pass by. She didn't stop and is still driving. Where are we going? I feel darkness wrap around my throat, I want to go home. I look back at her. She smiles.

"Curious? I have a surprise for you, for the birthday boy!" She is very excited and doesn't wait for me to ask her where we are going to tell me. "Earlier I was in town and I found a store that had bunches of piñatas, I couldn't pick one. So I figured that you're so excited about getting one that I will take you there and you can pick for yourself. Then we will go home for dinner, cake of course, and the rest of your gifts!"

I look over at her and smile, I can't hold it back. I forget about Mom for a bit and picture the biggest piñata hanging from the tree in Dorothy's backyard.

"That is the perfect plan, this is the best birthday ever, and we haven't had cake yet!!" Dorothy laughs and she messes up my hair. I like that the darkness stays away now when she touches me. I giggle and relax as the trees fly past the window. It takes about twenty minutes to get to town so I close my eyes and take a rest. I think of my mom and the way she looked the last time I saw her, lost and hurt. I hope I never see her that way again.

We pull back into the driveway, and I can't see over the huge piñata in my lap. I held it all the way home, I picked a huge Avengers one. It is perfect and Dorothy let me pick bags of candy to fill it, and we had to buy three big bags to have enough. Dorothy opens my car door for me and I climb out, careful to not hit the piñata on the car. We walk inside and I grab the candy bags. I am ready to fill it up with the candy for the party.

"Oh dear, it is too early to worry about that, we still have a couple days to get ready." She is setting her bag and things down on the table. "Besides, we need to make dinner, eat cake, and open the rest of your gifts!" She sets a pan on the stove and starts toward the refrigerator.

I forgot about presents, and cake, but I still want to get the piñata ready. "After we eat can I put the candy in it?" I give her my sad eyes and she laughs at me.

"Well, I guess so but we can't hit it until your party." She continues to open the fridge.

She pulls out a bowl with something in it and puts it in the pan on the stove to start cooking. It sizzles and steams. It starts to smell delicious. It makes my tummy growl and hurt. She makes quick work of cooking and then slides a couple cans over to me to open. Green beans. I love how she cooks them. I use the can opener and open them up and drain them how she showed me to. She dumps the cans into a skillet and they start to sizzle too.

"Dinner will be ready in about fifteen minutes, do you want to open gifts while we wait?" She starts to make hot water for tea while she waits for my answer. I think I want to wait, I don't want to be rushed.

"I will wait until after we eat, I don't want to rush through them, besides I am way too hungry!" I laugh as I rub my stomach.

Dinner is delicious as always. We eat and she tells me a funny story about her son when he was in preschool. Her giggle is so loud and just the sound of it makes me laugh with her. I finish my food and I am getting tired. I take my plate to the sink and start to clean the table. Dorothy gave me chores to help around the house, and wiping the table is one of them. She finishes up putting food away and she walks over to where the presents are sitting.

"Ok honeybun, it is time to open them up so we can eat cake!" She slides the gifts over to me. "Do you want some hot tea with honey?" She starts to make two cups of it before I can give her an answer.

The packages are wrapped nicely and the wrapping is cool to the touch. I pick up one and start to open it. This is the best birthday ever, I can barely remember the last birthday that had gifts and cake, plus birthday treats for the class. The thought makes me smile. The paper rips quickly and inside is a Lego set and a new book. It looks like the same type of book that Ms. Benson gave me but this one has Paw Patrol on the cover. I smile and start to try to read the book, but Dorothy's words distract me.

"Keep going now, we don't have all night to open them, it will be bedtime soon." She looks over her tea cup and takes a sip. She is smiling at me, but I better keep opening.

The next package I grab is small and has new socks, underwear, and Ironman house shoes in them. When I look up at her she starts to laugh at me.

"You had to get some needs too!" She pushes over another gift.

I start to open it, but the box doesn't have anything on it. I open one side of the box and then the other and I pull out a huge stuffed monkey with giant purple eyes. It is so cute and soft. I pull it close and rub the eyes with my fingers, they are cool and smooth to the touch. The only stuffed animal I have is Teddy. This is the best gift ever and the best birthday ever. I hug the monkey and then set him on the table. I walk over to Dorothy, who is now digging in a drawer, and give her a hug.

"Thank you, this is the best day ever, I am ready for cake!" I look up at her and she pulls out a butter knife and a triangle looking spoon and holds them up by her face.

"Perfect, because I am ready too!" She holds up the knife and spatula next to her face and wrinkles up her nose. It makes me laugh. She places seven candles on top, then takes a match to light them. The match doesn't work and she fumbles with the box to get another one. She says some funny words I have never heard before until finally she finds one that starts fire. She lights all the candles and starts to sing to me. I feel purple inside. Purple... I think that purple is love, maybe it is safe. I am not sure which or maybe both. She finishes the cake and I clap as she takes a bow.

The cake is the best I have ever tasted. There is a cookie dough filling in between the layers of dark chocolate cake. She said it was a new recipe that she wanted to try out, and I am glad she did. I had two huge pieces with ice cream of course. I am stuffed. She starts to put away the cake and I walk the plates over to the sink.

"Dorothy?" I pause and wait for her to turn around and look at me.

"Uh huh?" She turns and has a gallon of milk in her hand.

"Would you show me how to cook? And if you are already helping my mom, can you show her too?" I picture my mom cooking with me and us having fun together. Believe. It is like the poster at that visitation place. Mom can get better and if I learn how to cook then I can help her more. And I wouldn't have to eat gross food anymore, so that is a plus. I laugh at the thought.

"Of course, we will start tomorrow." She pours two glasses of milk and tells me it is about bedtime. I drink it gone and remember the book that Ms. Benson gave me earlier today. I quickly run into the other room to find my backpack. I left it by the door and pick it up to look through it. I really need to clean this thing out. After some shuffling, I find the book and don't bother to zip my bag before I race back into the kitchen.

"Can I read this to you tonight? I might need some help with the bigger words, but…" Before I can finish my words she interrupts me.

"I would love for you to read to me!" She smiles a big smile and then tells me to get ready for bed.

I climb into the fluffy soft blankets and put Teddy on one side and my new monkey on the other. Dorothy comes in and sits next to me and I am able to read most of the book. She helps me with some of the words but not that many, and when I am stuck she encourages me to try and gives me hints. Once the story is over she tucks me in and turns out the lights. I pull

Teddy close, and then roll over and hug the new monkey. I think of my day and it makes me feel happy. I had the best day and I think of the fun parts and it wasn't even my party yet. It felt like a party with the gifts and cake. I snuggle into my pillow full of happy and purple. It is a great feeling to have as I drift off to sleep.

CHAPTER 17

Singing. Singing fills my ears. It is soft and I can't hear the words. I get up. Covers fall to the floor and I kick them to the side. I need to find the singing. Where am I? I walk down the hall, I see a light at the end and it is bouncing off the walls. Darkness fills the room and the singing gets louder. I slowly walk toward the bouncing light. When I turn the corner, I see people, they smile and clap when they see me. The bouncing light is from candles on the cake, it makes shadows on their faces. Mommy. I see her smile, her eyes are happy and kind. She is next to my daddy. He is laughing and I try to run to him. I reach my arms out and when I close them in a hug, nothing. I feel nothing. The room is dark again and the people are gone. No candle, no light. I yell for help.

Dorothy's voice echoes in the room. I yell again and start to run. The door is locked and I grab the handle harder. Finally, the door opens and I fall on my face.

I OPEN MY EYES. I SEE MY CURTAINS, Teddy is next to me, and I am still under my covers. That was such a weird dream. Oh no, please no. I reach down to check the sheets and they are dry. I let out a sigh of relief. I didn't pee the bed. I usually pee the bed when I have such real dreams. I really like that I saw my dad's face. It really was a good dream and that is rare for me to have. I stretch out and feel like I should go back to sleep. Rolling over, I snuggle into my pillows and close my eyes. I try to go back to the dream and see my parents. It doesn't work. While I am laying still I hear rumbling in the other rooms. I am not sure what Dorothy is up to.

The party is today! How could I forget, I kick the covers off and climb out of bed. I run for the door but slide to a stop. I need to make the bed. Turning around, I see new clothes sitting out on the dresser. Dorothy is always shopping. I smile and pull the covers up and straighten the pillows. Looks good enough for me. I grab Monkey and Teddy. I decided to just call the monkey, Monkey. I couldn't think of a different name and it stuck. I walk out and the living room is moved around with an extra table set up against the far wall. I am not sure what that is for.

In the kitchen Dorothy has a mess everywhere. I was expecting breakfast but it was plates of snack food that covered the table. There are brightly colored Avengers treat bags piled up, and paper cups, plates, and napkins. Dorothy looks a bit flustered as she hurries around the room. She looks up and sees me and gives me her big kind smile that she always has.

"I couldn't sleep so I got up early to get things started for the party. Do you think this will be enough food?" She doesn't give me time to answer before she starts talking again. "I need to make room in the fridge and take the cake out to warm up." She walks over to the fridge and pulls out a huge box. She quickly slides it on the counter and I walk over to look at it. It is the most perfect party cake ever. It has two layers and the bottom has Avengers stuff on it and the top layer is Ironman's head. It makes me smile. She has done so much for this party. I hope people come. I hope Gavin comes.

"Honeybun, you need to go get cleaned up and get dressed. I will have breakfast ready by the time you get out of the shower." She doesn't look up and is still finding room for things in the refrigerator.

I turn and head to the bathroom. I better get in the shower right away, Dorothy means business today and I don't want to push her. The water is hot and makes the bathroom all smoky again. I hurry to wash up and get out. My tummy is angry and ready for food. I must have slept in late today. I get dried off and walk into my room. I pick up the clothes from the dresser. They are fancy looking. I don't like them. I let out a sigh. The shirt had one of those flappy things around the neck with buttons. It looks like the shirts that the Michael kid from school wears all the time. I don't hesitate and get dressed. I am thankful for the clothes, even if they are not my style. I don't bother with my hair and head to the kitchen.

"I am starving!" I tell her as I enter the room. "Can I help with anything?" I pull out a chair and sit down. I hope breakfast is ready. She turns around with a plate in her hand, and walks it over to me. "I will need some help after you eat up, sweetheart we have time before people arrive. I just want to be sure to not forget anything." She sits down with her cup of coffee and takes a sip. I pick up the breakfast burrito and start scarfing it down. It is yummy and one of my favorite things she makes. She also made a hash brown and sweet tea.

I walk my plate over to the sink and Dorothy doesn't wait to tell me what to help with. "Take these table covers and put them on the extra tables in the living room. Use that tape to tape them down so they don't fall off. One table will be for presents and one will be for snacks." She hands me some folded up plastic things and tape. I smile at her and walk into the living room to get started. I cover the first table and when I start on the second one, the doorbell rings and the door handle jiggles.

I move away from the door and when it jiggles again, the gray begins to swirl. Dorothy quickly walks into the room. Knowing eyes. She can see my gray.

"Oh, well now, it is just Jeffrey, he is going to hang the piñata for us. Breathe!" She smiles and opens the door.

He steps though the door and smiles at Dorothy. She welcomes him in and opens the door. He has his uniform on and has happy eyes.

"Good morning Austin, happy birthday. I do not have long. Can you show me where the pináta is going?" He looks at Dorothy when he asks the question.

"Oh, well of course. This way." She starts to walk through the house, pausing to grab the pináta off the dining table. They both walk out the back door and I go back to my job. The covers look great and are Avengers themed of course. While Dorothy is outside, I turn on cartoons and sit on the couch. I get to watch cartoons more since I live with her. She doesn't mind watching them with me unless it is time for the news. Paw Patrol is on and it is a super pup episode I haven't seen before.

Lost in the episode, I did not notice Jeffrey come back into the living room. When he walked to the door I looked at him, but didn't really know what to say.

"You have a good day now, Austin. Stay out of trouble." He reaches the door handle and nods at me.

"Thank you," I tell him and smile. He smiles back as he walks out the door. I wonder if he will come back for cake? I didn't know policemen help people, especially to hang up a pináta. The thought makes me laugh. I go back to my cartoon, but it is only minutes before Dorothy walks in.

"Ok we need to get all the snacks out and set up the snack table. And what games do you want to play?" She stops right in front of me and I can't see the T.V.

"Can I finish this episode, please? Then I will help. I don't want games, just the pináta." The idea of games makes me feel yellow and icky. I give her my puppy eyes when I ask to finish the cartoon.

"Oh, all right, I guess it is your party. But only this episode, then I need your help." She lets out a huff and walks back to the kitchen.

We get the tables all set up and once everything is in the perfect place, according to Dorothy, it is almost time for the party. Dorothy seems to relax and sits at her chair with a fresh cup of coffee. She looks exhausted and it makes me feel guilty. She has been running around all day just for me. For my birthday party. A party that my mom should be throwing for me. I feel red grow. I am not sure what sparked it but I feel it inside. I walk to the kitchen and get a drink of cold water and it helps back the red down. I watch the pináta swing in the tree out back and wonder where my mom is. I take a deep breath and try to not think about it. I am sure the party will be great but I feel gray poking at me when I think about it. Lost in my thoughts, I hear the doorbell ring. It must be time.

"Austin! Guests are arriving, come answer the door dear!" Dorothy sounds excited and gets up from her chair. The red inside me turns to gray and yellow. I wonder who it is, I run to the door and open it up.

"Hi Austin!! Here is your gift, it is not Ironman, but my mom tried. Hope you like it! Let's go play!" Gavin is as excited as I am and hands me the gift as he walks into the house. I follow him and put the gift onto the gift table. Dorothy said I can't open them until later. Dorothy welcomes Gavin's mom and starts talking to her.

"Hey, do you want to see the pináta?" I asked Gavin, who was looking around.

"Yeah! Is it outside? This is a nice house. Let's go!" He talks all the way out the door to the backyard. I really like him, and he talks so much that I don't have to. We head to the tree with the piñata, we both try to jump high enough to hit it. It is too high for us and we start to play tag in the yard. Dorothy's yard is huge and has a lot of trees to play around. I hear the screen door slam shut and look up to see more kids coming down the stairs.

"Happy birthday, Austin!" Nikki starts waving at me while she walks toward us. Behind her is Michael, he must not be mad about the fight at school the other day. We all start to play tag.

"Austin, I need a drink. Can we go in and get something?" Gavin is panting while he is trying to talk.

"Of course, Dorothy made some kind of blue looking drink for us, we can ask to have some." I start to walk toward the house and others follow me. In the kitchen, the adults are all talking and I notice Ms. Jennie and Mrs. Roush standing near the dining room door.

"What? You actually came!" I felt purple explode inside and run over to hug them.

"Austin, that was not a nice thing to say, can you fix it please?" Dorothy gives me the look she has when I am rude. I didn't mean to sound rude.

"I am sorry, I am glad you guys came. Can I get you something to drink?" I wait for their response.

"You can get me something to drink!" Gavin's voice is so loud. Everyone laughs and Dorothy starts to pour the blue stuff into cups for everyone.

"Where is this piñata that you have been talking about so much?" Mrs. Roush asks me.

"Oh, it is out here, come see." I grab her hand and Ms. Jennie follows. We walk out and I show them the piñata.

Gavin starts playing tag again.

"Thanks for coming, I am going to go play now." I start to run off and Ms. Jennie's voice stops me.

"We can only stay for a few minutes sweetheart. This is a great party! We are going to walk back inside to visit Dorothy, while you play." She smiles at me and I wave to them and join the tag game. I hear the screen door again and look up. My heart races and I stop breathing.

The darkness wraps around me. I try to keep it down, but it happens so fast. I can feel my heart beat echo throughout my body. I want to run but my feet are stuck to the grass. I am not sure if I should run to the house or run away. I can't believe what is happening, and my body is feeling so many colors. Lost in my thoughts, I feel someone run into me and we both fall to the ground. Gavin starts rolling around the grass and laughing. His laugh is so funny and it makes the darkness let go of me. We stand up, and he shoves me playfully, but I keep staring at her.

"Hey, what is your problem? Who are you looking at like that?" Gavin tries to push me again. Then he looks toward the house with me. I take in a breath and try to find my words.

"My mom," I say and feel the darkness turn to gray and blue.

"Your mom? I thought Dorothy was your mom, even though she is old," Gavin's voice sounds confused.

"No, Dorothy is not my mom." I let out my breath.

"Well, I guess that's why you call her Dorothy. And she is too old to be a mom!" He laughs again.

"Well, are you going to go see her? You are acting weird." Gavin nudges me again.

Am I going to go see her? I feel stuck to the spot and I am not sure what to do, a part of me wants to run to her. I picture her face, and him hurting her. Maybe she is better, maybe she can be my mommy again. The thought makes me feel weird, and I am not sure what the feeling is. I am lost in my thoughts and I don't notice Dorothy walking toward me until Gavin runs past me to the house. She is smiling at me and kneels down in front of me so that she is looking me in the eye.

"Sweetheart, your mom is here, and I know that is probably a surprise for you. I invited her, and didn't tell you in case she couldn't come." She is looking at me like I need to say something but I can't find the words.

"Austin, you don't have to talk to her if you are not ready too, but it is time for cake and gifts, then we will beat the piñata." She smiles at me and turns to walk toward the house.

I follow her but I can still feel my heart beating as I get closer to the stairs. Mom is still standing there, next to Ms. Bethany, she seems to be waiting. I need to say something, but I am not sure what. I start to climb the stairs and I think I might just ignore her and walk in. My head wants to ignore her and be angry with her but my heart feels different. She looks clean, her clothes seem to be new and fit her nicely. She has on jeans and a fancy looking shirt. I look into her eyes and she smiles at me. It is her. My mommy. Her smile, it is the one that makes her eyes squinty. It makes me feel purple and green and I can't stop myself from needing her. I take in a breath and picture her touch, how it used to be. When I open my eyes, my body launches toward her, I hold out my hands and wait for her response. She steps toward me and picks me up in her arms. Her touch and embrace fill me up with purple and I start to cry. She is warm and soft and my tears fall onto her shoulder. She squeezes me and I can feel her rock back and forth. Her touch makes me feel like I am melting. My mommy. She is getting better. She does care about me.

Mom's hug feels like it lasts forever, I didn't want to let her go but she puts me down. I look at her and she smiles again, I still can't find my words. She looks better, but can she be better? I am not sure what to feel or think, it is so confusing. She hurt me, but yet here she is and she looks stronger, healthier. She doesn't look empty anymore. I look around and everyone is inside. Dorothy's voice fills my ears. It is time for cake. I smile at my mom, I wait for her to say something, but she smiles back at me and has tears in her eyes. I think she lost her words too. She will find them when she is ready, the thought makes me smile and think of Ms. Jennie at school. She waited until I found my words. Dorothy yells again and it is her I-mean-it voice. I turn, open the screen door and run inside.

Everyone is gathered in the dining room and my eyes find Ms. Jennie. When she looks at me her eyes are kind, and they are knowing eyes. I bet she knows how mixed up I am feeling. Dorothy catches my attention and is demandingly waving her arms to come to the table. She already has the candles placed and is lighting them with a long weird looking lighter. I am ready for cake. This is the best day ever. I sit down in the chair in front of the cake, looking up, everyone starts to sing. I look up and I can see my mom's face smiling through the flames. She is standing next to Dorothy and she has her arm tangled up in Dorothy's arm. Dorothy, I can't help but think that she has a lot to do with my mom getting better. I take in a big breath and close my eyes. My wish. I wish for my mom to come back to me and for us to be a family again, with Dorothy, and her cooking of course. I laugh to myself and blow out the candles while everyone claps. Maybe wishes do come true. I want to believe they can. Believe, such a good word for a poster.

CHAPTER 18

I am running down the hall of the school and my footsteps echo and bounce around the walls. I see the office and see something hanging from the top of the door. There is my mom and she is hitting the colorful piñata and laughing loudly. I stop and watch her. Her smile is huge and her laugh makes me laugh too. Her clothes are clean and she looks happy. I hear a noise behind me and I turn around, the hallway goes black, pitch black. I can hear footsteps and I step in front of my mom. I see red eyes in the dark and his voice echoes off the walls. He reaches for us and starts to scream. I look back to see what my mom is doing, but she is gone. I yell for her and the cry for help only echoes and does not get a response. He grabs me and I see his fist coming at my face.

I close my eyes and wait for the pain. I fall to the ground and wrap my arms around my face. I am cold. I am wet.

I WAKE UP IN MY BED AND LOOK AROUND the room. I am safe. I let out a big breath and take in another. I had another bad dream. It was just a dream. I have had a bad dream every night since I saw my mom at the party. I guess it has only been four nights, but I wasn't having bad dreams before the party and now I am. I am wet again and peed the bed. I start to just change the bed myself, but I know that Dorothy will hear me and get mad because I didn't tell her. I turn on the light and walk toward her room, but her light switches on before I get there. She walks out and smiles at me. "I will grab the other sheets." She walks into the other room and comes back out with sheets in her arms. "Was your dream about your mom again?" Dorothy asks while she is changing the bed.

"Yes, and Don was trying to hurt her and me and she left me again." I look at the floor and can't help but wonder if she will go back to him. I let out a sigh and Dorothy pats the bed for me to climb back in. I lay down and she sits on the bed next to me. She looks at me and lets out a sigh, and then leans over to grab the covers. She tucks me in and then pauses. She looks so serious and then she starts to talk.

"Seeing your mom seems to have brought back your nightmares." Dorothy pauses and seems a bit lost in thought.

"Listen Austin, you never know what will happen in life, no one does. You have been through a lot, but you have a whole life ahead of you. We just have to keep moving forward, day by day and look for the positive. Positive in the world around us, positive in the people we meet. We can only have hope that the positive will outweigh the bad stuff. But we have to find it, the good stuff, we need to spread it and sometimes we have to create it ourselves. Austin, we have to have hope that people will choose to be better and choose what is right. Hold on to that dear, the hope that things will change." She gives me a hug and she has tears in her eyes. I can't tell what she is feeling.

"Goodnight dear and sweet dreams, remember you are safe and I am just a room away." She smiles and leaves to go back to her bed.

I look at the ceiling, it has some light bouncing around from the moon outside. I don't really want to go to school tomorrow. It has been a rough week for me, I spent a lot of time with adults. I even gave out Band-Aids in the office with Mrs. Marsha. It was hard to be in class, I felt all jumpy. Maybe tomorrow will be better. Hope. Another word that I don't understand. I wonder if it is on a poster like believe is. I pull Teddy close to me and feel around to find Monkey. I stick him on one side and hold Teddy in my arms. Can things get better? Maybe that is what Dorothy meant by hope and look for the positive. I close my eyes but my brain does not want to sleep. I roll over and it seems like just minutes before I hear Dorothy's alarm clock.

She always shuts off the alarm clock fast, she says she doesn't deal with that snooze button stuff. I can hear her in the bathroom and the shower comes on. I try to close my eyes for just a few minutes, but I can't sleep. I feel very tired and my head hurts. I roll to my back and think about the day. I have gym class today. I like gym. The teacher is very relaxed and lets us play a lot of different games. I am going to do better today, I am not going to take a break in the office, and I am going to go to recess. I hear Dorothy turn the shower off. I don't want to get up and I usually have a long time to sleep in after her alarm. My mind wanders to thoughts about my mom. I was so excited to see her. We did talk after Gavin and I took down the piñata and everyone left. She said a lot of words. The words I think of the most are that she wants to get me back and keep me safe. She said she stopped drugs and she is going to meetings and therapy. I don't know what meetings are, but it sounded like something she needed to do. I asked her about Don, and she said she was done with him. I do not know what to think about it. I guess in the words of Dorothy, I need to hope she can get better, whatever that means.

I smell bacon and decide to get out of bed. I am not sure what time I wet the bed, but I have not slept since then. I don't want to have nightmares anymore. I roll out of the bed and head to get cleaned up for the day, I know Dorothy won't let me stay home. When I walk into the kitchen Dorothy is smiling and breakfast is waiting on me. She made omelets and strawberries. She puts the paper to the side and takes a drink of her coffee before talking to me.

"Good morning, how are you feeling?" She takes another sip of her coffee.

"Hi, I am tired. I couldn't sleep after we changed my bed, my brain wouldn't stop." I take a bite of the omelet. Yummy, as always. I look up at her while I am chewing and she looks serious at me. Her look makes the gray bubble up. What is she thinking about?

"You must be tired then. That was around three this morning." She takes another sip of her coffee. "You have another visit with your mom today, I am taking you to meet her at the office. I think you should stay home with me until after the visit, how does that sound?" She still has a serious look on her face, but I am not sure why. I shake my head yes since I have a mouth full of food and go back to eating.

"All of your visits with your mom have to be supervised, which means there has to be another adult with you at all times. So, she could visit you at school sometimes too, or she could come here for dinner." She waits and keeps looking at me.

"Mmmmmm." I take another bite of my food. I am not sure what she is getting at with this, I just keep chewing and look at her.

"Well? What are your thoughts on these other visits? Ms. Bethany says as long as they are supervised and you are ok with them she can visit more." Dorothy seems impatient this morning, and I get the feeling she is not telling me something.

"I guess that is ok. Is Don still in jail? If she is visiting me can he find us?" I feel the gray build inside thinking about the night he showed up here pounding on the windows. Dorothy looks at me with knowing eyes.

"Austin, listen here, I will keep you safe and Don would be dumber than a bee in a rain storm to show up here again." She stands up to pour another cup of coffee.

"I know you will, Don was full of gray when he was here and you had that gun on the porch!" I smile at the thought that Dorothy makes Don feel that way.

"Well, no one is going to mess with this old hen!" She laughs and smiles. "Well I guess I was asking because your mom currently doesn't have anywhere to stay. I was thinking that if the next few visits go well, maybe she could stay with us. But only if you are ready for that." Her face is serious and she seems a bit lost.

Would I want my mom to live here with us? I feel colors start to form and swirl in my tummy. I think I would like that but what if she is not better? I look at Dorothy. I know she will keep me safe and as long as Dorothy is home with us, maybe it will be good.

"I am not sharing my bed." I can't think of other words right now but I know that I am not going to lose my bed. She can sleep on the floor or the couch.

"Of course not! I have another room downstairs that she can stay in, I would just have to clean it out. That room is yours and that bed is yours. Well, we will see how things go first and then you can let me know. I would not leave you with her and you would always have another adult with you when she is here." She takes another drink of her coffee.

"I think I would like that. She seemed better at the party." I finish up my food and take my plate to the sink.

"She is trying to make better choices and she started going to the same office that Mrs. Michelle is in to get more help. Ok, well, you go watch some cartoons while I clean up, it will be time to leave soon." She stands and walks to the sink.

I head to the living room and turn on the T.V. to some cartoons. I can't hear it because of my thoughts, but I watch it anyway. I like the idea of seeing Mom more, I think I do anyway. She seemed like she was happy at my party and said she was getting better. Maybe I will ask her more about it at the visit today. It would be fun to have her over for dinner, maybe Dorothy can show her how to cook. I picture her smiling and helping Dorothy. It makes me feel warm. Maybe I can get my mommy back and we can live together again. I close my eyes and picture snuggling with my mom and watching a movie together, maybe even eating Dorothy's milkshakes made with love. Dorothy walks into the room and I open my eyes, she is watching me. "Are you ready?" She smiles at me, walks closer, and opens her arms for a hug. I feel purple grow and I stand up and fall into her arms. She holds me for a minute and starts to walk out to the car. I am so glad I met her.

Seems like just a few minutes pass by and we pull into Ms. Bethany's office. The parking lot has a lot of cars in it and there are a lot of people walking in and out of the building. Must be a lot of visits today. I watch a car door open and a little girl gets out with a guy. I think it is the same girl I met here before. I get out of the car and walk with Dorothy toward the door. The girl seems clean and her hair is nice with a big bow in it. She has happy eyes. I wonder if her family is making good choices too. The thought makes me smile, maybe she found a Dorothy to take care of her too. Dorothy holds the door and we walk in after the girl does. I head over to the toys while Dorothy walks to the front window where the toad lady is sitting. The girl looks over at me and she smiles.

"I remember you," she said.

"Me too, I am here to visit my mom, is that what you are doing?" I wait for her to respond.

"No, my mom has not been coming. But my grandma has been and I have been visiting her. I miss my mom, but I am glad that grandma comes to see me." She lets out a sigh.

"Who is taking care of you?" It makes me feel blue, thinking about her mom not coming. I can understand how that feels.

"A nice lady named Amy. She has a house and cooks me food." Her eyes change to happy when she says this.

"That is great, I have a Dorothy," I laugh as I point to the front window. The girl laughs too. The guy that drove her to the office waves her to the door that leads to the visit rooms.

"I hope your mom makes good choices for you!" I smile and find a seat to wait for Dorothy. The girl waves at me before going through the door. I start to play with the Legos. It is not very long before Ms. Bethany walks in and waves to me to go visit with my mom. Dorothy walks over to a seat and nods as I walk past her. I can feel the gray swirl and bubble in my tummy, Ms. Bethany is talking to me but I don't know what she is saying. I am lost in my thoughts. I try to take in breaths to calm me down but I don't think it is working. I hope Mom is as good as she was the last time I saw her. I hope she will hug me. I let out a sigh.

"Ok Austin, your mom is waiting in here." Ms. Bethany opens the door and holds it for me to walk in. Mom is sitting at a chair in the corner. She has on jeans that look clean and seem to be a dark blue. Her shirt looks new and it is a bright green color. Her hair looks like she curled it and it is pulled halfway back. Her eyes meet mine and she is smiling. Her eyes look happy and her face is full and plump. She no longer has the lost look or the dark circles under her eyes. I start to walk toward her and she stands up and steps toward me. Briefly, the gray chokes me before my mom scoops me into a big hug. Her arms wrap all the way around me and purple stomps down the gray in my chest and tummy. My mom. I miss her so much. I try not to cry but I can feel my eyes getting heavy. I push them back because I do not want her to see me cry.

"Oh Austin, I have been waiting all week for that hug. I love you so much and miss you." She puts me down and wipes the tears from her face.

"Don't cry Mommy, Dorothy takes good care of me." I am not sure what else to say.

"I know she does, baby. Do you want to play a game?" She smiles and pulls Candyland off the shelf.

"Ok." I sit down on the floor as she sets up the game. I want to ask her about Don, but I need to get the words ready. She hands me the blue guy and she picks the yellow one. We giggle and laugh during the game. Her smile makes purple vine through me. I feel so warm seeing her this way. I think I have my mommy back, the real Mommy that loved me and my daddy. The one that laughs and her eyes get squinty when she smiles. I just stare at her and I know what I need to ask.

"Are you going to see Don again? I hate him, Mom. He hurt you and hurt me." I keep my face serious and want her to see how much I mean my words.

"Austin, I know he hurt us. And I hurt you when I didn't keep you safe. You are so brave. Way more brave than I was. I see how strong you are and I know I can get better and be the person you deserve." Her eyes fill with tears and she sits back and puts her face in her hands. "I am so sorry. I will never see him again. You are going to be my number one, no matter what."

She looks at me. Her eyes are sad but they look serious and strong. I believe her. There is that word again...believe. I believe she can stay better and we can be a family again. Plus, we have Dorothy to help us. And that reminds me about what Dorothy said about Mom moving in with us.

"Mommy?" My voice sounds small.

"Yeah?" She pauses and looks curious.

"Dorothy said Ms. Bethany said that I can see you more as long as I am not left alone with you. She also said that you can live with us and she can protect us from Don and teach you how to cook. Dorothy is an amazing cook and you need to learn from her." She starts laughing at me but I am serious.

Then she quickly reaches for me and I am not expecting it. My heart jumps and the darkness squeezes my chest. I move backward quickly and run into the table, knocking over the lamp that was on top. A loud noise echoes in the room as the lamp hits the floor and I jump away from it too. I close my eyes and try to take in a breath but his eyes flash in front of me and I need to get away. I stand up and Ms. Bethany walks toward me.

"You are safe Austin, your mom was just trying to hug you. Are you ok?" She sits in the chair next to me.

"Oh honey, I am so sorry…" she lets out a gasp and tears start falling. "I am not going to let anyone hurt you again. I..I…I..can't….just can't." She starts crying harder and seems to be having trouble catching her breath. Before I can say anything, she walks out the door but I can hear her cry bouncing through the hallway. I am not sure if I should go get her or if I should stay. I feel stuck to the floor and I don't understand what happened.

"It will be ok, your mom just really feels a lot of big feelings when she thinks about what happened to you." Ms. Bethany has calm, kind eyes and she touches my back. She moves slowly and it doesn't make the darkness grow.

"Do you think Mommy is better?" I look at her and I can feel the tears build.

"I think she loves you and is doing everything she can to stay better. It is a process and we all have a part." She smiles at me. "Your part is to keep doing what you can to heal and she will work on herself, and you need to go to school and do your best." She laughs when I look at her.

"I don't want to go to school!" I laugh. "So, Mom can really live with Dorothy and me?"

"Yes, as long as you are not left alone with her, and you are comfortable with it." She stands up and walks to the door.

"I think I am ok with it. I really like seeing her and I want her to learn to cook." I giggle and walk to the door with her.

"Oh, well I am sure she can learn! Why don't you sleep on it and discuss it with Dorothy tomorrow." She walks down the hall toward the waiting room.

I am not sure what sleep on it means, but I will talk to Dorothy more about it. I need to say bye to Mom, but I am not sure where she went. I start to ask Ms. Bethany about it but she walked into the waiting room before I could get the words out. I look over and Dorothy is sitting in a chair and her arm is wrapped around my mom. Mom looks like she has stopped crying and Dorothy's eyes are caring and kind. I am sure she told Mom some words to make her feel better. As we walk closer my mom stands up and gives me a look that is full of blue. It makes me feel blue but I have to be strong for her. She kneels down in front of me so that her face is the same height as mine. I don't know why adults do this so much, but teachers do it too. She holds out her hands and it brings me back from my thoughts. I put my hands in hers, they feel cold and rough, but comfortable.

"I didn't mean to scare you, I don't want to scare you. Austin, I love you and when I see what I have done, it makes me feel terrible. I will fix this, not the past but the future." She hugs me and I can't help but know that those are Dorothy's words. I look at Dorothy while Mom is hugging me and I see knowing eyes. She smiles at me, and purple fills me up again. Mom lets me go and says goodbye.

"Mom? Will you go trick-or-treating with Dorothy and me? We are dressing up as superheroes and plan to get as much candy as we can," I ask her with my small voice and I hope she wants to go with us.

"That would be a lot of fun. I would love to go if it is ok with Dorothy." She looks over at Dorothy when she says this, but I already know what the answer is.

"Of course you can sweetheart." Dorothy smiles and walks out of the office and the rest of us follow.

Mom hugs me and walks to a car that I don't recognize, I can see someone in the driver's seat and I can feel the gray grow in my throat. I walk over a bit to see better. Please don't be him. Please no. I lean forward, not really wanting to know but I have to. When Mom opens the car door I can see a ponytail and the person is wearing glasses. I let out a sigh and feel my chest loosen up. When I turn to the car, Dorothy puts her hand on my shoulder. Knowing eyes. She smiles and looks at me.

"He is in jail, Austin." She turns to the car and climbs in, I smile and follow her.

"Do I have to go to school?" I have to ask but I know what she is going to say.

"How about we go to lunch first, I think we have some planning and talking to do." She glances sideways at me before starting the car and backing out of the parking spot.

"Really?" I did not expect that answer, she always makes me go to school and I always ask to stay home but she still makes me go. Weird. What does she want to talk about? But lunch does sound good, my tummy is a bit cranky. I watch out of the window as we drive through town. There are a lot of people out walking and driving today. The car slows down and we pull into a restaurant, but I have never been here before.

"What is this place?" I ask and unbuckle my seatbelt.

"It is the pizza buffet, they have different types of pizza, salad, and chicken. I figured it is a place where we both can find something we like." She smiles and we both get out of the car. It is a busy place and the buffet smells yummy. I have never been to a buffet before. It makes my tummy poke and rumble. We pick a table and I am not sure what to do. I watch Dorothy and she looks at me. Knowing eyes; she can see through me.

"Come along, we have to get plates and we can get whatever food we want, but only take what you will eat. You can go back as many times as you want. I usually start with a salad and then dig into the pizza. Taco pizza is my favorite and they have delicious fried chicken." She smiles as we walk to where the food is. She hands me a plate and takes one for herself. I don't like lettuce, so I skip the salad and head for the pizza. After getting our food, Dorothy shows me where the drinks are then we sit down at the table.

I dig into my food. I didn't realize how hungry I was, and this pizza is really good. In between bites, I look at Dorothy and she is staring at me while slowly chewing her food. She looks lost in thought and I am not sure if I should say something or just go back to eating my chicken pizza, I think it has bacon on it too. I take another bite, but Dorothy is still looking at me. It makes the gray swirl and I need to say something. I don't like her looking so serious and when she is not talking, well, that is just not normal. I try to find the words and decide to just ask her what she is thinking about.

"What are you thinking about? You said we needed to talk about things and plan something? What was that about? This pizza is really good, you need to try it." I stuff another bite into my mouth and it is just as yummy as the first bite.

"Oh, well," she pauses and takes another bite of her salad. I have never realized how hard it is to talk while eating food.

"Well, I think that we need to plan our Halloween costumes more, and I think we need to talk about your mom moving in with us sooner than later. She needs a place to stay and I feel that my house is the safest place with the least temptation. You haven't given me an answer about her living with us."

"Yes, as long as I do not lose my bed, and you keep doing the cooking." I didn't have to think about the decision, and finished eating my pizza slices.

"Well, ok then. But you need to understand that you still have to follow my rules, even if your mom doesn't like my rules. I will have rules for her too." She smiles and eats more salad.

"I think I can handle that." I keep chewing.

"Then it is settled, after lunch we will go home and clean out the extra room for her and she can move in soon." She looks relieved and calm now. I think she had gray inside thinking about my mom.

"I can't go to school today?" I pause and for the first time, I am kinda bummed I can't go to school, but I know Dorothy needs help to get the room ready.

"You can if you want but that room is going to take some work to get ready."

"It is ok, I will help so Mom can be safe too. And I am thinking I want to be Ironman, you can be Wonder Women, and Mom can be Storm." I start in on a piece of fried chicken.

"Hmm, I am thinking I can be Cat Women." She lets out a laugh. I laugh with her and we both get up for more food. I get more of the pizza and then dig into the desert too. After we sit back down, I think about the school costume contest and wonder if we can have our costumes ready in time.

"Do you think we could have the costumes ready in time for the school fall party and costume contest?" I hope we can, Mrs. Roush said the whole school dresses up and the teachers do too. I am really excited about it.

"Have you met me? Of course we will have costumes ready! But first we need to get your mom's room ready for her. So finish up, we have a lot to get done, and we can stop at the fabric shop again to look for costume patterns!" She starts eating her food and stops looking at me.

I finish my last piece of pizza and walk up to get some dessert pizza. I have never had blueberry pizza but it is yummy in my tummy. We head out to the car and climb in, Dorothy tells me that if we can't find a pattern then we will stop at the costume shop to see what they have. I bet Dorothy can make anything work. I might have a chance to win the contest. Thinking about us in our matching costumes, makes me smile. Mom and Dorothy are both going to go to the school party, it is going to be great. I didn't get to wear a costume to school last year. It was only me and one other kid that didn't dress up. But not this year. I can't help but be excited for it, maybe I should have Dorothy make an extra costume for me to take to school in case someone in my class doesn't have one.

I like the idea of Mom coming to my school. I picture introducing her to my teachers and to Ms. Jennie. I can even read her the book that Ms. Benson has been helping me with. The thought makes me feel warm. I wonder if we can win the contest, that would be perfect. Things are going to be great with Mom at Dorothy's house. I know that Dorothy will keep both of us safe. Mom will have to make good choices with Dorothy around, because if she doesn't, well, I just know Dorothy can take care of that too. I look at Dorothy and remember her words, hope; hope that things will get better. I do have hope and it seems like it's working out, I smile and can't help but feel like Ironman, ready to take on whatever happens next. The thought makes me happy inside.

CHAPTER 19

IT IS LATE. I AM NOT SURE WHAT TIME IT is but I know I have been in bed for awhile and Dorothy shut her light off a long time ago. I can't sleep and my brain will not shut off, I have so many thoughts flying around. I really need to sleep, I roll over to try to get more comfortable. Tomorrow is the Halloween party at school. Dorothy finished up the costumes today and I got to try mine on. It looks so cool! It is way better than the ones in the store. She tried hers on too but wouldn't show me. I hope Mom will like her costume. She hasn't seen it yet, but she is meeting us at school and said she will change once she gets there. She is coming home with us after and it will be her first night living with us. The thought makes the gray swirl. I hope she likes her room.

Mom's room turned out great. It took us forever to get it cleaned out and organized. My legs hurt by the time we got done moving stuff upstairs. It really was a hot mess in there.

She had things piled in every corner. When Dorothy said it needed to be cleaned, she wasn't kidding! We ended up taking a bunch of stuff to the thrift shop. We had to stuff her car full of things at least three times before I could see the bed. I am just glad it is finally done. The look on the thrift store worker's face when we pulled up a third time made me laugh.

After the last trip, Dorothy took me to the store to pick out a new blanket and sheets for Mom's bed. I picked green because that is her favorite color. The bed looked great when it was made with the new stuff. I hope Mom likes it. I helped Dorothy make curtains for the window too. I roll over again and try to picture my mom being happy here. It makes me feel green. I start to fall asleep and feel myself sink into my bed.

The sun warms my face as it pushes through the curtains. Morning. Already. I can't get up yet. I am so tired. I try to fall back asleep and as I am about to drift off, Dorothy comes in and sits on the bed.

"Good morning Austin, it is time to wake up. Come on now, it is a big day today." She starts to rub my back to get me up. "Breakfast will be ready in about fifteen minutes, so get in the shower." She walks to the door and leaves.

I need to get up, I need to get in the shower. My head feels heavy and I force myself out of the bed. The shower feels nice, wakes me up and seems to make my head feel better. When I get out, the smell of breakfast finds me. My stomach growls and I can taste the cinnamon rolls already. It makes my mouth water. I quickly get ready and head to the kitchen. I actually feel awake and excited for the day after the shower.

Dorothy is at the table drinking her coffee and reading the paper. She already has my food on a plate waiting for me with a glass of chocolate milk. I sit down at the table and start to eat. She looks at me and sips her coffee. I can tell she has something to say, and it doesn't take long for her to start talking.

"How are you feeling about the day?" She pauses. I stop chewing and think about the question. How am I feeling? It is mixed up and I am not sure how to describe it.

"Well, it is yellow mixed with gray and purple." I start to drink my milk. I know Ms. Jennie and Mrs. Michelle would make me find names for the colors but I am not feeling up to it this morning.

"Are you scared to have your mom live with us?" She pauses but doesn't give me time to answer the question. "Oh, well, Austin, remember that I will be here and we will work through this together. Your mom has to continue going to counseling and going to her support groups. She is doing much better or I wouldn't let her come here." Dorothy looks so serious. "Remember, adults make mistakes too and they can make the choices to get better, it sounds like your mom is doing what she needs to for you and her to move forward." She sips her coffee again. She always has good words to share.

"I am not scared. I know you will keep me safe." I don't have any more words and go back to eating my food. As I take my last bite, I remember that I need to wear my costume. I feel excited and can't wait for my class to see it. I stand up and Dorothy looks confused. "I need to change into my costume. You have to wear yours too but it doesn't start until after lunch." I do not feel like talking. I put my plate and cup in the sink and head to my room to get my costume.

I look awesome, I keep looking in the car mirror at myself. Dorothy seems quiet. I think she is lost in her thoughts. We pull up to the school and there are a lot of kids in their costumes walking into the school. I feel bubbles in my tummy, gray bubbles. I look over at Dorothy and she looks back at me with her kind, knowing eyes. Her smile makes the bubbles fade. It is going to be fine, the day is going to be fine, and Mom moving in with us is going to be fine. I can't find the words, but I know that without Dorothy...well, I let out a sigh and try not to think about it. I smile back at her. "Thank you," I tell her as I reach over for a hug. I open the car door and start to step out.

"I will see you after lunch and I will have your mom with me in our costumes. Have a great day, sweetheart." She smiles at me as I close the door and walk toward the school. I take in a deep breath and put on my mask. I want to show Ms. Benson and Ms. Jennie to see if they can guess it is me. The office is busy as usual and when I walk up to Mrs. Marsha, she gets a huge smile on her face. I wait for her to guess who I am, but it doesn't take long for her to start talking.

"Austin, your costume is amazing! You look just like Ironman, but short!" She laughs at herself and then hugs me. "I hear it is a big day for you today, I can't wait to meet your mom and see her costume too."

"She will be here with Dorothy after lunch, I will make sure she meets you. She is coming to live with us too, it is going to be great and her room is all set. And I get to keep my bed." I take off my mask as I talk and smile at the thought of my mom being here. It makes me feel warm and purple inside. "Have you seen Ms. Jennie or Ms. Benson?"

"Ms. Benson is in her office and Ms. Jennie is running around the hallway somewhere saying hi to kids. You can go see Ms. Benson in her office." She smiles and goes back to answering the phone. I slip my mask back on and walk into the office.

"Well look who we have here, Spiderman!" She laughs and has a big smile on her face. I shake my head no. "I meant to say we have Ironman and a super Austin inside. I love your costume, it is so detailed!" She continues to smile and holds her hand out for a high-five.

"Dorothy made the costume for me, and she made my mom a costume and herself one too. They will both be here today, and then my mom will be living with us at Dorothy's house, but Dorothy said she will keep me safe." The words roll out before I can even think about them. It is so nice to not have to hide words anymore.

"Sounds like a big day for you, how are you feeling about your mom living with you again? It is a big change."

"I feel yellow, gray, and purple, Dorothy already asked me that this morning. I am glad I get to keep my bed. I don't want to have to sleep on the floor again. And I plan on showing Mom how to cook and we are going trick-or-treating together, with Dorothy of course." I smile and picture trick-or-treating with my mom, I don't remember trick-or-treating with her before.

"Austin," Ms. Benson pauses, she has kind caring eyes. "I am so proud of you and how hard you have been working." She smiles but is serious about this.

"I haven't done anything." I roll my eyes, she is crazy.

"But you have, you are talking about things, recognizing your feelings, and look how much you have grown academically. You have worked so hard in such a short time and I am proud of you. I bet your mom will be proud of you too."

"You are weird." I didn't mean to say that out loud. I smile at her and laugh. I am not sure what proud means but I like it. She smiles back at me. I am glad she doesn't get mad at me. She still has kind eyes and she doesn't fake-care like other teachers at my last school. I feel warm inside and green and purple grow. I am not sure how it happens but I wrap my arms around her and give her a big hug. I don't know how to thank her but I put a lot of words into that hug. She squeezes me too. When she lets me go, I quickly turn and head to class without looking at her or waiting for her to talk.

The hall is full of students in lines walking to class. I must have missed the bell again. I feel my heart pick up and beat faster, I don't like to be late. I start to run and zig-zag between people so I don't run into them. I can't wait to show Mrs. Roush my costume. I start to turn the corner and I hit someone, hard. I fall back onto the floor and the darkness starts to choke me. I look up and see a pointed nose with cold angry eyes staring down at me. I feel the darkness grab me and I see him. His nasty grimy hands reaching for me and my heart freaks out inside. I close my eyes. I take in a breath, *I am at school, I am safe, he is not here.* I repeat this in my head and the darkness lets go of me. I hear her shrieky voice and open my eyes again. I look at her and can't help but laugh out loud.

She is dressed as a witch, with a hat and everything. It is so fitting. Her words are angry but I ignore them. I stand up and can't help but look at her. "Your costume is perfect for you," I try to say this without laughing, but I can't hold it back. I laugh and the look on Mrs. Gentry's face is so funny. I start to walk off then Ms. Jennie's voice fills my ears.

"Ironman! I knew you would dress up as Ironman, it is fantastic! I heard what you said to Mrs. Gentry." She pauses and I start to feel like I am in trouble. I look at Ms. Jennie and her eyes are calm and happy. She doesn't seem to be upset.

"You are so right that her costume is perfect." She laughs and reaches for a hug. I hug her back and start to laugh with her. She must remember me calling Mrs. Gentry a witch. Ms. Jennie is dressed funny. She has her hair braided and it is sticking out from her head in pigtails. The pigtails are stiff and pointing out from both sides of her head. She has big freckles painted on her face and a funny looking dress with big boots on.

"What are you?" I ask her because I have no idea.

"Well, I am Pippy Longstocking of course! The strongest girl around." She flexes her arm to show muscle. I roll my eyes and laugh, I like her silliness.

"Oh, ok. I have never heard of her." I smile at her and realize, I need to get to class. I start to walk toward my room.

"I will walk with you." She walks next to me. "I hear I might be meeting someone today?" She glances sideways at me.

"How does everyone know about today?" I put my hand on my forehead.

"Because you have been telling me about it for a week!" She smiles. "I know we have had many chats about her moving in, but how are you feeling now? Since she is moving in today?"

"I am ready for her. We have a lot of catching up to do, and Dorothy will be there too so she can help Mom. I need to get to class." I start to open the classroom door and then remember something. "Ms. Jennie?" She turns and looks at me. "When I fell in the hall, I used that positive talk stuff you have been talking about, and it worked!" I smile and walk into the classroom without giving her time to answer.

The class is putting stuff away in their lockers and I hurry to get ready for class before Mrs. Roush notices I am late. I quickly get to my seat and start my journal while she takes attendance and lunch count. She walks past my desk. "Good morning Austin, I love your costume." I look up at her and smile. She is dressed as a huge green crayon. It even has a pointy hat on top to look like she is sharpened. She starts going over the calendar and I can see her mouth moving but I can't hear the words.

I keep thinking about my mom coming and us winning the costume contest. It would be so fun, but it is ok if we don't win too. Mom will be coming to Dorothy's today. I try to picture what it will look like. Laughing and smiling. I can see her face with her squinty eye smile and us dancing in Dorothy's kitchen. I hope she is happy, and can stay happy. I don't want to lose her again. I hope she can stay in her counseling and groups like Dorothy said. She seems like she is making better choices. I guess if she doesn't, I will always have Dorothy to take care of me. But I think Mom can be better, and now she has Dorothy to help. I think Dorothy can do anything. I want to make milkshakes tonight, I am going to ask Dorothy if she will help me make them for Mom and her. My brain is going really fast and I lay my head on my desk to feel the cool on my face. The smooth surface feels good on my cheek and my hand. I start to want to get Teddy, but I know it is going to be ok. I feel a hand on my back and it makes me jump. I look behind me and it is Ms. Benson.

I look back to Mrs. Roush and she is lining students up for reading groups already. Ms. Benson sits down with me and gets out some books to start reading. She tells me that the office is busy and that we can have reading groups here. I am able to read the first book she has and then the second I need a lot of help with, but she teaches me some new letter sounds. Reading group is over fast and it is time for recess. I am not sure I want to go outside today. I am having big feelings and it is probably not a good idea to go.

"Can I stay in the office for recess today?" I ask Ms. Benson while Mrs. Roush walks the other students outside.

"Of course you can, we can walk that way." She turns to head out the door and is looking at her phone. She has a black shiny jacket on and boots that make a lot of noise when she walks. I don't really feel like talking. I hope my mom comes today. I think about kindergarten when she said she was coming and then didn't show up. It was not a good feeling and then this other kid started making fun of me for not having a mom. I ended up in a fight with him and got into trouble again. I try to not think about it.

The rest of the morning goes by quickly. I am not sure where the morning went. Next thing I know, Mrs. Roush is nudging me on the shoulder asking me to line up for lunch. I sit by myself at first but Gavin sits next to me, which I don't have to talk much because he doesn't stop talking. He dressed up as Batman and has on a t-shirt and some bat ears. I go back to the office to sit with Mrs. Marsha during recess. She is busy which I don't mind because I don't feel like talking much. I look at the clock and then out of the windows to see if I can see Dorothy's car. I can see a lot of parents pulling up but not mine. I feel gray swirling around and take in a deep breath. She will be here. When the bell rings, I head to class without waiting for Mrs. Marsha to tell me. I can't help but let the gray grow as I see parents checking in at the office. What if she doesn't show up or Dorothy can't find her? I squeeze past a lady standing in the doorway to get to the hall.

When I look up, the gray disappears and I feel green and purple explode inside. Dorothy and my mom are standing there in their costumes talking to Ms. Jennie and Ms. Benson. Ms. Jennie and my mom are laughing and smiling while they talk and Dorothy reaches out and hugs Ms. Benson for some reason, which looks a bit funny in her costume. I look around and notice that the other parents are not dressed up except for a couple people. I run up to them and give Dorothy a hug and then turn to my mom. She smiles at me and her eyes look happy and full. Then she gives me that squinty smile and I wrap my arms around her, she picks me up in a huge hug and I lay my head on her shoulder. She is back. My mommy is back.

When she puts me down I grab their hands and walk them to the classroom.

"Mrs. Roush, Mrs. Roush!" I say her name a bit louder than I wanted to, but I am so excited to introduce her to my mom. I pull my mom's arm and run toward Mrs. Roush, who is talking to another parent. I wait for her to finish up talking and then she turns to me.

"Mrs. Roush, this is my mom! She came with Dorothy." I keep Mom's arm in my hand.

"It is so nice to finally meet you; Austin has been so excited for you to be here today. Help yourself to some refreshments and goodies," she motions to the table full of food and juice boxes.

"Thank you for everything you have done, I know Austin really loves your class." My mom continues to talk to Mrs. Roush and I walk over to Dorothy to see what she is doing.

"Thank you for bringing her today," I say and wait for her.

"Of course, love. Now pass out these bingo sheets. It's almost game time." She hands me some papers to pass out.

"When we get home can you help me make milkshakes for us all to drink?" I ask her as I straighten up the pile of bingo sheets in my hand.

"Well, yes, but now you need to get those papers to your friends." She smiles and goes back to making plates with treats to pass out.

I pass out all the papers and look toward Dorothy and Mom who is now sitting next to her helping with the treats. They are talking to each other and then Dorothy laughs. They seem like they get along really well. I smile and walk over and sit in between them.

"Time for bingo, so students please sit at your desk and we will pass out treat plates and get bingo started!" Mrs. Roush walks to the front of the room. I head to my desk and sit down. Mom and Dorothy help pass out the treats and I look over at Gavin. He is covered in orange icing and is stuffing a cupcake in his mouth. I start laughing at him and then grab mine. We giggle as we both have icing all over. This is the best party ever. Mrs. Roush starts calling out numbers and everyone is eating and playing bingo. I didn't win, but Gavin and I laughed and talked the whole time so we didn't really hear the numbers anyway.

"Class, class, it is time for our school's family costume contest announcement. The mystery judges walked through the classrooms and looked at everyone's costumes. They will be announcing the winners and they will get an ice cream gift card. But all of your costumes are so festive and fun!" Mrs. Roush is talking and walking to the front of the room at the same time. She looks around the room and takes in a breath.

I can hardly wait for her to announce it, I can feel my heart beating and I look over to Mom and Dorothy and they are still talking to each other. I wonder if they are as excited to hear who won as I am. Gavin leans over to me.

"Austin, who do you think is going to win? If you do, can I have the gift card?" He looks over at me and smiles. I don't have to answer because Mrs. Roush starts talking again.

"Our classroom winner is Austin! Yay Austin, come up and get your gift card!" Mrs. Roush is smiling and claps for us. I jump up and I can't help but smile. I hold my head up high like Ironman and walk up to get my prize. Mrs. Roush hugs me and hands me an envelope. I quickly skip over to Dorothy and Mom.

"We won!" I hand Mom the gift card and turn to hug Dorothy. "Thank you for making our costumes so awesome!" I turn to my mom and she still looks happy. I hug her too. "Thank you for being here mom." I let go and walk back to my desk to finish the games. Gavin is so excited, and keeps talking about his favorite ice cream flavors.

The party ends and it is time to go home. I show my mom my locker and where I keep my stuff. I grab Mom and Dorothy's hands and tell Mrs. Roush goodbye with a hug. We start to walk to the office.

"Mom, you have to come meet Mrs. Marsha, she is the nicest lady and the best secretary, nothing like that witch at the other school."

"Oh yes, I forgot about her. I am so glad everyone at this school is so nice and it seems like they take good care of you, sweetheart." She smiles at me and then looks over at Dorothy.

"Mom, it is because they care, not fake-care, but they really do care," she needs to know this. The office is busy, but Mrs. Marsha stops talking to another family and walks over to me.

"We have been waiting to meet you! I am so glad you could come today. You have such a sweet, kind, and wonderful boy here." Mrs. Marsha reaches out and hugs my mom. It surprises me and I think it does her too. When I look at Mom, she has tears in her eyes.

"Thank you for caring for him so much," Mom's voice is shaky.

"Of course we care, and we are here for you too." Mrs. Marsha smiles and walks back to her desk to get the phone.

We turn to leave and Ms. Benson walks in. She smiles at us and then my mom suddenly hugs her too.

"I can't thank you enough for being so kind and patient with him." Mom is all weepy and I am starting to feel embarrassed. While they are talking, I see Ms. Jennie and she still has her hair sticking straight out. I walk over to her and show her my gift card.

"Austin, I am happy for you! You are going to have the best weekend with ice cream, trick-or-treating and your mom being home with you now." She hugs me and one of her pigtails hits me on the head.

"It really is going to be a great weekend, and I am going to tell you all about it on Monday. Can we have hot chocolate and donuts in your office in the morning?" I smile at her when I let her go.

"You know it! I can't wait to hear about it!" She gives me a high-five and I hear Dorothy's voice calling for me.

I walk out the front door of the school. Dorothy and Mom are in front of me walking to the car. It is crowded, and kind of feels like slow motion. Kids and parents are all leaving, some holding hands and others talking. I look back through the school doors and Ms. Benson is standing with Ms. Jennie. I feel purple and I am so glad this is my school. They smile and wave to me. I turn back to start walking toward the car. I see Dorothy put her arm around my mom's arm and she leans in for a side hug. They are smiling and laughing. I feel something new and I see it. Hope. The hope that Dorothy was talking about, and hope feels great inside. It really should be put on a poster. As I start to run toward them, I realize something. I take off my Ironman mask. I don't need to be strong like Ironman, or strong like Dorothy. I just need to be strong like me, like Austin and I can do anything.

ABOUT THE AUTHOR

CHELSA HAS WORKED IN THE MENTAL health field since 2008. She is an LCPC and elementary school counselor in Great Falls, MT. She believes every student deserves to be loved, cared for and safe. She believes that words matter. Adults in and out of school need to remember the impact they can leave on students.

Chelsa's roots are in a small Ohio town where you can always find sweet tea and fried taters. When she is not in school, she enjoys the outdoors including riding bikes, horses, and new adventures with her family. The inspiration for her book, Colors In Me, came from the many struggles students have shared with her over the years and her experience working in the school system. She hopes to help every student believe in themselves and have hope for their future.

Made in the USA
Coppell, TX
30 November 2020